RAVAGE MC #3

CONSUME
me

WALL STREET JOURNAL & USA TODAY BESTSELLING AUTHOR

RYAN MICHELE

Fourth Edition Published: October 13, 2019
ISBN-13: 978-1-951708-02-3
ISBN-10: 1-951708-02-4
ASIN: B00SEZC5KQ

Previous Edition Information:
First Edition Published: 2015
Second Edition Published: 2016
Third Edition Published: November 17, 2017
ISBN-10: 1505605350
ISBN-13: 978-1505605358
ASIN: B00SEZC5KQ

CONTENTS

Blurb	vii
Prologue	1
Chapter 1	3
Chapter 2	23
Chapter 3	57
Chapter 4	77
Chapter 5	97
Chapter 6	117
Chapter 7	151
Chapter 8	187
Chapter 9	201
Chapter 10	217
Chapter 11	229
Chapter 12	241
Chapter 13	261
Chapter 14	277
Chapter 15	281
Chapter 16	285
Chapter 17	291
Chapter 18	299
Epilogue	303
About the Author	315
Acknowledgments	317
Thank you	319

RAVAAGE MC FAMILY TREE

1. Ravage Me
2. Seduce Me
3. Consume Me
4. Inflame Me
5. Captivate Me
6. Bound by Family
7. Bound by Desire
8. Bound by Vengeance
9. Bound by Affliction
10. Bound by Destiny
11. Bound by Wreckage
12. Connected in Pain
13. Fueled in Fire
14. Sealed in Strength
15. Connected in Code
16. Bound by Consequences
17. Bound by Redemption
18. Bound by Fate
19. Bound by Temptation

COMPANION BOOKS

POPS & MA

PRINCESS
1

CRUZ & PRINCESS

COOPER
& BRISTYL

AUSTYN
8
& RYKER

NOX
11
& CARSYN

GT
2

GT & ANGEL

DEKE
7
& RYLIE

EMERY
10
& JACKS

DAGGER & MEARNA

TANNER
4

DAGGER & MEARNA

TUG & BLAZE

MICAH
16

& ENSLEY
17

RHYS & TANNER

RYLYNN
12 13 14 15

MAZIE

BREAKER & SHAINA

BOOKER

BUZZ & BELLA

AXTON
19

RAIDEN

BOUND

GREEN & LEAH

RAIDEN

DRYERSON & KATIE
18

BLURB

The past is never far from the surface...

Being a stripper at Studio X was never **Blaze's** dream, but it pays the bills and puts food on the table. Having it owned by the **Ravage MC** is both a blessing and a curse.

She's worked hard to get where she is to let anything detour her. Not even the **hunk** of man who won't seem to leave her alone. He's a **temptation** she doesn't need.

Tug is prospecting to become a member of the Ravage MC, doing everything he can to **prove his loyalty** to the brothers.

His mind is also set on a sexy brunette whose **eyes set him on fire**, even if she keeps pushing him away. Tug loves a **challenge—bring it on**.

When **secrets** are revealed, it will be the ultimate test between the two.

Sometimes the only way to beat the demons back is to look them **straight in the eye**.

Come and join the ride with the Ravage MC!

To you — Thank you.

PROLOGUE
Blaze

I knock and there's no answer, just as I expected. I smile to myself as I open the creaky door, slowly, not wanting to disrupt her rest. I walk over to the bed, noticing that only her beautiful head is poking out from under the covers. God, I love her. I love her more than anything in this world.

Oh no... her lips. Her lips are a weird color; they're so pale. I place my hand on her head. Cold. Ice cold. No. God, no. I rip the covers away from her body and put my ear to her chest. Nothing. No. Please. No. I open her mouth and breathe inside of it then begin pumping her chest. This can't be happening. Please, God no.

Tears stream down my face as I scream at her to wake up, to just fucking wake up. Pumping and breathing feverishly into her lugs, I will her to open her eyes. My stomach drops to the floor. She's gone. Holy shit.

My tears become sobs after long minutes that feel like hours, and then reality hits me and I stop myself.

I take a moment to kiss her forehead. "I love you," I whisper to her still form.

Survival kicks in as I take in my surroundings. I have to get out of here. Now. If I don't, there's no way I'll ever escape...

CHAPTER ONE
Blaze

THE LIGHT FLASHES ON, ITS HEAT PENETRATING MY SKIN, illuminating my body from the top of my overly done hair to the tips of my pointed heels. My barely-there clothes offer little protection from the warmth, but they are not intended for that. Their sole purpose is to entice, to leave the audience wanting more—more of my body, more of me. And I will make sure they'll be begging for more. The coolness from the metal pole alleviates a little heat as I rub my back against it. Catcalls and whistles fill the air as the music blares through the speakers. I close my eyes, breathe in deep, and allow every cell of my body to absorb the music. *His* eyes are on me only, ratcheting up the fire.

Showtime.

Tug

"AMERICAN WOMAN" pumps through the room as Blaze takes the wide stage. She doesn't just take it. She owns that shit. She exudes confidence from every inch of her body and fuck if it isn't the biggest damn turn on. Her gaze smolders, laced with unadulterated sex appeal as she silently scans the crowd. Her eyes draw each of us in more, leaving us craving her, desiring her. Blaze's body is a vision from the gods: all curves, toned, long legs, silky hair the color of brown sugar, and a huge fucking rack that I can tell from sight is all real.

Blaze hooks her leg around the metal bar, her hand grasping it as she swings around the pole, stopping just short of the floor. The way her muscles flex with each movement tells of her strength and skill. She does things on that pole that weightlifters wouldn't dare.

Her arms reach up the metal rod and she locks her ankles tight around the bar then hangs upside down, the rest of her body falling down the pole's length. She hangs there for several seconds as her arms reach down, almost touching the floor; her ample tits come close to spilling out of her flimsy red top. It would be nice if they did.

She releases her ankles slightly and slides down the pole until her hands are firmly planted to the floor, her bare ass staring me in the face. Whoever invented thongs needs a fucking award. Only thing better than a thong is nothing at all.

Blaze's ass is something that men dream of fucking and women dream of having. Those taut, curvy globes beg to be spanked and then fucked repeatedly.

Kicking her slender legs out, she lands on the black stage and sensually stretches her arms above her body. Her hips sway to the music as she turns and faces the crowd, her beautiful face shining. Every contour is perfection, from her small nose to her sexy as shit eyes... *perfect*. The only problem is her smile. It's not real and doesn't reach her silvery-blue eyes. From the screams, obviously others haven't noticed.

I do.

She continues her seduction of the crowd. My cock thickens. I grip the front of my jeans, adjusting to relieve the pinch from my zipper. Damn I hate when that happens. Nothing worse than a dick pinch.

Her eyes connect with mine and those silvery heavens bore into me. My heart rate picks up, beating rapidly. A small smirk plays on her lips, not the fake smile, but a genuine one. She knows exactly what she's playing at, including what she's doing to me. The entire crowd is eating from of the palm of her hand, but to me they don't fucking exist. It's only her. Her teeth pull her plump bottom lip into her mouth and she touches it with her finger, so fucking sexy. Aligning her back with the pole, she stretches her arms above, arching her back, tits poised for my viewing pleasure, and she closes her eyes. This woman definitely gets a fucking *A* in seduction. My already hard cock twitches inside my jeans, aching to be free and inside of the buxom brunette.

"What can I get ya?" Misty, one of the new dancers at Studio X, asks us—*us* being myself, and Buzz and Breaker, my fellow Ravage Prospects that happen to be identical twins. We all sit staring, mesmerized by the woman on stage, not taking our eyes off her for a second. With the spotlight on Blaze, nothing else in the room exists, but I answer wanting to get rid of the woman.

"Shot of Jim and a beer." My words are barely heard over the pumping music as Buzz and Breaker yell their orders in as well. We spent the damn evening cleaning up Jace's fucking corpse. Stupid motherfucker. I'd like to have him alive just so I can kill him again for what he did to Casey. No one should lay a hand on a woman, ever. I don't give a shit what she has or hasn't done. In this case, Casey didn't do a fucking thing except be part of GT's life; loving a Ravage brother made her a target. Damn. Growing up with that shit day in and day out, I will not stand for it. Having witnessed my father hit my mother repeatedly, I won't stand for it ever again.

The brothers caught Jace and took care of the problem, even if I got the shit job of cleanup at the end. Being a prospect, I get all the fun. Right. Cleaning the clubhouse from top to bottom isn't fun at all, but it's shit that has to be done and as low men on the totem pole, it falls to the prospects.

I've never said shit or complained once about cleaning whether it be the clubhouse, blood, or the brothers' bikes. Everything I've done this past year has been out of love and respect for the Ravage MC. And I know that each of the brothers did this exact same shit to become members and they wouldn't have me do anything that they wouldn't do themselves. It's all about respect and I have it for all of them tenfold.

Snapping to the here and now, I see her drop down into a split, her ass hitting the shiny floor. She bows her head, hair falling all around her, and extends her arms over her legs. The music plays its last notes as she flings her hair behind her, one arm up in the air, and locks eyes with me. I lick my lips at the intensity of her stare. Her eyes flare as she rips the top away from her body. Fuck me.

The damn stage lights go dark all too fast and I pray the fuckers come back on. Whoops and whistles ring through the room and cash flies all around, like green leaves scattering in a blur as the lights come up revealing an empty stage.

Blaze and I have been playing this cat and mouse game for the past few months. Her taunting me from on stage, her beckoning eyes, everything calling to me, drawing me in. One time, she came out on the floor of X and talked to me briefly. Her hulk of a guard, Cali, stayed glued to her side the entire time. She was short and to the point with me, not giving me a fucking inch, and damn did it turn me on.

Thinking about the way her metallic blue eyes bore into me has me craving to see them again. Sure, I've fucked many women since the first time I saw her, but it's been a while. That always-there-pussy isn't tempting me as it once did. I've had enough and decided Blaze will be mine.

I've made it my mission to be around this past week. Every night after she gets done dancing, I either go backstage to say hi or meet her by her Jeep in the lot. She's a strong woman, but there's something in her eyes when she's not on stage that says otherwise. I want to find out what's behind them, and I intend to do just that.

It's been made very clear by the entire club that Blaze is off limits, and I'm pretty sure Princess is behind that order. She makes money for the club therefore she's protected, but no one is to lay a hand on her. First Diamond and then Pops clarified that Blaze is not a club momma and will not be treated as such. And damn it if it doesn't just make me crave her more—knowing my brothers haven't touched her, knowing that I'm the only one that will. And I will. I'm patient and determined.

I've always gone after what I wanted. Life is too short not to. It can end in a flash and I intend to end it happy with Blaze at my side.

Tonight, I'm making a stronger move. I'm normally a take life by the balls because of my life's too short policy, but with Blaze, I've made a slight adjustment. She may come off confident as shit, but from the looks on her face sometimes, she's hiding inside and even a bit scared. The confidence she shows everyone is a front. I'm sure she doesn't want me to know that, but it's not hard to figure out if you pay attention. And I pay attention. I also intend to find out what, why, and who did that to her. Then decide who I need to kill.

My brothers' eyes are transfixed on the next dancer. I glance up. She's not bad, but does not hold a candle to Blaze. Mossy blonde hair, okay curves... but nothing.

Buzz, Breaker, and I have known each other for years. All the way back to basic training. They may not be blood, but they are my brothers.

"I've got shit to do." I throw some bills down on the table.

"Where the hell you going?" I nod to the door that leads backstage and snag my beer, gulp a final pull, and set it down on the table. "You haven't got a shot in hell with her," Buzz smarts, shaking his head, and the corner of his lip quirks up.

"We'll see."

He's been with me long enough to know how persistent I can be. The words *giving up* are not in my vocabulary. He's giving me shit, which is normal, at least for him. What are brothers for?

I rise without another word and charge through the crowded room. Princess sure has done a bang up job with this place. Hordes of men and women line the tables, waving cash like it's nothing, ready to throw it at the dancers. Good for the club. The deep red she chose keeps the place sexy and the damn bar is crammed with people waiting to get drinks.

After Babs trashed X, Princess pretty much had to start from scratch. Even with red carpet, somehow the blood still showed through.

I shove the thick, red curtain aside and force my way

behind it, blinking a few times to adjust to the lights. It's much brighter than the sultry atmosphere in the front. One of the new bouncers, Doug as the nametag on his shirt says, stands in my path blocking me and I come to a halt. With his arms crossed over his beefy chest and his long blond hair tied in a ponytail, he tries to throw around his bulk. Not fucking happening.

"Where ya headed?"

His words piss me off. I should drop his ass right here for even questioning me. The club owns this damn place, owns him. He has no fucking right to question anything I fucking do here.

"Move your ass to the side. I'll go any-damn-where I please." Fury bubbles in my veins as I clench my fists tight. I fucking hate being questioned, especially by pissants who think their shit doesn't stink, but my face stays blank, my tone low and fierce.

He looks me up and down, trying to intimidate but only pissing me off more. Wrong fucking move.

My fist connects with his stomach in a flash. Doug lets out an *ugh*, uncrosses his arms and bends at the waist, but doesn't go down. He gasps for breath, but not enough for my liking. It was only one hit though. Tough motherfucker, glad Princess hired him.

"You work for us, motherfucker. Remember that shit. This is Ravage's club. You see men with leather, you'd better move the fuck out of our way. Don't you fucking forget it." I may not be a full-fledged brother yet, but I will not be disrespected by anyone. No. Fucking. Way.

"Why'd you have to do that?" Doug shakes off the punch, his eyes narrowing as he stands to full height, which is an inch shorter than me. What is wrong with this fucker? My hands open and shut, ready to land another punch, as his posture is anything but demure. If he wants to fight, let's go.

I learned to fight from the best in the military. Even if he wanted to go at it, he wouldn't last five seconds with me. I trained relentlessly for hand-to-hand combat. When my muscles couldn't function, only then would I be allowed a break. I won't even begin to discuss the weeks on end of torture simulations. If I can get though that shit, I can get through anything and anybody.

"If you don't get the fuck out of my way, you won't walk for a fucking week," I growl, seething from anger. Another part of my military training is the motto "Never Back Down." The motto goes the same for the club and my future brothers. I stand by them, they stand by me. Trust, honor, and loyalty till the end.

"Fine." He begrudgingly steps aside, and the ladies in the room, primping for the stage, give me their I-want-to-fuck-you-now eyes.

I ignore each and every one. I don't give a shit that I've fucked most of them at one time or another over the past year. They're easy and don't hold any appeal for me anymore. Always-there-pussy. I direct myself toward Blaze's dressing room in the far corner. Her days of skating around me are over. This time, I'm not allowing it. I'm done with games.

The white door is closed and Cali stands in front of it with his arms crossed, his eyes swinging to me. Cali is six-three, has cropped, jet-black hair, and is built like a fucking tank.

I step toe-to-toe with him. "You gonna be a problem too?" The coolness in my voice is not reflective of the anger leftover from Doug's idiocy. I'm damn sure that Cali can feel the pulses bouncing off of me.

Cali holds his hands up in mock surrender. "I'm not a dumb shit like that one." He motions to Doug behind us. I made my point with him and if he needs clarification, I sure as shit will give him that. What I won't give him is the satisfaction of getting my attention again. "Blaze is changing, though. Give her a minute?" His brow rises, as he wonders if I'll listen to him. At least Cali has respect for the club; that's more than I can say for the other asshole.

"No problem. I'm gonna knock and tell her I'm here." He steps to the side, but stays near the door. Definitely going to have to ask her why all the security. None of the other women have this and I've never asked at the club. I need to remember that.

I knock, allowing any lingering anger to dissipate, and get ready to get to my girl. Yes. She's mine and I don't give a shit who thinks otherwise. She may only be mine for a night or a few days, or maybe a few months or a year, I'm not sure yet. But for me, she is mine.

"Cali, I'm changing. I'll be out in a minute and we can go," Blaze's honeyed voice calls through the door. Desire consumes me from just the sound.

"I'll go wherever you want me to, darlin'." The noises stop and she inhales so deeply that I can hear it from out here.

"Tug?" she utters, breathily.

The way she says my name has my cock throbbing. I

can't fucking wait to hear that when I'm balls deep inside her.

"Yeah, sweet lips. Get your fine ass out here."

Rustling noises on the other side of the door pick back up, along with shuffling of feet and *ughs* coming from her beautiful lips. I wonder what she's changing into. It could be a garbage bag and she'd still be hot. The door flies open, sending a whoosh of air past my body. Blaze has the slight sheen of sweat from her dance still covering her skin, making it glow in the light. Her black shorts hug her hips, her damn legs are a mile long and perfect for folding around my back. The bright pink shirt fits snug around her boobs, stretching the material and giving a damn great view. She's fucking gorgeous. I lick my lips, lips that are suddenly so damn dry.

"Sweet lips? Are you serious?" Her hand latches onto her cocked hip, showing off her curves as she tries to give me attitude. Little does she know, I love the fucking attitude. I eat that shit up. *Sweet lips.* I can't wait to fucking kiss the shit out of them.

I have a difficult time taking my eyes off her body, and when I reach her face, they lock with her glittery blue ones and the fire blazing inside them. It's there, hot and vibrant. She shuts her eyelids then opens them up a second later and the fire is almost extinguished. Fuck that. I will have that fire back.

"Give me a taste of those luscious lips and I'll tell you if it's true or not." Her mouth opens slightly as she sucks in a breath so deep her tits rise, her nipples pebbling under her shirt. Gotcha.

Her arms wrap around her body protectively. Scared?

Horny? The puzzle pieces aren't coming together yet on her.

"No. What do you want?" she blurts out, but the small hitch in her voice is not lost to me. She feels this shit, this connection, but she's fighting it. I need to find out why.

"To talk." For now.

"So, talk." Her demeanor screams I am a confident woman hear me roar, but her damn eyes tell a whole other story. What that is exactly I can't put my finger on, and damn, I wish I could. But that is part of the fun. Challenges turn me on like no other.

"You want to talk here?" I quirk my brow, hoping to remind her several dancers are watching our interaction. Not that I give a shit, but I want her alone.

Her forehead wrinkles and she tilts her head. "Yes, where else are we going to go?"

"There's a diner up the road, let's go have something to eat and talk." A sinister chuckle leaves her lips and damn it if isn't one of the sexiest noises I've heard in a long time. I have no doubt I'll be turned down. I expect nothing less.

"Not happening. You've come to me every night for the past week, aren't you tired of being shot down?" She pauses. "And I'm sure your idea of *talking* and mine are two totally different things."

I won't dispute that fact one bit, but I ignore the other comment. I place myself directly in front of her, bending my knees to be eye to eye with her.

"Honey, I'm not throwing you up against the wall and fucking your brains out until you beg for it." Her arms tighten around her body and from the corner of my eye, I see her pebbled nipples tighten to tips. Fuck yeah.

"Good thing I'm not begging." That's what spews from her mouth but it isn't what her body is screaming. I'm going with her body; her mind can catch up later. Being this close to her, I'm dying to crash my lips to hers, but Pops' warnings flash through my mind and I resist. Barely. I need her to want it. More like admit she wants it, but she's not there yet.

Her eyes shift over to Cali, who stays silent and pretends to ignore us, though I know damn well he's listening to every word.

"This isn't going to happen. No dinner, no coffee, no nothing anywhere. Stop wasting your time. I need to get home, it's late." She steps back and starts to shut the door.

"Congratulations are in order, I hear," I say, remembering a conversation between Princess and Casey the other day.

The door stops mid-swing and I raise my brow, knowing I have her attention. I will get her full attention one way or another. It's a bit more effort than I'm used to, but it'll be well worth it when my cock is plunging into her tight pussy.

"Where'd you hear that?" Her eyes narrow, probably thinking I had the guys check up on her, but that's not the case. Being Princess and Casey's tag along means that I overhear some interesting conversations. They gab all kinds of shit, not thinking about the listening ears around them. Everything they say, I file away. Never know when I'll need it.

"Princess and Casey talk a lot." I shrug. Her face heats

to a rosy blush. "I overheard. Graduating college is a huge deal." Way huge in my book since graduating high school was hard enough, but I did get that far at least. It was touch and go there for a while.

A smile like I've never seen before graces Blaze's face, lighting up everything around her and making her already beautiful face gorgeous, extraordinary. So much so, it's punching me in the fucking gut, but I don't allow it to show. This smile is not the forced shit she gives on stage. No. It's pure and genuine. Fuck, I will make sure she does it over and over. "Thanks. I'm pretty proud of myself."

"You should be. I went into the service right after high school. After I got out, the military said they'd pay for my school, but it just wasn't for me." It wasn't. Nothing interested me anyway, but no way in shit do I want to go into too many details about my time in the military. Not exactly the best time in my life, though not the worst either. Just prefer it stay under lock and key.

She leans against the doorjamb and puts her hands in the front pockets of her shorts, her posture somewhat relaxed. A halo of light glows around her long brown hair as it falls below her breasts, landing like a veil across her shoulders.

"What branch?" Her question surprises me, only because I didn't think she'd care and the fact she has an interest in me is a good sign. Patience and determination can get anything.

"Army." Memories of my times there creep through me, stilling my actions, but I tamp that shit down fast and change the subject. "Did you go to the ceremony?"

Pain sweeps across her face, contorting it in a way I never want to see again, and I instantly regret the question. She abruptly masks it, the clouds in her eyes clearing. Not quick enough that I'll be able to forget it, though. "No. I just got the certificate from the office the next day. Really your transcripts are all that matter." Her flippancy regarding the subject eats something deep down in me.

"You want to talk about it?" I ask, not wanting her to relive the pain, but wanting to know her.

She waves her hand nonchalantly, flapping it up and down. "Nothing to talk about. There's no one to celebrate with, anyway." Shock registers all over her beautiful face. No way did she intend me to catch that little tidbit of telling information. Too damn bad.

"I have to go." Rapidly, she tries to shut me out with the door. I place my black-booted foot in its path, bringing it to a halt. None of this shit will get rid of me. She needs to learn that lesson quick. Blaze starts to talk, but my phone rings inside of my prospect rag and I hold up my hand. She silences instantly, surprising me and giving me a rush. The display reads *Dagger*.

"Yeah?"

"Where are you?" Dagger clips impatiently. When I first met Dagger over a year ago, we instantly clicked. I don't know why, he was just a guy that I could talk to. He made it easy. Each prospect has a member for a sponsor that teaches them the way of the club and club life. They kick your ass if you go too far. Luckily, I haven't had that problem. With Dagger being mine, I have no doubt he'd put my ass in line at the slightest misstep.

"X," My eyes lock on Blaze's unreadable ones. *What is going through your head?*

"Good, get as much whiskey as you can carry on your bike and get your ass back to the clubhouse now." Dagger's short, low words tell of the anger inside of him. Something must have happened.

"On my way." When I first started prospecting, I learned quickly to never question a brother's request. I never have from day one. They tell me to do something, I don't care how shitty it may seem, I do it in a heartbeat. Each thing they have me do is to prove my loyalty and respect to the club as well as each brother. I will never let them down.

I swipe the phone off. Worry lines form around Blaze's silver blue eyes. It's nice to know she actually gives a shit. So close, almost there. "Everything okay?" The concern in her voice is the icing on the cake.

"Always. Gotta run. We'll continue this soon, sweet lips."

"There's nothing to continue, Tug. Take care." She tries shutting the door, obviously forgetting my boot is there halting it. She lets out an aggravated sigh. "You can move your boot now."

"Babe, there's a lot to talk about. Later." I wink, moving my boot from the door. Blaze says nothing, but closes the door, giving her the escape she thinks she needs. If I didn't have to go to the club, I wouldn't have given her such an easy out tonight. Smirking, I lift my chin in Cali's direction and make my way back into X.

Luna, one of the dancers I've fucked before, saunters up to me as I step through the red curtain.

"Hey there, stud. Wanna have some fun before you go?" she coos, trying to be seductive. At one time, it would have worked, but Blaze has her beat by leaps and bounds. Luna's blonde hair is cut into a short bob that frames her face. Her blue eyes sparkle, but not like the radiant ones I had mine on a few seconds ago. The clothes she has on leave little to the imagination. My dick doesn't even harden a bit. Fuck me.

"Nope. Gotta run." I sidestep her. I barely hear the huffs and puffs behind me. This leather attracts women like bees to honey. It's been damn nice for over a year. I have no complaints about the amount of pussy thrown my way. Now, there seems to be only one my dick wants. Fucking shit.

After getting the booze, I ride directly to the clubhouse. The wind whips all around me as the roar of my bike soothes me. When I was in the service, I rode in Humvees all the damn time. All boxed in and, at times, suffocating due to the amount of men jammed inside. I told myself that *if* I got out, which there were times when I didn't think that shit was gonna happen, I'd get a bike so nothing would be around me and I wouldn't be confined or caged. So, I'd be free and damn if that isn't true. Being on my Harley is the best possible high in the world. Nothing else matters but me, my bike, and the open road.

The large gates of the clubhouse are open and Doc, the club's doctor, scurries across the parking lot carrying his big black bag. The clubhouse is on the left side of the lot and the garage, where we work on cars to earn the club's legit money, is further toward the back with a separate entrance there for customers. Next to the clubhouse is a large courtyard filled with tables and chairs surrounding a fire pit. There's also a huge playground that I helped build when kids started coming around more often.

I park my bike in the prospect lot, hop off, and clutch all the booze. Buzz and Breaker's bikes are already here so I go in search of them. What the fuck is going on?

As I enter the clubhouse, a flurry of activity surrounds me. Men are moving every which way, most covered in dirt and grime.

"I'm fucking fine!" Rhys barks from the couch when Doc approaches him. From this distance, nothing appears to be wrong; he's just covered in black soot of some kind, but judging from Rhys's temper, who the hell knows.

"About fucking time." Dagger approaches, snatching one of the bottles from my arms. I hold tight to the others, not wanting to drop them. He turns the cap and swigs from the bottle, not flinching though I know it has to burn going down his throat. Must have been a hell of a night.

"What happened?" I ask as we amble over to the bar.

I give the bottles to Buzz who nods and gets right to pouring shots. "Bomb exploded. Knocked us on our asses, but everyone's fine. Rhys is too big of a son of a bitch to stay down for long. Knocked him out cold though for a bit. Fucker's being a jackass not getting treated, but that's him." Dagger pulls from the bottle, the liquid swishing against the glass as he drinks.

"I take it ya didn't find Paine." The guys were going out to find that asshole while Buzz, Breaker, and I cleaned up the mess from Jace. Pops told us to hang behind and he would call if they needed us. Guess shit got rough.

"No. Fucking son of a bitch. Jace gave us an address. We went and it blew. I'd love to dig that fucker up and put a bullet in his head," he growls, gripping the bottle so tight his knuckles turn white, his expression contorting into one nobody wants to be on the opposing end of. I'm surprised he doesn't crush the fucking bottle or throw it across the room, but that would be a waste of perfectly good whiskey. Dagger's smarter than that.

"What do you need me to do?" I scan the room, taking it all in. Rhys is sitting up on the couch, wiping his face with a rag, some of the black coming off his skin. His anger radiates through the whole room like shockwaves seeming to set everyone off and put everyone on edge.

"See if Doc needs anything, after that, get us some food."

I nod, and head off to talk to Doc.

CHAPTER TWO
Blaze

I SLAM THE DOOR AND LOCK IT AS SOON AS TUG REMOVES his big ass boot then sag against it, my head hitting the hard wood with a thump. God, that man is gorgeous, like he should be modeling in some biker magazine for the world to see, gorgeous. His shoulder-length dark hair and smoldering chocolate eyes lure me in every time. Damn man. It's getting harder and harder to escape the fog that seems to envelop me each time he's around. He doesn't hide the fact at all that he wants me. A huge part of me wants to give in, wants to feel his hands on me, his soft lips kissing up and down my body in what I imagine is the most sexy thing ever. Unfortunately, I can't. I won't allow anyone to get close to me. Even if he wants a quick fuck, I can't. To me he's different. I don't know why, but inside somewhere deep is telling me so.

It's already hard enough that I've become friends with

Princess and Casey. I love them and would do anything for them. If I have to leave all of a sudden, it would kill me to split from them, but that is always a possibility for me. I've been lucky for the past four and a half years, staying low.

Princess helped me out huge when I showed up at X for the first time, without even knowing my name. I don't know how she did it, but one day I went into her office as Paige McMillion and the next came out at Taryn McKnight. That's who I pretend to be. Since dancing, my X name is Blaze and I go by it more than anything.

I actually like the name. At first, I didn't think it fit me at all. I was so damn scared to get up on that stage and show my body off to men. It felt like my old life was trying to creep into my new, having my body exposed for men's pleasure. I even threw up when I got off the stage, but I kept at it. I didn't have a choice. I didn't puke after that, but panic attacks set in at times. I made it through and now it's like second nature to me. I flash my tits at the very end of whatever song is playing and wear a thong to cover that part of myself. The men at X don't get all of me. No one gets all of me, but me.

At the same time, I realize that I'm on fire when I'm up there. I may not like it or get off on it at all, but when the music plays and the lights flash, I'm on top of my game. The money is what keeps me going, though. The tips have allowed me to have some security in this life as Taryn.

I stand and grab for my things, and slowly open the door. My shoulders sag; Tug is gone. I can't handle another run in with him tonight. Every night for the past week has been wrecking my defenses. Each time, I want to give in. If he keeps this up, I'm not sure my resistance will.

I motion for Cali to follow me. The air around me smells exactly like Tug, sending my hormones into hyper-drive. I've gotta get out of here.

As I walk through the brightly lit dressing room, the other girls glower at me from their seats along the mirror-lined walls. I couldn't give a shit less. I straighten my shoulders and stiffen my spine, not allowing anything they dish out to faze me. None of these women are my friends, and I wouldn't even consider one an acquaintance. I've gotten a reputation over time of being stand-offish and not wanting to be part of their clique. Truth is, I didn't want to deal with their shit, deal with their entanglements, or get close to anyone. Every woman here has some sort of problem they want help fixing and I've got enough of my own to deal with. I sure as hell am not the one to ask advice from—I can't even figure out my own life, let alone someone else's.

When Princess recently cleaned house, she got rid of some of the women who were the bane of my existence for a long time. They were caught with drugs, but their attitudes were what got me. The holier than though bullshit. They were always better no matter what. Me, I didn't care. I just wanted them to shut the hell up.

The new girls aren't any better with their cattiness, but I brought that on myself. My purpose was clear for doing it and I still stand by it. When *those* women were still at X, I requested my own dressing room, so I could lock the damn door and get away from them. I wasn't running, I just didn't think that beating the shit out of those women every night was healthy, for them or me. I may not want the entanglements, but I wouldn't let their words get too far and they were getting to that point. It's also why I didn't find out about the drugs until right before Princess did; I was never around them.

I may not like conflict and will avoid it as much as possible, but when pushed to my limit, I will fight back, hard. I didn't want that at my job or in my new life. When I requested my room, Princess needed a reason. The one I gave her was pretty lame. Just the fact that the men in the club wouldn't leave me alone and I needed privacy. She knew it was a load of shit. Men can't get into the dressing area because of the bouncers, but she gave it to me anyway and never asked about it again.

When I first showed up at X, I lied to her. Which I swiftly learned was something you didn't do to *the* Princess. At the time, I had no clue who she was, but followed my aunt's advice. When I left home, I went to my aunt. She told me to come here. I listened.

Princess knows so many people and I'm not sure how she did it, but she gave me a completely new identity.

She took one look at me and for some reason, decided to help me. I have never been questioned about it. She never asked of the past and I didn't offer the information. The less people that know, the better.

I've never actually thought about it until this second, but I'm sure Princess has searched. Shit. Wonder if she's ever pieced me together. If she has, she's never let on in the years I've been here. I never gave her my real name, but with her connections, who knows?

Coming to X has proven to be my saving grace and I am nothing but grateful.

The downfall of her helping me with the ID and then later the private dressing room is that her cautions are up with me. I see it in her eyes and actions, but she's never said a word and hasn't to this day.

The women here snicker, saying I'm a stuck up bitch or think I'm too good for them. The best was that I was fucking Princess and that's how I got my own room. It doesn't matter; this is for the best and soon enough I will be done with all of this. I need to find the right job and sadly, around here, there aren't too many to choose from that pay the kind of money I make here. It's not a bad job, if you overlook the fact that I take my clothes off for men that get woodys and jack off to me later, it's just not the one that I want as my career. Luckily, when Princess got me an ID, she also got me a Social Security number and birth certificate so I could get an honest job if I could find it. I majored in business and minored in accounting. One would think my range of jobs is large, but not here in Sumner and I really don't want to leave. I've thought about it, but never too hard.

I stride by the women and swing the door open, the night air hitting my skin like a cool caress. Cali, as usual, is right behind me as I reach my four-door Jeep. I love this damn thing, bought it all by myself, and the best part is that it's paid for thanks to X. I added KC lights to the top and extra rugged wheels; right now, they're for looks, but one day, I'm going out mudding. That's gotta be a hell of a lot of fun. I saw on it on a show once and the people seemed like they were having a blast. I haven't had fun in I can't remember how long and it's nice to dream.

"Thanks, Cali." This man took on a very boring job protecting me, but does it with no questions asked and I seriously like him. When I got the dressing room from Princess, she said that if I needed my own room then I'd need my own guard too. I didn't care one way or the other and I thought she was just trying to prove a point, but he's stayed with me. I really like having him around to escort me out to my car, if nothing else.

"You're welcome, Ms. Blaze. Safe driving." I lock the doors, not out of paranoia but out of safety—at least that's what I tell myself. There is that possibility of one of the men from the club coming out and starting shit, thinking that I'll have sex with them and even offering a shit load of money, but I don't roll that way. I may strip but I am not a prostitute. There were a few instances when I first started, all right several, but I handled them. Come to think of it, they are probably the reason Princess demanded Cali, whatever.

Out on the road, I roll my window down and the crisp air filters inside as the streetlights pass by in a blur. Tug. Built, rugged, tatted, and sexy man. My heart thumps in my throat. From the first time I laid eyes on him in the club, I knew he was going to be trouble for me. God, he's gorgeous. He is the total package. Bulging biceps covered in tats, sexy, brown hair that curls slightly at the ends where it brushes his shoulders, and chocolate-colored eyes outlined with a hint of green all called to me from that moment. It's no different even now.

When I came in to meet Princess for a job about four

years ago, the place was loaded with big, strong men all wearing leather vests. Each one had this aura of dominance, control and a bit of danger. Scary actually. They all had their own unique brand of hotness, which sent off loud warning bells. That kind of man reminded me of my old life and I had just left one bad situation. I sure as hell didn't need another. I made a vow then to keep to myself and stay away from them. Princess told me they actually owned the club and were part of the Ravage Motorcycle Club, whatever that meant, so I have been cordial, but that's as far as it got. I even talked to Princess about it and she said she'd deal with it. Whatever she did has worked, until Tug.

When he came along to prospect, which I found out meant he was in training to become a member of the club, I couldn't keep my eyes off of him. I'd glance down at him every so often while on stage, that in and of itself was a huge no-no for me, but I couldn't resist. I don't interact with customers and the fact he caught me excited and scared the shit out of me.

That first night I ever saw him, on my way out of X, I caught him fucking a girl named Cindy up against the building. Their moans filled the night air, his jeans around his ankles and Cindy bent over, her hands pressed onto the brick of the building, ass sticking out. They were fucking hard, both obviously enjoying themselves, yelling and grunting. My heart sank and I didn't stick around. I doubt he even saw me standing there or knew I saw him. Not that he would have cared one way or the other.

The sight of him in that situation actually helped me.

Every time that flutter came to my heart, I'd picture him fucking Cindy and my heart would deflate, which is what I wanted. There was no room in my life for him then and there is no room for him now.

I bought my three-bedroom, brick ranch house two years ago. I pull up to my sanctuary and instantly feel relieved. I've never had a stable place to call home. Growing up, my mom moved us from place to place because she couldn't afford the rent, and each spot we went to she tried to make a home, but it never felt like it. The place we ended up was definitely not home, but this place is totally mine. Paid for and the deed's in my name only. *Home*. It's not much but it's *my* stable place and that means the world to me. That's why tears spring to my eyes at the thought of ever leaving it. This small piece of property means the world to me, one that my mom could never give me.

I'm lucky enough to have a home that is surrounded by trees. The park is next to it, giving it a secluded feel, but I have neighbors down the block. This house used to be the caretaker of the park's home, but budget cuts made them sell it. Luckily, I had money saved up and was able buy it on the spot. It needed fixed up, badly. I watched internet videos to try to learn how to do some of it, but ended up hiring contractors. It was for the best.

I had a security system installed and added all the amenities that I wanted, including a jacuzzi tub in my bathroom which, unfortunately, is rarely used. I need to relax in it more. This home is my peace. It is my calm. It is mine.

After showering X off me and changing into my

comfy purple heart fluffy pajamas, I'm still wide awake from the night, pumped actually. Serious adrenaline rush. Some night I get them, while others I come home and just pass out. A movie is in order. Action, I need action and hot men. *Hmm... Fight Club* with sexy Brad... Oh yeah.

Throwing some popcorn in the microwave, I search the freezer for my rocky road ice cream, and find it lodged between two damn icebergs that have formed around it. I jimmy it out with a knife, working up a slight sweat. Guess it's been a long time since I've eaten it or opened the freezer at all. Taking a spoon from the drawer and yanking the top off the icy heaven, I rest my hip against the large kitchen island. I totally gutted and remodeled this space as well. When I first bought it, the avocado green appliances, orange tile and faded linoleum had to go. In their place, white cabinets line the walls along with sleek stainless steel appliances. Not that I cook much, but it's all there if I ever want to. Chucking the orange tile and replacing it with a light gray was a must. It made the space more open and brighter. I am not a fan of orange, except for Halloween and even then, it's stretching it.

The microwave dings, drawing me from my delicious creamy confection. I gather everything up and move to the living room, placing everything on the coffee table. This space is wide open and connected to the kitchen. The brown L-shaped couch and chairs are the most comfortable, pillowy things I've ever sat on and normally, I fall asleep in them within minutes. I indulged a bit and bought a huge TV that takes up most of one wall and is centered between two windows. I had the walls painted a light blue then added the same color to the pillows and throw blankets on the couch. I rub my feet over the soft plush carpet, loving it beneath my toes, and after a night of heels, it's heaven.

I flick through Netflix to find *Fight Club* and start the movie while shoving a piece of popcorn in my mouth. Yum, I love buttered popcorn. It was a great day when popcorn was invented. I settle on the couch, prop my feet up and pull the blanket over me, snuggling into the pillows.

As I lie staring at the screen watching Brad's muscles flex, my mind drifts to Tug and I close my eyes, envisioning him in Brad's place. His abs flexing with each throw he slams into his opponent, his biceps round and hard as he shuffles his feet around the man, ready to bring him down. The other guy throws a punch, but Tug easily fends him off, slamming his fist into the guy's face and sending blood splattering through the air.

My hand drifts down my body and under my fuzzy pajama bottoms straight to my sopping wet pussy where my finger swirls around my clit. My hips join in as the movement quickens. Heat invades me and my breathing becomes shallow.

With my eyes still closed, Tug lands punch after punch, sweat dripping off his face, and rippling down his defined muscles. Oh God.

The tension in my body curls up like a coil. My other hand grips the couch hard while my climax races through my body and everything in the world stops. Panting, I open my eyes and a pang of disappointment hits when the man of my fantasies is nowhere to be found.

Brad is on the screen in all his bloody glory beating the hell out of his opponent. Fuck. What is wrong with me? I rip my wet hand out of my pants and throw the blanket off of me. Either I need some serious damn help or to get laid, probably the latter.

X IS HOT, steamy, fiery smoking tonight. The full crowd means lots of tips and lots of horny drunk men and women. One would be surprised how many women come to check us out on any given night. Some come to get tips and tricks for their man at home. Some come with their man and I bet don't even make it to their car before they're screwing like animals. Some just come to watch for enjoyment.

I've already been on once tonight and I fully admit that the energy out there is electric and exciting. I even felt a little more sway in my hips and more sexy from the energy. Everyone out there is pumped, which can be good or bad and is why I stay in my room waiting for my next dance. Luckily, in this club, Princess wants the men to *crave* the women, as she calls it, therefore it's each of the dancers' choice to *work* the floor after dancing. Most women want to do this because the majority of private dances come this way, but some like me opt out. Cash is so good on stage that I don't need to. Yes, I'm that good. That's not me being cocky, I'm just judging by my bank account. Not to mention with the cocktail waitresses and the girls on the floor, it gets a bit much with this many people here. On top of that, I can't be in private with a guy I don't know. Some things I know I can't handle, and that is one of them.

I flip through the latest gossip magazine, reading stupid shit I don't care about. I mean, who cares if a woman is on her nineteenth kid? Seriously. Or that some woman is an internet craze for showing her ass, which I'm sure is photoshopped beyond recognition. A loud bang on the door rattles the walls and I jump. Tug? My room instantly goes up thirty degrees. I try to shake it off. No use in getting my hopes up. Dammit. I don't want that. I swear my body and brain are on two different playing fields and need to get their shit together.

"Yeah?" I set down the magazine.

"Blaze, open up," Princess says almost in a panic, which is not like her. Her even-keeled approach to business is why X is so successful. In hurried motions, I throw the lock on the door and open it wide, the blast of air rustling both Princess and my hair. Her face is panic-stricken, eyes wide and almost bugging out of her head. Her fists are balled up like she's itching for a fight and ready to punch, contradicting the panic. She barges in as I shut the door and lock it.

"Casey's gone," she blurts out as she turns to me. This time fear greets me and I don't like that from one of the strongest women I know.

"What are you talking about?" I haven't talked to Casey in a really long time. She went off to school and I just... shit, I should have called her.

Princess turns to the tall rectangular mirror, its bright round light bulbs illuminating the worry lines on her face. "Some asshole took her. The brothers are going to bring her home. They have Shaina, too."

My stomach plummets and I cross my arms around my body protectively. God, I'm going to throw up. Someone took her? "Why would they take her? Is she all right?" I sputter.

"Club business, but I'm pretty sure it was to get to my brother. Fuck!" she roars, turning to the wall and connecting her fist with a hard thud. Drywall dust scatters to the floor from the force. Her chest rises and falls in slow repetitions, anger emanates off her. The slight wetness in her eye catches my attention, though. What the hell? Seeing Princess mad isn't a new thing, but having her almost in tears along with it? It's just not right. It doesn't happen. It also proves this situation to be dire. Shit.

"Are they going to hurt her?" I whisper, trying to block out the memories I keep locked down deep inside but failing miserably. With each second that ticks by, they creep in one at a time.

Princess breathes in deep, gaining some semblance of calm. "I don't know." My attention jerks to her, thankful for the distraction from the memories but pained by her words.

My insides twist into knots as I recall a time when I had no power and felt helpless. I never want anyone to feel that way especially someone who I've come to love dearly. I try to clear my thoughts, as if by some stroke of luck, they could fall out of my ears and I'd never have to think about them again. Wishful thinking. "What can I do?" My voice is soft as I get closer to Princess.

"Watch over the club. I've got Doug, Jimmy, and Steve on the floor managing the crowd. I called in Travis and Rick to help. Ace is behind the bar. He can handle that. I need you to take care of the girls." Ever since Princess's assistant Liz turned out to be a homicidal maniac and tried to kill her and hurt Cooper, her son, she hasn't attempted to find a replacement. She's been handling everything on her own, and I'm not sure how she does it with a man and child, but she says she needs to trust the person fully and hasn't found them yet. I hope for her sake that she does soon because she is wearing thin and this doesn't help.

"Of course." I need to help in some way. Even if it's not helping Casey, it will give me something to focus on and take my mind off the situation. Hopefully, it'll keep my past at bay as well.

Princess paces around the room like a caged animal ready for a fight. Her hands clutch behind her back and I have no doubt the one she punched the wall with is hurting like a bitch. "DJ knows the lineup and Doug will come in and get the girls when it's their turn. I need you and Cali to make sure there's no shit going on."

"Where are you going?" I ask carefully.

She faces me, her eyes a mixture of anger, fear, and sadness. "I'm going to the club to wait for Casey. I want to be there when they bring her home."

"You think they will?" Since my mom died, I've had very little hope in happy endings. I lost everything when she was taken from me.

"Yes. In what shape, I don't know. But they will bring her home." The confidence in her voice is welcome and puts me slightly at ease. Slightly, because I have to deal with the women who I've given every reason to hate me, but that is nothing compared to the hell Casey is living right now.

"I'll take care of the girls. We'll be just fine."

Princess rubs the back of her neck with her hand, seeming lost in thought. Feeling the need to comfort her, I place my hand on her shoulder, knowing the love between her and Casey is real, blood or no blood. I only wish I had half of what they have with each other. True, I am a friend of both of them, but their bond is something that stories and Hallmark movies are made of. They include me and I'm grateful for that, but I'll always be on the outside looking in.

"Go ahead and go." I squeeze her arm softly, trying to transfer to her whatever strength I have.

She wraps her arms around me, surprising me. I stiffen but relax and reciprocate swiftly. If she needs the comfort, I'm more than happy to provide it for her.

"Be careful tonight. The crowd is rowdy and don't take any shit from the girls." She maneuvers me to an arm's distance. "I don't know what the hell is going on or who exactly has Casey, but keep your eyes and ears open at all times. You hear me?" Warmth fills me at her caring words. It's been a long time since someone gave a shit about me. "Come on." She strides to the door and I'm fast on her heels.

Her high-pitched whistle as soon as she steps over the threshold of my door has my ears ringing. I close my eyes, the sound echoing in the back of my head. When I open them, everyone in the room stops and their full attention is on the woman standing next to me.

"Listen up! Blaze is in charge." She points to me as if these girls don't know who I am and their eyes widen. This will for sure cause some rumors. "You need anything, you go to her. All you have to do tonight is get out on that stage and dance. No extra bullshit. No private dances until Rick and Travis show up." The girls groan at the money they could lose. "You'll be fine. It's for your safety. No shit tonight. Got it?" Princess stares down each one of the girls like a mother scolding her children and they nod in agreement.

"I'm serious as shit here girls. She tells you to fucking jump you'd better say how high." We've hung out enough that she knows I'm strong and won't let anyone trample over me. I won't take any shit. "I'm out." She turns and faces me, eyes serious. "I'll call you as soon as I hear something." I nod and she breezes past, leaving me in a room full of slack-jawed women.

I square my shoulders, hold my head high, and turn to the girls standing before me. "Everyone good?" A few snickers come across but no one talks and all eyes are on me. "All right. When I'm not dancing, I'll be dressed and monitoring the floor. No shit." I think about my bag and hope I brought clothes that I can change into to wear on the floor.

"Like you'll do anything about it." Luna, the blonde with huge tits and an obvious chip on her shoulder, grumbles under her breath. My eyes snap to her. This is the moment. I didn't think it would happen this fast, but it's here nonetheless. I need to show them I mean business. If I let it ride and don't squash this shit now, they'll never perceive me as someone they have to listen to. I'll be damned if Princess comes to work and there's a fucking shit storm because these women have a problem with me.

My heels clack on the hardwood floor as I stride closer to Luna, her face turned as she whispers in one of the other girl's ears. Stupid on her part, not paying attention to her surroundings. Not paying attention will cause her problems, like right this second. "Stand up!" I bark.

Luna sits at her makeup table, her back snapping at my words. Her eyes sweep up and down my body, sizing me up. Good. She reclines in her chair with utter defiance oozing off her. She thinks I'm not a threat. Whatever she saw wasn't what I thought she would, all right. Time to step it up.

"I said, get up. I *won't* repeat myself again," I clip hard, my tone leaving little room for her to ignore. Cali steps closer and I'll have none of that. This is not his battle. "Cali, back off." He retreats slightly, but my eyes stay locked with the blue ones in front of me that are screaming for me to smack the hell out of her.

"Nah. I'm comfortable here." She crosses her legs, her body still pretty relaxed. With her arms crossed against her chest and her feet not locked with the chair, I grimace. I'm not happy about what I have to do and luckily her chair is out far enough that it can be done.

I shrug, lift my foot, and kick the chair underneath of her hard. She falls to the floor with a thud as the chair flies behind her, crashing into the makeup station and scattering things. The women around her stand in shock, moving away from the flying items. Luna's gasp and wide eyes tell me that she is surprised by my actions. Good. I may appear small, but after years of strength training on the pole, my legs can pack a powerful punch. I refuse to give her a hand to get up. She can do that shit on her own.

"What the fuck?" she roars, shaking out of her shocked stupor. She rises, dusting off her thong-covered ass that is now dirty.

"Thanks for standing up."

Luna's face turns as red as the inside of a watermelon. Anger or Embarrassment. Who knows? My own anger creeps in and I silently count to ten and school my features. I stare her dead in the eye so she knows I'm serious as a heart attack. Tom Petty's song "Don't Back Down" pops in my head. Shit. Focus.

"Let's get something straight. *I'm* in charge. You don't like it, there's the damn door. Don't let it hit you in the ass on the way out. You don't like me, tough shit. Right now, I don't like you so much either, so we're even. You give me one ounce of shit, I'll do a hell of a lot more than kick a damn chair out from under you."

She interrupts me. What in the hell is wrong with this woman? Stupid. "Who in the fuck do you think you are, whore? You think just because you eat Princess's pussy it gives you the right to look down on all of us?" Even through her anger, a small smirk plays on her lips like she thinks that comment is going to affect me. The bitch has to know that Princess will flip her shit when she learns about this. She's either brave or incredibly stupid. I'm going with stupid.

I shake my head, ignoring the pussy comment. It's so not worth my energy. "See, right there is where you're wrong. I don't look down on you. I know you fuck men for cash among other things outside of here. I don't give a shit. I don't know you and you sure as shit don't know me."

"Luna, you're up," Doug yells from the doorway and she smirks, sashaying around me. No fucking way.

"No." I call out, not turning around but keeping my gaze on the other women in the room. "Do whoever is next in line. She doesn't dance until I say so." The room is so quiet all I can hear are the faint catcalls from the men and women on the main floor. That rarely happens with all the commotion back here. It probably has to do with the fact that the other women have their jaws hanging and can't yap them.

"Ms. Blaze. I know you're in charge, but Princess said to keep to the list." Doug's impatience pisses me off.

I turn around and actually let some serious anger come into play. I've kept it in check, but...

Luna's evil eye does nothing for me and the apprehension in Doug's expression makes me want to laugh but I don't. "Like you said, Doug, I'm in charge. Luna doesn't dance until further notice." I'm clipped and to the point, leaving no room for argument.

"You can't do that!" Luna wails and stomps her feet like a petulant two-year-old, her arms crossing over her chest. I seriously thought we were past the tantrum stage.

I ignore her and focus on Doug. "Who do you need?"

He removes a little card out of his pocket and stares at it. "Brandy, but give me a minute to let the DJ know the change. Be right back."

My eyes land on Luna and I clasp my hands behind my back. "You obviously have an issue with me and I don't care. If you want to dance tonight, get the stick out of your ass. You do as I say and keep your damn mouth shut. You open it again spewing your vomit, you're gone." I turn to the others behind us, not giving Luna a chance to respond. "Anyone else have anything to say?" Heads shake no as soft vocalized no's come out of their mouths. I turn and brush past Luna, but stop. "And don't think for one minute that if I kick your ass out, Princess won't fire you in a heartbeat." I wait a mere second, seeing if anyone is brave enough to take me on, and then jet to my room.

Once there, I find my bag and unzip it. Jackpot. I change into my worn boot cut jeans and a V-neck navy top, way more covered up than I normally am in this place, and I like it. I put my hair up in a messy bun and dig in my purse for my reading glasses. Not really a disguise, but it may help. Trial and error.

I can't help but be a tad bit nervous being on the floor. If one of the guys recognizes me, who knows what will happen. That's why I have Cali.

A soft knock comes and I open the door. Luna is standing there, looking at her shoes. "What do you need?" I ask, sweet as pie and not giving her an ounce of anger that she deserves.

"I need to dance. I need the money." She sighs loudly. "I'll keep my mouth shut and listen."

"I know you need the money. So do I. That's why we're both here. Keep your mouth in line and I'll let Doug put you on the next rotation." She nods and skirts away. I nudge Cali. "Let's go."

First problem solved.

SEVEN HOURS LATER, my feet are barking from the nonstop rotation in these killer heels. When I wasn't on the stage, I was circling, making sure everything went smooth. I had the occasional ass grab and those assholes were greeted with a raised brow from me along with a warning from Cali. He didn't like me being out there at all. His guard was so far up it would take him years to climb over it. I think he's more relieved this night is over than I am.

Luna got her stick out of her ass and straightened up, so I allowed her to dance. The rest of the girls were respectful and the only other problem we had was lost shoes, which were later recovered. All in all, considering the rowdy crowd, it was a great night and none of the customers put two and two together regarding me. Thank you alcohol.

I wave off Cali as I lock my Jeep doors and check my phone. I haven't had a chance to all damn night. It reads 3:37 a.m. and has voicemails, missed calls, and text messages. I scroll through, all from Princess.

. . .

PRINCESS: Brothers got Casey. They are bringing her to clubhouse.

PRINCESS: She's in bad shape.

PRINCESS: Shit Blaze.

MY STOMACH PLUMMETS as I think the worst. I've been there and if what happened to me has happened to her, I hope she's strong enough to get past it. I listen to the voicemails which are mostly Princess repeating herself, but the fear and uncertainty in her voice is desperately conveyed.

I chew my lip. I don't want to go home yet. I'm too revved from the night and worried about Casey. I put the Jeep in drive, pointing it straight for the clubhouse. I'm not sure what I can do, but if there is anything, I'll do it in a heartbeat. Even if it's just being there for Princess.

The night passes by in a cascade of streetlights. One good thing about it being this early in the morning, most people are still in bed and traffic is scarce. With each bright light that I pass, my mind wanders to what Casey might have gone through.

MY BEDROOM DOOR CREAKS OPEN. Oh God. I keep my eyes closed, hoping he thinks I'm sound asleep and won't wake me. Not that it's stopped him or his miserable son before, but anything at this point is worth a shot. A second pair of foot-steps follows behind the first and I pray this is not like before. It took a week last time to be able to pee without it burning.

I lie on my side and keep my breathing steady, giving no signs that I am awake even though I want to scream at the top of my lungs, not that anyone will hear. My mom is out with some of her friends tonight and the house is practically sound-proof. I could fight, but the last time I did he beat me so bad that I had to miss several days of school because of the marks, and with it being my senior year, I hate to miss. It's the one thing I'm actually good at. I told my mom that I got into a fight with another girl, but it was all a lie. One that if he said I didn't say, he'd end up killing my mom and after what he's done to me, I have no doubt he would.

"Aww... look at her, son. So sweet. I get first dibs." I cringe. Please, no.

"Damn, Dad, you got it first last time." As they talk as if this whole situation is a normal thing, bile rises from my stomach threatening to escape my lips, but I choke it down silently.

"Stop being an ungrateful little shit. I could withhold her from you all together. I'm not fucking her mother for the fun of it." That fucking piece of shit.

"Wake up," someone growls and the covers are torn off me, but I don't move. I lie there paralyzed. Please go away. Three harsh slaps to my hip and my eyes open wide from the pain. He flips me over, lying me flat down on the bed. I wish my clothing would deter them, but that's just a pipe dream.

"Get her clothes off." I press my legs together, not wanting trouble, but not wanting to give in either. "Open those thighs, bitch. You're fucking ours tonight." Something snaps and the

fight wins out. Even though I know the consequences, I can't play dead. I scurry from the bed yelling no, but it's too late. An arm comes around my waist, pushing me back onto the bed and a head punch has my world spinning.

"Shut your fucking mouth or I cut your mother's treatment off. Then she dies. Or I can kill her. Either way she dies. You want that on your conscience for the rest of your life?" From the grittiness in Santos's voice, I shake my answer, no. There isn't anything I wouldn't do to protect and help my mom. Even this.

A LOUD TAP on my window catches me off guard, snapping me out of my thoughts. I jump in my seat, turning to the sound, shock flowing through me. My breath catches at the handsome man staring at me, beer in one hand and eyes dancing with lustful humor. I realize quickly I'm in the clubhouse lot and have actually parked my Jeep. Shit, when did that happen? Rolling down the window, the quiet sounds of the night crickets chirping and a fire crackling form in the distance. Peaceful.

"You gonna get out of the car, sweet lips?"

I growl as Tug says those words, pretending the pet name pisses me off when in actuality I kind of like it. I'll never tell him that though, and the thing is, I think he likes me pissed. It's as if he gets off on it.

"Get out of the car, Blaze." He swings the door open wide. The indoor light flickers to life, cascading a glow around me. I blink a couple of times from the harsh change, also taking a second to put on my armor. When it comes to Tug, any extra strength I can get, I need.

I follow his bidding and step out of the Jeep. "I came to see how Casey is doing and if Princess needed me." Even with only the moonlight, his milk chocolate eyes suck me in and draw me to him in a way that scares the ever-loving shit out of me. I break from his gaze, needing a reprieve. How can one man pull me in so much with a damn look?

"Come over and let's talk, they're with their guys, hopefully sleeping." I shouldn't go. I should stand my ground. Truth is, I really don't want to be alone either. I nod and he leads me over to a set of white lawn chairs scattered around a big fire pit in the courtyard. This space is large and open, mostly grass and includes chairs and picnic tables scattered around haphazardly. Bikes are parked in the side lot. There is also a kids' play set that I'm sure belongs to Princess and Cruz's boy, Cooper. With no one around, it's eerily quiet, the only sounds coming from the flickering flames. I sit next to him, and his energy comes off loud and clear. It's a combination of frustration and anger. I don't like either.

"How are they?" I'm scared to know the answer to the question, but I need to know for my own sanity.

He sighs loudly and swigs the beer. Gripping the bottle between his hands, he rests his elbows on his knees and bows his head. "Casey and Shaina are in bad shape. We think that Shaina got the worst of it, but don't know too many specifics as Doc doped them both up so they could sleep and I haven't heard the final report. One thing's for sure, the fucker who took them won't hurt them again." With tight eyes and grim lips, danger is pouring off of him. A small slice of fear creeps in as I have yet to see this side of him.

"What can I do to help?" I focus on the fire instead of his features. Luckily, I get entranced in the flames turning from yellow to red to orange, going high then low. I love watching fire burn, not like a pyro or anything. It has always calmed me and right now, I need any and all distractions.

"Nothing right now. There isn't anything any of us can do." Helplessness draws in his voice. He and Casey have been close over this past year. Casey has repeatedly told me how easy he is to talk to and this whole situation has to be hard on him.

Instinctively, I reach over, placing my hand on his thigh and give it a gentle squeeze, hopefully letting him know that I'm here for him too if he needs me. The big problem with my hand touching his hot heat is it burns like it's getting scorched by some flame that isn't even there, shooting tingles up my arm and engulfing my body. His face turns to mine and the same fire burning my skin is blazing in his eyes. Shit. Shit. Shit.

I tug my hand away from his thigh, but he stops me and places his hand on top of mine. If I thought it was electric before, it was nothing compared to this. I'm pretty sure he caught the full body tremble that ensued, judging by the smirk playing on his lips.

"I should just go." I stand from the chair in a rapid movement and sever contact with him. I wipe my hands on my jeans, thinking I can rid the touch, the feel, but it doesn't happen.

"No." Tug sets his beer on the ground and stands next to me, so close I can smell the beer on his breath. I wonder what it would taste like on his lips. "Stay with me," he pleads, and damn my heart aches for him. The anguish is so raw. Even a tough guy like Tug isn't immune to it. "Just stay and talk to me." My heart clenches and I fear it will burst from my chest.

Talk. What the hell are we going to talk about? We have nothing in common, at least that I know of. He's involved with a motorcycle club, I strip. Not a lot of similarities there, but the pain and ache in his eyes crush me. If it will help him, I'll stay, even if the consequences could be difficult for me.

"All right," I breathe out, taking my seat. The flames of the fire dance and little pops coming here and there echo through the night sky. I could almost get lost in it.

"How's it going at X?" He breaks the comfortable silence, but I notice he asked me how it's going not how did I do tonight running the show. I'm sure with everything going on Princess didn't fill him in. I roll with it.

"All right. Princess cleaned house with some of the girls. That helped a lot. Those women were nothing but trouble." Trouble and a pain in the ass.

"Princess runs a pretty tight ship over there. What do you do when you're not at X?" He picks up his beer and sits fully back in the chair. His ankles cross and I realize just how long the man's legs are. Damn.

His question catches me off guard. For some reason I didn't think Tug was interested in me as a person. I figured I was a challenge, another notch to put on his overwhelmingly full bedpost. But he actually wants to know me? His sultry eyes beg me to talk to him, tell him about me. How can I not?

"Read mostly." He coughs as his beer bottle reaches his lips. I swear he's laughing at me and that pisses me right the hell off. I grip the plastic chair, wanting to scream at him but for some reason hold back. "What? Just because I'm a stripper, I don't read?" I bite out. There is nothing worse than assholes thinking that all we are is a body; of course, that is what we are to them, but still. I am so much more than that. He congratulated me on my degree last night, surely he didn't forget that already.

"It ain't that. I know you got a brain up there," he turns to me, "and I like that." My heart goes weak. Dammit.

He stays quiet like he's reading me or is inside my brain, going through the files of my life, before he speaks. "So what do you like to read?"

"Really. You want to know that?" I challenge, my curiosity piquing. What man gives a shit about this? Are there guys out there that care about this stuff? It would be nice if there were, but I'm sure he just wants in my pants.

"Really," he replies, and I think about my answer carefully because I sure as shit am not blurting out that I read books with sexy men riding motorcycles who have lots and lots of hot sex. Uh... no. That'd be like handing me over on a silver platter. Not happening.

"Romance books." Each one of my books has romance, a love story. Mostly love stories that have so much heartache you cry and so much sex you get hot and bothered. Perfect combination.

I watch with interest as his lips mold around the top

of the beer bottle. He smirks, catching me, and I retreat my gaze as my cheeks heat up, no doubt red. "Like those ones with that Flableo guy on them?"

I laugh and it's not a fake one like I muster for others, this one is true, genuine, and it's good to let out. It's been a long time since I've really done that. "His name is Fabio and no. A lot of what I read is written by indie authors." He stares at me, confusion written all over his face, so I drop it.

"They got lots of sex in 'em, like that book I see on TV they're making a movie about?" Amusement litters his words. His white plastic chair is so close to mine. With one little inch, I'd be touching him or he touching me. My pulse kicks up. What would it be like to feel it?

Another creep of heat comes to my cheeks, spreading throughout every cell of me, and I'm thankful that the darkness is hiding it. Not that I am nervous about sex or have issues with it, at least not anymore. I just can't put sex and Tug in the same thoughts. I fear it will have disastrous consequences.

The first guy I was with after leaving home thought I was totally crazy and he wasn't wrong. When his hand skated into my jeans, I screamed and jumped off the bed, moving far away from him. My world tilted and everything went blurry. I thought for sure I was going to pass out. Looking back, I'm surprised I even gave the guy a shot, but thankful I did. Even though I freaked, the guy, Ben, talked me through it. I never told him what had happened to me, but he helped ease my fears and eventually I was able to go all the way. It surprised me that sex wasn't meant to hurt. It wasn't meant to terrify. It wasn't meant to control. It was meant for pleasure, and it was the first orgasm I ever had. It ended up not working with Ben, but I am grateful to him because if he had freaked, screamed, called me names or anything negative, my view on sex would have been permanently marred. Thanks to him, it is not. I see the positive in it when it's done with care.

"Yeah, sex is normally in them." Since I get none in real life, what's better than to read about it?

"Hot damn!" He slaps his hand to his knee, and I jump at the loud noise penetrating the quiet of the night. "Wanna read to me? Only the fucking parts." I turn to him as he chuckles and wiggles his eyebrows at me suggestively.

It takes all I've got not to roll my eyes and tell him that there's no way in hell that will ever happen, but the sweetness of it is not lost to me. We sit in silence, but it's comfortable and I like it. It's like we don't have to say anything, we can just be and that's okay.

I take him in while he's staring into the fire. His black t-shirt caresses every muscle of his chest and arms while his leather Prospect vest hides the bulges, but not the tattoos. Mouthwatering. His body is relaxed, calm and at ease. Comfortable with me.

"So, sweet lips, when you gonna let me take you out?" His question breaks the silence and snaps me away from my ogling. I'm surprised it took him this long to ask or bring it up, but with him, I'm realizing he likes to be spontaneous.

"Never." I try to muster authority, but come on, this is Tug.

"Aww. Come on, babe. Don't lie to me and tell me that shit." I stare off into the distance. I get hit on all the time on stage, but tune it out. Those men just want the fantasy, the sexy woman on stage, never the real me and even if they wanted the real me, I'm pretty sure I wouldn't be able to give it. Not the way a man actually deserves anyway. Sex, I could give a man that, but never the real me; the one that is hiding so far down that I don't even know if she's in there sometimes. The one that holds the past, one that I really don't care to relive, ever, and that is not fair to Tug, or anyone.

"Tug, I don't date, but thanks." Those words have never been truer and I'm pretty sure they shock Tug because his mouth slightly opens and his brows lift to his hairline.

"You mean you don't date brothers or those of us associated with the club?" he clarifies and I want to laugh.

I peer into his milk chocolate depths. "That too, Tug, but I don't date. Period." The comfortable silence we shared earlier isn't so comfortable anymore and the weird feelings going on inside of me are turning to panic. I need out. Need to get away. I rise and the plastic chair tips a bit from the bumpy ground beneath me, but right myself in time before it and I tumble to the ground. "I've gotta go," I blurt a little louder than anticipated, sounding like an idiot.

"You mean to tell me that you don't date anyone. Ever? I call bullshit cause with a body like that, babe, it's screaming for a man."

My pussy quivers, sending shocks through my body. If

he only knew. He stands and enters my space. The energy between us is combustible, like zaps of lightning bouncing off of the two of us repeatedly with no end in sight. My knees weaken and it takes all I have not to wobble. My breathing picks up, my lungs suddenly having trouble getting air. I place my well-manicured hands in my pockets. With him so close, I have this undeniable urge to touch him, feel him. It doesn't help. I grip the fabric inside my pockets, trying to steady them. God, he turns me inside out.

I breathe in deep, drawing up the strength that has gotten me through these past few years. I square my shoulders and give him a sly grin. "Nothing my vibrator can't handle but you don't need to worry about that," I smart, coming off tons more confident than I actually feel.

Fire flashes, taking his milky chocolate depths to hot molten. My pussy does a full out quiver and dampness coats my underwear. Shit.

"Sweet lips, I'd be more than happy to help you out with that." His hand sweeps across my cheek and everything is lost. I forget that my guard is firmly in place. I forget that I'm not supposed to want him. I forget everything but him and lean into his hand, closing my eyes and enjoying the warmth of his rough touch, and damn it's better than I could have imagined. My heart squeezes and I let it. I let myself feel. A noise I don't recognize escapes me, but it doesn't distract from his warmth. "That purr you got going on, sweet lips, is the sexiest fucking sound I've ever heard."

I startle, his words breaking the moment. I mentally

shake and step out of his touch, his hand falling to his side. What in the hell am I doing? All my guards snap firmly into place like a lock clicking inside of me. I'm seriously pissed off at myself for that brief lapse because now I know the fire in his touch and I want more.

"I'm leaving." I extract my keys from my pocket but he plucks them from me before I get a good hold. "Give me my keys!" I bark as he holds them up in his hand, dangling them with a sly smile. Bastard.

"What, these?" He jiggles the keys in my face. He's playing with me, toying with me, taunting me. Damn him. "On one condition. Tomorrow after work, you have coffee with me." Coffee? Big bad biker man wants to have coffee with me, really? And at two in the morning? Umm... no.

"No, give me my keys." I hold out my hand, expecting my keys to plop in them, but it doesn't happen. He jingles them again. I'm learning quickly how stubborn this man can be and somewhere deep inside I freaking like it.

The wonderful sound of his deep chuckle causes my belly to clench, but I hold on to my irritated stance, barely. "No isn't an option. I'll be there when you get off. Be ready." His tone is controlled and firm, leaving no room for disagreement.

"I'm not fucking you," I blurt out. I guess my mind decided to take a break. A vacation is more like it, but it is the truth. I'm not. Won't. Even if I want to, it's not happening.

Tug steps closer and places the keys in my hand, his touch electric. His mouth is so close to mine I can practically taste the beer on his hot breath. I like it. My eyes grow heavy as the lust takes over. I so desperately want to kiss him. "I said nothing about fucking. I said coffee. Don't hide, cause I'll find you," he whispers softly and I have no doubt that he would.

Shivers prick throughout me, and by the intensity in his eyes, he means serious business. Shit. "I'm leaving." I need to get out of here. Need to breathe. I turn, but a strong hand seizes my arm, gently turning me back to face him. A small gasp leaves my lips at the closeness, his hard body pressed up against mine. His steel length pokes into my stomach and I barely hold back a groan. My breath hitches and I think he's going to kiss me, I so want him to kiss me. Instead, his succulent lips dance on my cheek, giving me a soft kiss. I close my eyes and allow myself to enjoy it. It'll be the closest I get to him.

He peels away and I instantly miss the heat of his body next to mine, but I'm lost. "Sweet lips, open your eyes." His words are so soft. His eyes are warm, soft, and I want nothing more than to melt in them again. "Tomorrow." I'm unable to talk. Words will not form in my mouth. Why won't my mouth move? All from a kiss on the cheek, damn I'm pitiful. With every bit of power I can muster, I step away from him as his hands drift from my body. I escape to the confines of my Jeep and take off, not looking back at the club.

CHAPTER THREE
Tug

BLAZE'S TAIL LIGHTS LEAVE THE LOT AND I FOLLOW THEM until I can't see her anymore. Fuck. The hard-on from being that close to her is pressing against my damn zipper painfully and I'll be lucky if there isn't an imprint of it there. She's had this effect on me since the first time I saw her. Then when she dances on the damn stage it's more like stone, hell she has that effect on me and every other man in Ravage and around Sumner. The difference is her reaction to me. Yes *me*. I saw it the first time we met. I saw it tonight.

And I'm fucking going to call her out on that shit.

When I amble into the clubhouse, the lights shine bright, but all is quiet. The brothers must be in their rooms or have gone home for the night. The only reason I stayed is in case I could help Casey, but I'm pretty sure nothing *I* could do would help her. But for some reason I needed to stay.

It's strange how only knowing these men and women for a little more than a year, I am closer to them than the "friends and family" I grew up with. But that's what Ravage is, *family*, and I'm more than fucking ready to be a full-time part of that. Have been for a while.

I lumber directly to the two sleeping club mommas on the couch. *Blonde or Brunette.* Doesn't matter, won't be thinking about her anyway. I only need a warm mouth. The blonde stirs at the sound of my approach. Bingo. Her eyes flutter open.

"Hi Tug. What cha need?" Her voice is too high-pitched and her mouth definitely needs something shoved inside of it.

"Open," is all I say, unzipping my pants to let my cock spring free. "Teeth." When my piercing clatters on their damn teeth, it makes them stop sucking. I fucking hate that shit. She scoots to the edge of the couch and opens her willing mouth wide as I press my dick into her heat.

Her hands snake up my legs and I still. "No hands, put them behind your back." I sure as shit don't want her touch me. She complies. I thrust in and out of her mouth as she sucks in earnest. One thing is for sure, the woman sure can suck. I close my eyes and picture the vivacious brunette swinging around the pole, eyeing me like she's going to eat me alive.

I grip the woman's hair and thrust my dick in and out of her until I explode, sending cum down her throat, and she swallows it down. The release is good, but nothing mind blowing, just something to scrape the edge off for a while. I open my eyes and stuff my dick in my pants. "Thanks."

Her eyes sparkle up at me, trying to be sultry, but it falls totally flat. She swipes her finger on the side of her mouth. "Anytime. You need more?" She bats her big brown eyes up at me and my dick doesn't stir. If it hadn't been for Blaze a few minutes ago, I wouldn't have been up and ready.

"I'm good. Thanks." I turn to the bar, nab a beer, and sit on the round stool. The coldness from the bottle seeps into my hand as I stare at the wall behind the bar. Lights, bottles, and glasses line it. Nothing spectacular, but it's comforting.

When I first got out of the Army, I had a rough time adjusting to life outside of the military. They try to prepare you but those are just words. Living out in the civilian world is foreign after you've been where I've been. After being in hell. I initially went home to my mother and sister. *Home.* But it wasn't home anymore. Granted the home-cooked meals were a perk after living on MREs. But I couldn't stay there, not when five and a half years prior, everything in my world changed in that house and the two women there still couldn't get past it.

"Calm down, Jimmy." My mother's terrified pleas come from her room as I stand in the hallway. Not a-fucking-gain. I clench my fists, my knuckles turning white.

"Shut the fuck up, bitch. This is all your fault." My father growls and the sound of flesh hitting flesh along with my mother's yelps come through the closed bedroom door loud and

clear. This isn't the first time that I've tore my father off of my mother and I'm sure it won't be the last. Since I was fifteen and Dad lost his job, he's been pissed at the world and blames it all on my mother. The booze doesn't help either. I don't know why she stays, but she does.

In two months, I'll be eighteen and I'm getting my mom, sister, and myself out of this hell hole and away from him. I'll do whatever it fucking takes. I've saved up enough cash to get us an okay apartment for a few months and if I continue to deliver pizzas and Mom gets another waitress job, we should be good.

Opening the door, I find my mother is curled in the far corner of the room, arms up in an effort to protect herself from the blows. She's terrified and breathing heavy. My father's pudgy ass head snaps to the door and he snarls, "Get the fuck out of here, Andrew." His eyes stay on me; he's not a stupid man. I'm getting better at taking him on.

"Get out of here now!" I demand. My veins throb in my neck and my body shakes with undiluted anger. Tears stream down my mother's face, along with red marks marring her beautiful skin. My anger turns to an inferno.

My father chuckles and steps in front of my mother, crossing his arms over his chest, blocking my view of her. "What the fuck are you gonna do? Huh? Lock me out of the room again. Stupid fucking punk." The last time this happened, I did exactly that and was utterly grateful that I didn't have to beat on him, because I didn't know if I'd have the willpower to stop.

"Get out." I try my damnedest to allow my anger to show through in my words and hope that he just leaves. Even though I'm pissed as shit, it's hard to stand up to the only man *you've had as a role model. Even a shitty one like him, but I do it.*

"Fuck off." Dad charges at me and I step to the side, evading him by moving my body swiftly. The second time he lunges, my fist connects with his jaw in a biting crunch of bone on bone. I pay no attention to the jolt it gives me up my arm. I shake it off, but his foot meets my ribs before I see it and the pain is intense. I don't back down. With my hands in front of me, I block shot after shot, getting in a few good licks to my father's face. He's not backing down this time either.

His blow meets my temple hard and the lights flicker as I stagger, trying to get my bearings. Dad kicks me and I stumble to the floor next to Mom with a grunt. I shake myself, trying to get the fuzziness out as Dad yells.

"You think you can fucking take me, you stupid ass?" Spit escapes his lips as he speaks. "I rule this fucking house! You, your bitch of a mother and stupid ass sister will follow what I say!" The dizziness fades and I know he's right. He won't stop because he doesn't have to. I will not let this happen anymore. I'm done. Smirking, Dad backs toward the door. My eyes grow wide at the sight of my sister's frightened face behind him.

"Mom!" she yells and starts running into the room. My father yanks her by the hair hard enough that she cries. A lamp sits on the nightstand and I clutch it, the adrenaline fueling my body. Standing, I allow the anger to boil over and no words leave my mouth as I swing the heavy solid lamp into his skull.

"TUG!" I jump to my feet, turning around hastily, my hands in fists as I search the room and blink through the invading memories. My pulse races and my vision clears from the fog of the memory. Princess holds her hands up in front of me, her brows furrowed together in obvious concern. "You all right there, buddy?"

I give myself a mental shake, the balled up tension leaves my body as I blow out a small breath, releasing the death grip my fingers formed. "I'm good." She nods and slides up to the barstool, reaching around to grab a bottle of Jack and a glass from the side bar. I sit next to her and draw a hard pull from my beer. Shit, I didn't mean to snap like that at her. Damn memories.

"Wanna talk about it?" she asks, pouring the amber liquid into her glass and I sure as shit don't want to breathe a word of that shit.

"Nope." I take another drink from the beer, draining it. Some shit is better left alone. "How's Casey?" I change the subject.

Princess downs the shot, not even flinching at the burn, only the small tick of her eye gives away that she took it and felt it. "A fucking mess. I hear her screaming through the door, but GT's in with her so I'm trying to stay back. Shaina is worse. Thank God Doc left some meds to knock her all the way out." She pours another, tosses it down her throat, and slams the glass on the top of the bar when it's empty. "That son of a bitch fucking tore her up. She needed fucking stitches."

I grip the bottle in my hand until my knuckles turn white. I didn't realize it was that bad. "That bad?" Maybe I didn't want to learn the extent of the injuries Shaina has.

"Oh yeah. Had to sew her up. Guess Paine liked a bit of pain in his conquests." Princess twirls the glass in her hand, spinning it on the bar, the clink echoing through the clubhouse.

"Too bad he's dead. I'd love to string him up and show him what pain is," I growl the words, sure and focused. Any man that preys on women is a fucking piece of shit. I'd make sure his torture was the most painful it could be, for hours, even days. Son of a bitch.

"Yeah. Shaina's not like us," Princess almost whispers. "She's not built to handle this kind of thing. This life. I'm not sure how she'll do."

Being raped and tortured would fuck up any woman for the rest of her life, and being in a club or not wouldn't change that. Either way, there isn't a damn thing I, or really anyone, can do about it. "I'm sure you'll help her through."

Her silent confirmation hangs in the air around us. "Why you still here?" She shoots another drink then screws the lid on the bottle.

I shrug. "Thought I could help Casey, but that's doubtful."

"You're a good friend to her. Thanks for that."

Her words take me back a bit. "Why you thanking me?"

She blows out a ragged breath. "I wasn't here for her and I'm just glad you were. The friendship you two built while I was locked up, I'm pretty positive kept her sane."

"She didn't tell me anything about Mia, if that's what you mean." I reach over for another beer. I'm not sure Princess is thinking clearly because all I did with Casey was listen. I'm not sure I helped much at all.

"Don't mean that. She told me about your talks, she

needed that." Her eyes meet mine. "You're a good guy, Tug."

I scoff. "Good guy," I mutter under my breath and then drink. That's one phrase I wouldn't use to describe myself. Long minutes pass and we sit in comfortable silence. The term good guy didn't even apply to me in the service. Taking guys out repeatedly never felt good. It was necessity. It is a necessity. But I never felt good about it. Just like I never felt good about... my mind drifts off, but the clicking of buttons dissipates my thoughts. Princess on her phone.

"Did Blaze come by?" The mere mention of her name has my full attention, not that I let it show.

"Yeah. For a bit, just checking in on things." I twirl the bottle with my fingers, little beads of water slide down the glass. Blaze's face is burned into my mind.

"I put her in charge of X tonight. She say anything?"

"Nope, not a word. Just that you got rid of some of the girls and made her life easier. But nothing about tonight." Which seems odd. Surely she's not so nervous around me that she can't talk to me? I did only ask her how X was, I wasn't specific.

"Shit. I hope everything went okay. Those women can be bitches, but I'm sure Blaze handled it." She nudges my arm. "It was kind of a test. I needed her to be in charge of X. Tonight threw that chance at me. I've been wanting to do it for a while."

"What kind of test?" The snideness in the way I said test has Princess smirking. Call it protectiveness or any damn thing you want, but testing her doesn't fucking sit well with me.

"Need to determine if she can handle the women. I know she can, but she stays cooped up in that damn dressing room of hers all the time. I need to know she can take care of the business. Hands on."

"Why, you handing it over?"

"Fuck no." She snorts. "I need help. I can't do this shit all by myself anymore. I got a man, a kid, and a club to take care of. I need someone I can trust. Someone smart. Someone loyal. And after that fuckwit Liz, I have to be in deep with the person I hire. The fact that she graduated and is smart as shit with numbers is another bonus."

"Better hook her before someone else offers her something."

"Gotta see how tonight went. If it went as expected, I'll take it to Pops." She pauses. "Your time's about up prospecting?"

"Yep." I know better than to discuss club business with anyone other than members, even ol' ladies.

"Smart man." She pats me on the shoulder and rises. "I'm gonna go get some sleep. Cruz and Cooper both snore like hell." No matter what words come out of her mouth, she wouldn't change it for anything. She loves those two.

"Night." I trudge outside, the fire slowly dwindling with only a few embers still lit. I lie on the picnic table, even though the harsh wood could splinter my back. As I stare up at the stars, the peaceful night calms me. I've always loved being outside at night when everyone is asleep and nothing seems to exist besides the crickets. It seems to take everything wrong in the world and still it, right it, if only temporarily. I calm and I drift off.

THE SCRAPE OF WOOD, the ting of metal, the flick of a lighter... all these indicators mix together as I try to open my eyes, but the bright light makes it difficult. Shit.

Pop... Pop... Pop... Pop....Pop... Loud noises, like gunshots ring in my ears. What the fuck?

I immediately go on alert, calming my breathing, and jump up with my gun aimed in the direction of the noise. I squint, trying to adjust to the sunlight as more pops go off. My entire body is on high alert, moving left and right, trying to find the damn shooter, but when my eyes focus, they land on my brothers roaring hysterically to the point of bending over and tears escaping their eyes. Motherfuckers.

I breathe in deep and put the gun back in my waistband, rubbing my hands over my eyes.

"Wake up, sleeping beauty," Dagger calls from the corner, his voice filled with laughter as my brothers surround me, giving me pats on the shoulder.

There is a pot on the picnic table with red papers and singed wicks from several firecrackers. My body calms. "Ha, very funny"

"We thought so." Rhys crosses his arms over his chest, feet apart like the badass he is, but there is a crinkle in his eye.

"Damn right, we needed a good laugh," Cruz says from the other side of Dagger.

"How're the girls?" The faces on the men change,

hatred, anger and death start to pulsate off of them in droves. Anyone else would have probably cowered from asking, but I refuse.

Pops steps forward. "Let's have a seat." I help Dagger drag over another table and we butt it up to the first, all of us taking a seat while Pops sits in a white plastic chair at the head of the table. Everyone's here except for GT, which is to be expected. I must have been really out of it to not hear Buzz and Breaker's bikes come in. I rub my hand over my face, pressing my thumbs in my eyes and adjusting to the sunlight. I need my fucking sunglasses. I pat my rag. Nothing. Shit.

"GT will be with Angel the next few days. You need him for anything, come through me first." Everyone nods. "Dagger, Buzz, and Breaker go over and make sure everything is clean." Pops is referring to the house that blew up and the reason Rhys got knocked on his ass.

"You got it," Dagger says with Buzz and Breaker nodding in agreement.

"Becs, Cruz, and Tug go meet up with good old Randell." Randell is one of the very few informants we have on the Sumner Police Department, and from what I heard the last visit to him didn't end up so well. He had to take a leave of absence for a while. A broken leg will do that for a beat cop. "Any information on this explosion he's got, I want it. No blowback."

We wait for Pops to continue, but he is obviously done. "Go!" he commands and we scatter. Pops' fuse with all this shit is very short. Pissing him off is not in the cards for any of us.

"Give me ten and let's roll." Becs pats me and eyes Cruz who gives him a chin jerk instead of words.

"Gotta piss and I'm ready," I grunt, the damn man better have some information.

"I DON'T KNOW NOTHING," The officer in plain street clothes mumbles. My fists are gripping his shirt at his chest, his feet still on the ground. The man's body is stiff, as if that would intimidate me. Not.

"Randell, somewhere along the line here, you stopped the information track. You have gambling debts, we pay them, you give us information. That's how this deal works. I talked to Cassius." At Becs' words, Randell's eyes widen, disbelief crossing them. Cassius is a bookie that Randell turned to when he needed cash. "Yeah, motherfucker. You've racked up over thirteen grand. How are you gonna pay for that?"

"I'll pay it back." I release the shithead and throw him to Cruz who wraps his arm around his neck from behind. The living room we are in has thin walls that are covered in a dark paneling and the carpet has track marks in it from the wear of many sets of footsteps over the years. The entire room is dusty and in serious need of someone to pick up the litter of pizza boxes spread around the place. Pictures line the walls of a woman and a few kids, but there is no way those people live in this house the way it is.

"Wife leave ya, Randell?" I ask as he whips to me.

"I don't got shit left." He's visibly pained to say those words, but it also proves he has nothing left to lose. This could go either way at this point. Good or bad. But it does give him a reason for dropping off the grid and not being a rat and giving us to the higher ups. Cruz tosses the man into a recliner and it rocks back and forth from the force.

"Yeah. Whatever. Information. We want it about the building on Waters that burned down. We want all information on it by three o'clock," Becs says, lighting a cigarette and sucking in a drag from it.

"And if I have to come back I sure as fuck will get some shots in on your ass," Cruz warns.

Randell looks up at Becs from his chair. "You gonna pay the debt off?"

"Five, if the information comes back right. If it doesn't, I'll put a bullet in ya and save my money," Becs replies.

Randell is a tricky one to read. His eyes show of desperation but his body shows of giving up, like all the fight's left him. Maybe he needs some more motivation. "You see your kids?"

His eyes dart to me as I stand stoic. "No, she won't let me."

Becs nods in agreement. "We'll try and help you out there." A small spark of hope enters his eyes, but it's short. He nods. I can't do shit about his kids, but Ravage just needs his information and I'll say whatever to get it.

Becs kicks the chair, giving Randell a jolt. "I'm calling at three." Cruz tosses Randell a burner phone that he catches. "Have the information." Becs lifts his chin to me and Cruz. We move.

I place my sunglasses over my eyes, blocking out the glare of the sun after shutting the door with a click. "Gonna do it?"

Becs strolls to his bike, me and Cruz on his heels following. "We'll see. If not, we put the bastard out of his misery."

"LADIES AND GENTLEMAN... Give it up for *Blaze!*" The announcer's long, drawn-out version of Blaze's name does nothing but rev up an already ignited crowd. The guys and I just got here in time for her last performance and I'm assuming since Princess is at the clubhouse, Blaze is in charge again tonight. Up on the stage, a light shines directly over her from behind, pointing out to the crowd and giving us a tantalizing view of every curve of her body.

As the lights flash, my mouth drops. Tight black leather surrounds her body, her beautiful tits held up by a vest similar to a rag. The buttons down the front are connected with stones that sparkle, amplifying those beauties. The small little shorts below crisscross over her hips, her legs appearing longer than normal. Damn.

The music blasts and her hips sway to the sound, rolling in seduction. Those killer heels on her feet define each muscle in her very toned legs. Her signature smile is in place, but behind her eyes is a void. She's not enjoying this, not one bit. She's trying to mask it for the crowd and doing a damn good job, but I've been seen the real thing.

And damn if I don't want to dig inside that brain of hers and find out more about her, not her physical appearance, she's already got that shit down pat, but her. What makes her tick? Fuck me. I must be losing my shit.

Her body sways on its own accord, never missing a beat. Her legs hug the pole as she slides down slowly, and then she thrusts up and down once her feet hit the floor. She unbuttons the vest one tedious button at a time, giving the crowd a slight peek. Her eyes meet mine and a small wink comes my way. My dick throbs and pinches inside my jeans. I adjust myself as the leather falls from her body, her voluptuous breasts on display. Fuck.

All too soon, the lights disappear and all I can think is I have a date with that tonight. It is good to be me. I rise, giving Buzz and Breaker a grin.

"You're really hitting that tonight? I mean, really seeing her, not this going to talk to her bullshit?" The skepticism in Breaker's voice pisses me off. It's like he thinks I couldn't get something that is considered unattainable.

"I fucking told you I was," I bite.

He holds his hand out in a calming gesture. "Easy there, brother. No need to get your panties in a bunch."

"Back off, Breaker," Buzz chastises, but has a smirk grazing his face. He says no more about it. "Eight a.m., clubhouse."

"Got it." Like I could forget. Pops called church, not that we'll be sitting in on it, but it's mandatory that we are in the clubhouse during the meeting. I do know what will be discussed, though. Randell said the fire was deemed accidental. Some pipe in the basement broke giving off gas and when the water heater kicked on, it blew. I think it's a bunch of shit and the guys do too.

I nod at the guys and blow through the crowd that parts like the Dead Sea as people catch me coming.

I wander past the red velvet curtain and Doug stands guard. "Doug." I wait for him try to stop me. I'm pretty sure he got smarter from the last time though, at least I hope.

This time his eyes do not waver and he steps aside, allowing my entrance. "Tug." I smirk, at least he can learn that's more than I can say for some people and cross straight to Blaze's door ignoring the women in the room, but they watch me. I nod at Cali which he reciprocates and knock on the door.

"Be done in a minute, Cali. I gotta do another sweep and then Doug said he'd stay and lock up." I stay quiet and listen for movement inside the room. It sounds like a damn tornado breezing through it. If I had feelings that could get hurt, I may think that she's trying to escape me. Surely she knows better than that. I place my hands in the front of my jean pockets, waiting. "Then I gotta get out, Cali. The girls are all square and there's only two more up, probably one now that I'm dressing," her voice rings out.

Her rambles are pretty fucking cute. The door whooshes open, but Blaze is too busy with her belt and doesn't realize I'm here. Her soft body collides with mine. I grip her hips and her eyes swing to mine, shock registering in a flash. "Tug," she says so soft only I can hear her. She tries to school her facial expressions, but it's too late.

"Hey, sweet lips. Ready to go out?" She steps out of my grasp, finishing with her belt. The button-up white shirt she has on is rolled at the arms and tucked into her jeans, which fit her like a fucking glove. The tears in them are strategically placed, giving a hint of skin in all the right places. Fuck yeah. She has the sexy business woman thing down pat, she may want to include that in her act. A low growl resonates in my throat at anyone learning this of her but me.

"I have a job to do, Tug. Maybe some other time." She focuses on Cali, obviously trying to dismiss me and scurry away as fast as possible. Inside I want to chuckle. She has no idea. "You ready?" she asks Cali.

"Whatever you need, Ms. Blaze." Cali pushes off the wall and Blaze tries to sidestep me, but she doesn't get far as my body blocks her.

"I'll wait." Her body tightens, shoulders rise and her luscious tits puff out. Damn that's a great view.

She breathes in deep, whether to control her anger or the fact that she's turned on I'm not sure which, but I can tell her body is aching. Her nipples are at peaks through the thin white cloth and her breathing has increased. She probably doesn't even know it's happening. Or she totally does and is avoiding me like the plague. Not going to happen.

"Tug, seriously. I don't know why you're doing this." She shakes her head, the wheels inside her brain turn so fast I'm surprised steam doesn't roll out of her ears. I wish I knew what is consuming her. "I work for the club and I'm not a momma. Anyone here will be happy to fuck you and send you on your merry way. It's not me, Tug."

"Did I say I was fucking you?" I place my hand on her soft cheek. Her whole body quivers beneath my finger-tips, calling her a liar. I don't let her answer as I continue, "No. I said coffee, maybe food. I want to know more about what's up here." I remove my hand and point to her temple, tapping it two times.

She scoffs. "Right Tug. You just want to fuck me, add me to your list of conquests, and be on your way to the next. I know men and your type." I won't lie and say I don't want to be between those thighs, because that is where I will be soon, but I want to know more about how she knows my type. I will know. The emptiness in her eyes is compelling me to find out. Better just to ignore her comment.

"Go do your thing and hurry up." The evil glare she gives me only sparks my fire more. My hand reaches to the small of her back, smashing her up against my body, and air leaves her lungs in a whoosh. Her hands snake to my pecs, trying to push, but I don't give an inch. Her body is strung so damn tight. I can think of several ways to loosen her up lips, tongue, hands...

I lean in close to her ear as she tenses and whisper softly. "Baby, you smell so fucking good." A mix of sweat and something floral turning my overriding libido up higher. "Tonight, we have coffee. Sit and talk. You find out I'm not such a bad guy and we go from there." I can't resist. My teeth nip her earlobe and she jumps away from me, eyes wide.

It takes her a few seconds to find her words and I love the fucking fact that I did that shit to her. "Coffee, then I'm going home. Alone," she concedes.

Keep telling yourself that. I swear those words are more of a reminder for her than a warning for me. But, I'm in this shit and I don't back down. Won't. Really I can't. Not now.

I step out of the way, nodding to Cali who follows behind her.

CHAPTER FOUR
Blaze

STUPID MOTHER FUCKING PIECE OF MONKEY ASS SHIT. I growl, pacing the floor of X with Cali on my heels muttering about the stubborn man in my dressing room. I should call him a worm since he's worming his way into my life and damn if I don't give in. I'm angrier at myself than anything, but being angry at him is easier, so I'm going with that. I can't help but be pissed at the Neanderthal who thinks he can dictate what I'm doing and when I'm doing it. And the problem is, I'm freaking letting him just like I let what happened to me all those years ago happen. I can't do this. I won't do this again. I clear my mind and focus on the task on hand.

My scowl must be turning people off and luckily with my hair secured in a bun and my change of clothes, I don't get many long stares. Shit, I almost forgot. I drag my reading glasses out of my pocket, placing them on, anything to help disguise myself. The good thing is most of these guys are pretty damn drunk. That helps too. They recognize me with my clothes off the fantasy, not fully dressed. Kind of a blessing.

I go through all my rounds in the club, allowing my anger time to calm down. Truth is, I want to go with him, but I know I shouldn't. Wanting and having are two entirely different things. Entering the dressing room, relief washes over me. No Tug. I breathe not realizing I was holding it. I'm not scared of him, for some reason I know he'd never hurt me, never force me to do anything I didn't want, but it's him. The overall him, Tug. Even at sight and I'm a huge ball of knots. I can't afford to let my guard down. I can't afford to let anyone too far in and he definitely wants it.

No one can know my real name. No one can know the things I did to survive. No one can know the hell I lived through. No one. I escaped it and it's behind me. I moved on.

I open the door, my eyes darting around the room, and my breath catches. Sprawled out on the couch, his head resting on one arm and his feet propped up on the other is none other than Tug, with fire burning behind his eyes and directed at me. His arms are linked behind him like he is in the most comfortable place in the world. "Make yourself at home." Sarcasm drips from my words as I wave my hand at him. But I admit he looks hot, so damn hot. *Shit*.

"Don't mind if I do." His boots hit the floor with a thump as he sits up. "You ready?"

His body sucks me in. From his jeans that seem made

solely for him, molded against every muscle, to his black biker boots, black t-shirt, and his leather. Yum. I break my gaze from him and skitter around the room, putting my things in a bag. Get it together. "Just a minute," I weakly grumble. Why does one man have to look so damn good? Boot steps come my way and his hard body presses against my back, his steely erection into the curve of my ass. He clasps my arms, halting my movements and my body stills.

Everything flares to life in a way I have never felt before from one touch. An invisible shroud falls upon us and my whole world is him. The sexual tension is so thick a chainsaw couldn't cut through it. He leans down next to my ear and whispers, "Hurry," and steps away. That bastard turns me on and then leaves. I slam my purse inside the bag and turn to him. Why am I letting him get to me this way? *Because you want him.* Shut up!

"Let's go and get this over with." I glare at him, partially from arousal and partially from anger.

He chuckles, his eyes sparkling with enjoyment. "Don't sound so excited." My freeze out obviously had no effect on him whatsoever. I swear, he even thinks it's cute. Damn, man.

"I'm driving myself." He doesn't respond, surprising me with his agreement and I huff. Wait. I stop close to the door. "Where am I going?"

"Right up the road to Sam's." His voice is directly behind me, any closer he'd be against my ear. How the hell is he so fast and quiet? Like he appeared out of thin air.

"Fine." Why I'm acting this way, I really don't know. I

shouldn't be and even that is starting to piss me off. My mom would be utterly disappointed in me, but she hasn't been living this life for the past few years, running and trying to hide. If I let him in and have to leave, it will kill me.

After Cali leads the way outside, I jump in my Jeep, not glancing back at Tug but the heat from his stare is palpable against my skin. Saying goodbye to Cali, I drive to the diner, which is a short distance from X so I don't have much time to think. Good. The rumble of his bike never left my ears all the way here and when the engine stops I turn. He removes his helmet and places it on the handlebars. He runs his gloved hands over his thick brown hair as he throws his leg over the bike and takes off his clear riding glasses. Every hormone in my body decides to come to this party, leaving me almost out of breath before I can even get out of the Jeep. I swear to God there should be a warning label on him: *stand back will cause ovaries, pussies, and panties to spontaneously combust.* He is that good.

His full out smile is an immediate trigger for my stomach to clench. His teeth aren't perfectly straight with his side tooth having a slight angle to it, but damn near close. He stalks over to my Jeep, movement fluid as if he's on a mission, and opens the door swiftly.

"Sweet lips, why am I always getting you out of cars?" His joking tone should set me at ease, but instead it shocks me with nerves. I don't want to like him. I don't want him to joke with me and be a gentleman. It's much easier if he is a figment of my imagination. A guy I imagine in the audience that is with me but really isn't.

But I think that time in my life is up. The imagination is becoming reality and damn if that doesn't scare the shit out of me. Get a grip, woman.

I break away from his intensity and hop out of the Jeep. "Maybe you should give up," I whisper, passing him but saying it loud enough that he can hear me.

His hand clasps around my arm and he brings me to a halt, whispering in my ear, "That's not the kind of man I am." Shivers ripple intensely down my spine. My pussy screams *show me, please.*

He loosens his grasp and leads me into the diner with his hand on the small of my back, burning me with his touch. I step and try to shrug from his hold, but he doesn't allow it and never severs contact with me.

Tug reaches around and opens the door in a chivalrous gesture that I'm not sure how to read. Most men I've been around, which really aren't many away from X, wouldn't give a care in the world about doing something like that. The simple gesture warms my heart as I step through the threshold and into the twenty-four-hour diner.

The wide open space is filled with booths that line the full-length-window-covered walls in front and tables that surround a half moon shaped counter. The chairs and benches are covered in black vinyl with chrome accents. Behind that is the cook's area with workers hustling and bustling around even though there are very few people here. The smell of bacon emanates from the griddle and my stomach rumbles.

A waitress with light brown hair in the tightest ponytail that I am sure is giving her a hell of a headache and soft eyes focuses on us. "Have a seat wherever. I'll be with ya'll in a minute." I love the sound of her southern twang. It's one thing coming from Colorado to Georgia that I love is hearing the accents in their voices. Tug's accent is there, but more subtle than others from here.

"Come on." Tug guides me to the far corner booth, leaving no room for me to choose any other seat but the one he wants. I'm a mix of frustration and turned on by the control he has, that I'm allowing him to have.

I choose the far booth seat so my eyes can focus on the room in front of me. I hate having my back to people. You never know who could sneak up on you. Tug captures my arm gently. "What?" His chocolate eyes smile at me.

"I need to be there." He points to the booth I was going to enter. "Gotta keep my eye on things." I allow his words to sink in. How long has it been since I allowed anyone else to *keep an eye* on things for me? I always have done it. He doesn't not know the struggle I'm having in letting him do this and I won't let him know. But this is rough. I inhale a deep breath. This isn't a bad thing. It's doable. I slide in, sitting cockeyed so I can see the door and everyone else in the place, but at a weird angle.

Tug's large frame slides into the booth, his rough hands clasped together on the white tabletop. I notice the ring on his thumb, a simple silver band holding a large skull that covers part of his knuckle. The skull has red stones for eyes and is pretty fierce.

"Didn't know you'd give me trouble just sitting down in the booth. You sure you're not part hellcat?" I didn't think he saw my trepidation, but no matter what my inner thoughts were, giving him the upper hand isn't in the cards.

"I just like to keep an eye on things. I guess like you." My stomach takes that moment to growl. I grab the menu, putting my focus on it and allowing his hellcat comment to slide. Forgetting to eat while I'm running things for Princess is going to wear on me. I have to remember to eat. My luck I'd pass out on the damn stage one night.

"Good to know, babe. But when you're with me, I'll take care of you." My eyes repeatedly read the words *tomato, lettuce, mayo, and fries* off the menu while my mind races with his comment. One thing I for sure don't need is a damn man to *take care of me.* I've been doing it myself for years and have no intention of stopping. I have learned one solid true thing over the years, the only person I can trust in this world is myself. While I may feel safer with Tug and know somehow he wouldn't hurt me, trusting him is a whole other issue that will not ever happen.

"I..." my words trail off as the waitress, her nametag says Rose, comes up to the table with cheeriness oozing off of her.

"Hey, Tug. What can I get ya'll?" My eyes sweep to Tug. Surely, he didn't fuck the waitress. Right? The smirk on his face tells me he's in my brain, damn him.

"Hey, Rose." He winks, making a show. "What do you want, sweet lips?" He pauses for me. I'm off kilter, but restrain myself.

The menu catches my attention. "Can I get a bacon cheeseburger with fries and a diet coke please?"

"Sure thing, sweetie. You?" She nods at Tug.

"I'll have what she's having, but I want a Coke instead."

The waitress scribbles the words on a paper. "You got it, be right back." She scurries off.

Placing the menu behind the napkin holder, I sit back in the seat. Awkwardness surrounds us. I don't have a clue what to say to this man. *Oh yeah, how's the weather.* That does not sit right.

"How was work tonight?" Tug cuts through the bullshit and opens it up. Deep down, I'm pretty grateful for it. While I'm used to the silence at home, being out with someone and not hearing anything doesn't sit right with me at all. And talking about X is safe.

"Same old, same old. Wardrobe malfunctions that required a little needle and thread, a sick dancer causing me to rearrange the lineup, and a few unruly guys wanting to touch and getting their asses thrown out." I shrug. "Pretty typical night."

"You like running things while Princess is helping at the clubhouse?" he questions. Ah, Princess did tell him.

I pause, my brain rolling around the question. "Yeah. I do. It's only been two days so I'm sure that can change, but it's not bad." The only thing that I didn't really care for is the floor. The crowds of people everywhere made it very difficult for me to keep my eyes on everyone around, but that is what Cali is there for.

His steady gaze sweeps over my body, heating me. If he keeps this up, I'm going to combust. My appearance has never been the problem. It's the fact that it's the only thing men see when they watch me. But it's for the best.

Keep them dreaming, I keep denying. Keeps everyone at bay, been going good so far. I wish his intensity didn't cause me to melt right into him and didn't make my heart pulsate each minute I'm in his presence.

When he's not pissing me off, that is.

"Glad you like it. So why you got Cali on your heels all the time?" Since he's part of the club, I figured he already knew, but maybe Princess doesn't share the daily comings and goings of X with the club. Interesting, learn something new every day.

"Protection. Some of the guys get a little touchy." His hand rubs over his chin and he appears to be thinking. I focus on his every action with curiosity. What does his skin feel like? Is it hot? Is the stubble rough or soft? What would he taste like if I ran my tongue along it?

"Why you and not the other girls?" He shakes me out of my glorious thoughts.

"I asked Princess for my own room, said the guys had grabby hands. She said if it was that bad, I needed Cali. I took her up on it." His head tilts. His eyes bore into mine like he's inside my brain again, searching. He's going through every inch of me and reading every damn thing at lightning speed. It is unnerving so I close my eyes and try to block him out, but it doesn't help. I can still sense him in there rummaging around. Shit.

"Guys still give you trouble?" He placates me, but he's not buying it. I can tell by the furrow of his brow and the crinkle of his eyes. Something in me snaps.

"They weren't really bothering me, at least no more than usual. The girls there were giving me shit and I was sick of it so I wanted my own space. I told Princess about the guys and I'm pretty sure she didn't buy it either but she gave me the room. Then she made the point that if I needed to have my own room, I needed Cali." All my words rush out of me so fast that I don't even realize I told him the whole truth until it's over. My eyes widen as the shock hits me.

The damn man snickers and I jump when he places his strong hands over top of mine on the table. He holds them steady, even when I try to remove them. "Now was that so hard?" He rubs his thumb on top of my hand, the coarse touch of each stroke against my skin forcing butterflies in my stomach to fly.

I'm pissed at myself for blurting that out like I intended all along to tell him what's on my mind. What the hell is wrong with me? Inside, I steel my doors and walls, locking them up. He's not getting anything else. He can't.

But when his eyes soften even more, the steel becomes a bit more pliable. Damn.

"Well, I for one am happy as shit Cali has your back." I nod, grateful too. "You don't sound like you're from around here. Where'd you come from?"

I want to lie. Everything from the past few years has conditioned me to be fast with the lies and know exactly what to say and at what moment to say them. But I can't. The words won't spill from my lips. Only half-truth will. "Up north." It's like I'm in a Tug fog or something and he's scrambling me.

"I see." His ministrations on my hand continue and the electrical current flows up my arm and my nipples tighten. I hope my thin bra doesn't give too much away. "Tell me about your family there."

My entire body stiffens and all the heat that he just gave me fizzles like cold water splashed down, extinguishing it completely. Family. What family? The one thing I haven't had in years. The one thing that I'll never have again. I can't hide the immediate despair and try to remove my hand from his grasp, but he holds tighter, not allowing it.

"Talk to me." The gentleness in his voice caresses over my skin like a warm blanket, getting rid of some of the coldness but not nearly enough.

"I have no family." I straighten my spine and muster every bit of confidence.

"None at all?" I ponder what I should tell him. I gotta give him something.

"My mother died. So I have no family." His eyes narrow as if he doesn't believe me, but whatever he notices in me causes him to relax. "But I don't want to talk about it, Tug. I mean it. Please don't push." I'm begging him. Shit.

"Got it." He nods in confirmation and I'm relieved I won this battle. A small one, but definitely a win.

"What about your family? You from here?" His intensity doesn't change even at the sound of me asking.

"Got a mom and sister close to here."

Rose drops off our drinks and is gone wordlessly. My eyes focus on the swirling liquid in front of me as the bubbles float up to the top. Suddenly, I become very interested in his family life. "You close to them?"

"Not like go to dinner all the time close, but they

know I've got their back." Tug's brows are furrowed like he's deep in thought. Too bad I didn't study psychology in school, would have been useful with this guy.

We sit in silence, but his intense stare bores into me again. He cannot figure me out. Surely he can't. Having anyone slash through my layers is a bad thing. They don't know what the hell they'll get themselves into inside there. Sure I've managed over the years, but even I know there is some deep shit that can't be fixed no matter what I do.

"So, I read online that you were top in your class." My eyes shoot to Tug's and shock doesn't even seem to cut it. My breath seizes and at his smirk, I gradually exhale. How in the hell?

"You checked up on me?" I glare as the shock wears off and anger boils. How dare he check up on me, not that he'd find a whole lot thanks to Princess.

"You're adorable when you're pissed. It's amazing what someone can find out on the internet." His vague response has the fire in my veins turning to ice in a flash. Damn. Does he know? I need to get the hell out of here.

I rise from the seat. "I've gotta go." Tug's hand grips mine on the table, startling me.

"Sweet lips. Sit." My fight and flight are waging war inside me. If I run, he'll know I'm hiding. Who am I kidding, he already knows that. There's only one thing to do. Fight. I plop down in the seat and close my eyes briefly.

After regaining myself, I think quickly. "Did you find everything you wanted to know?"

"Not much. Just your degree and where you went to

school." His eyes are questioning me, trying to put me together like a puzzle. Good luck with that, buddy, I still can't figure me out.

"That's all there is to know then."

"Babe." He leans into the table, his elbows resting about halfway in. "There is so much more to know and I will find out what makes you tick." I try not to panic and think about what he will find. Part of me wants to blurt it out so he doesn't but I can't. My lips won't allow the words to slip from them.

Rose saves the day by stepping forward with the food, placing it on the table with a plop. "Ya'll need anything else?" The burger smells delicious with the juices coating the meat, the cheese all gooey and melted. My stomach rumbles at the smell of the bacon. Everything in life tastes better with bacon.

"No, thanks," I tell her as Tug says nothing. Rose leaves and I bite into my sandwich. One thing I've never lacked, even in stressful situations, is an appetite. The rich taste of the meat bursts on my tongue and a small moan escapes my lips. My eyes flit to Tug who is staring at me appreciatively.

"Sweet lips, can't wait to make you moan like that."

The meat that I swallow gets lodged in my throat and I cough it down then drink to wash it all the way down. As I gasp for breath, a hand taps my back and I jump at the touch, turning. Tug. Besides the coughing, I settle when I know it's him.

"You all right?" Tug's concern is evident as his hand does wicked things to my back, rubbing up and down continuously.

"I'm fine." I cough and wipe my mouth with my napkin. The air flows through me, finally reaching my lungs. Tug must have been satisfied as he sits down in his seat, never taking his eyes off of me. I ignore him and the sultry smell of him that lingers on me from his touch and resume eating. I will not think about the kindness he showed in making sure I wasn't choking. I will not think about the fact that him doing that totally puts him in the good guy category. Nope, not me. I will not think any of that.

"Glad I have that effect on ya, sweet lips," he says, snapping me out of my thoughts. I shake and process his words. Ugh, ego much. My eyes water from the coughing fit and I dab them with a napkin repeatedly to stop the water. If I didn't, I'd be glaring at him.

"You just caught me off guard. One minute we are talking about something the next you're making lewd comments." Lewd, sexy and hot as shit comments that drive me crazy. *Stop!* I chastise, not wanting these thoughts even remotely distracting me.

He chuckles and gives me a full out sexy half-smirk. "Babe. That was nowhere near lewd. You want me to do lewd?" His brow raises in challenge.

My burger stops right before entering my mouth and I contemplate his words as a chill runs down my spine. I don't answer verbally, but non-verbally I shake my head, not needing anything like that coming out of his mouth. I'm already on edge as it is and if I can stop him I'm going to do it. He sits up in his seat and picks up his burger, scarfing it. The way his strong chiseled jaw moves with each chew has me mesmerized. The movement of his

Adams' apple and the way his lips swipe side-to-side as he chews, make me think of all the places I'd like his lips on my body. I rapidly turn away, not wanting him to decipher my thoughts. I don't dare look at his face because the ass will know. He seems to be able to read me and I really don't like that.

I need to get this conversation off of me and off sex before this night ends up in ripped clothes on a bedroom floor, or maybe the diner's bathroom. "What made you want to join Ravage?"

He sets his food down on the white plate and leans against the seat, almost like he's proud that I asked him. His eyes gleam with happiness. "Family. Brotherhood. I wanted that."

"But you have a family." To me it seems a bit jaded if you have one but want to find another, but who the hell am I to talk? I have no one and would love to have some type of family to spend holidays with or even talk to. But it is an honest question.

"Having a family and being part of one are two different things. I have a mother and sister, but shit happens." He lets his words drift and doesn't finish them. "With Ravage, it's like a team and each member will have your back no matter what."

"So you wanted to be on a team?" My eye quirks as I try to figure this man out. I get wanting to have a family, hell I'd love to have one, but the team part is throwing me off a bit.

He scoots his food off to the side and the air around us changes. The seriousness of what he's about to tell me rolls off of him in waves. I'm captivated by it and I want to know what it is. Need to know what it is. Why is up for discussion another time. I set my food down and listen intently.

"When I was in the service, I had a team of men." He pauses. "That team was there through everything. We counted on each other and every single one of those guys I knew would have my back. When a guy gets out and has to join civilians, it's not easy." He shakes his head as if he's clearing away a bad thought. "When you come back and there are so many laws dictating you, after not having them for years, the adjustment sometimes doesn't work out so well."

I start reading between the lines of what he's saying, but not really saying. Tug had a very difficult time adjusting. I wouldn't know the first thing about what he saw or what he did in the military. I take him at his word.

"But how did you meet up with these guys?" Sure. I found the place because my aunt gave me a card with X's address on it. I'm not judging just curious.

"Buzz. He was in my unit. Didn't know him growing up, but come to find out we only lived about an hour from each other. Anyway. After we got out, we went our separate ways, didn't last long. He knew the Ravage brothers and that's how it all started."

I am not going to pretend to know exactly what they do in Ravage because it's none of my business, but the brotherhood sounded good for him. The pride in his voice about it isn't hidden to me. At least he saw something and went for it. Shows his determination and persistence.

"But you're not a brother yet?" I dip my fry in ketchup and then shove it in my mouth. Yum.

"Nope. Prospect. Been that way for almost a year." He scratches the scruff on his sexy as sin chin and my damn mouth waters. Yes, waters. If I could kick myself in the ass I would so do it.

"What does being a prospect mean exactly?"

His eyes narrow and I don't like that look on him at all. "Means I'm trying to be part of the club, anything else is club business." That's pretty much what Princess said.

I read many erotic romance books about motorcycle clubs. But who knows if they have a lot of real information in them or not. One thing that is consistent in all of them is that women are not part of the club, they don't know the comings and goings inside of them, and they definitely are kept in the dark. And to be frank, thank God for that because I really don't need to know. I should have remembered this before asking the question in the first place, but it was conversation that didn't revolve around sex.

"Understood." His eyes quirk up in surprise almost like he thought I would challenge him on this. Like I would pester him to get information. There is no need, especially considering after this, we will not be seeing each other again and his Prospect/Brother status will be moot.

"Does it bother you?"

"Does what bother me?" I repeat, confused.

"Me being with Ravage MC."

"Oh," I breathe out, "I don't care one way or the other,

Tug. This is only dinner and then we are parting ways. You live your life. I'll live mine."

He leans back in the booth, putting his arm on top of the seat. Confidence oozes off him in thick waves, almost knocking me off kilter. His long brown hair frames his face. I flex my fingers. What would it be like to run my fingers through it? Would it be tangled or sleek? I blink and try to get myself under control. This night needs to be over soon. I can't take much more of his hotness.

"Sweet lips, I'm just getting started." Before I can speak, his phone rings. He holds up one finger as he answers it swiftly. I quiet without thought.

"Yeah." He stays stoic, not giving any body language away throughout the short conversation. Only hearing one side sucks, not that I care.

"Be there in fifteen." He pauses, gazing at me with eyes full of disappointment.

"I'm with Blaze. Gotta make sure she gets home." He winks at me and heat rises up my cheeks. I breathe out, willing it to go away, willing my body to stop this reaction to him.

"Yep."

"On it." He turns the phone off. "Gotta go." He throws some bills on the table and rises from the booth.

"You go on. I'll be fine." Really I just need a breather and if he goes I can have it, get my wits about me.

"Nope. I'll follow you to your road and then I gotta go." The steel in his voice leaves little room for discussion or argument, but he's only following me so there's no reason to argue. Wait.

"How do you know where I live?" Because I know sure

as shit I didn't tell him. I rise from the table at my question.

He smirks and leads me out the door. "Google." How in the hell can someone find me that easily, especially with my *name*. I really need to brush up on my technology.

Something niggles at me so I ask, "This happen a lot? You get calls and have to leave?" He stops. The moon shines down the side of him, making his face glow and his hair shine. I bite my lip as the shadows play on his cheeks and his eye lashes shadow them too.

"Yeah, sweet lips, part of it." He says no more and leads me to my Jeep, ushering me in, while holding the door open. Another nice thing for a man to do. Damn.

I stand next to my seat, my back turned to it facing Tug. Hot. So very hot in this small space. He steps closer and I need to breathe. I try to hop up in my seat, but his arm catches me around the waist. His hold is snug and he keeps it while turning me back into him. My breath catches as his warm, hard body presses up against mine. Every muscle of his body from legs to groin to chest invades my space. Hard. Hot. Sexy. Time seems to stand still and my lips part. He's so close that if I stood on my tiptoes our lips would lock in what I'm sure would be a ferocious kiss.

His lips come down on mine in the softest peck I've ever had, surprising me, or disappointing me, I'm not sure which. The kiss is more like a butterfly kiss, a flutter of a wing caressing my skin. My eyes lock on his and part of me wants him to devour me, consume me. It's as if he can read the desire in my face as his eyes light with a fire I have yet to see. "Another time, sweet lips. Next time I get a real taste."

He releases me on unsteady legs, but I hastily climb up into the Jeep, shutting the door as soon as he steps away. *Shit*!

CHAPTER FIVE
Blaze

"GET ME THE NEEDLE AND THREAD." I PAUSE, THINKING ON my feet. "Oh and the boob pads, hurry." Another wardrobe problem; this time from one of the newer dancers Star. She's been here a couple of weeks so I consider her new. Her routine tonight has something to do with stars and her top, or lack thereof, broke, spilling her tits out, which would be fine, but not the right time for that.

Luna, who has turned over a new leaf, brings me the things rapidly. Suzie homemaker was not on the job description and considering I am no seamstress, I do the best I can. Luckily, it's one of the things my mother taught me back when she wasn't sick. When she was vibrant and could do all the things a mother does with her child. Until the sickness ate her up inside, taking my whole world away from me.

"Ouch!" Star shouts and my focus goes to the pin I have obviously stuck her in the chest with. Shit.

"Sorry." I have no idea how Princess did all of this by herself every night for so long. Stupid shit like no tampons. Really? Everything is easily fixable and normally doesn't take long to deal with, but it does get tiresome. Sometimes I feel like their mother.

I remove the top off of Star and continue to sew so I don't poke her.

Princess hasn't been around and I haven't heard much from her except to tell me that Casey is hanging in there. She's popped in a few times, but never stayed long enough for any real conversation. She did tell me that she wants to have a meeting, but doesn't know when that will be yet.

It's fine. I can handle pretty much anything at this point. And what's better is the women don't give me shit so much anymore. They listen, do what they're supposed to do and we all make money. Pretty simple concept. Glad they figured it out, saved us all from headaches and drama that I do not need. That doesn't stop the cattiness between the girls, but I have learned in this short time to handle each situation as it comes.

"There." I finish stitching and hand Star the garment. She slips it on and it fits like a glove.

Star jumps in her spot excitedly. "Thank you!" She rushes off to get ready for her set. I do a sweep of the room, nothing is out of place. Women doing makeup, chatting with one another, everything is good. I've gotten much more practical in my shoes since starting my new tasks. Those first nights with heels were killer to my poor feet and since I've been doing a pretty good job of being incognito, flats work so much better. Guys that come here expect the women in heels and all done up, helps me fade into the background.

I weave through the crowd with Cali trailing behind, and people shift out of the way as they focus on the dancers, waving money and catcalling through the room.

My eyes land on the table in the front row and a small pang of disappointment settles at the three guys in business suits sitting there. Tug hasn't been to X for two days. I thought for sure I'd have him up my ass, and the fact that he's not kind of eats at me, considering he had been here the entire week before, not that it matters. Who am I kidding? That night after our *coffee* that I didn't have, all I've thought about is that man. Even had a few orgasms in the process. I swear he's gone in and scrambled my brain.

It pisses me off that he's a nice guy. Why can't he be a fucking jerk and have me hate him. It would make all of this so much easier.

A hand on my ass stops my thoughts and I turn. Cali seizes a pimple-faced kid, probably just turned twenty-one, and drunker than shit, eyes partially glazed over. The grin on his face instantly fades and terror replaces it. Cali picks him up, escorting him out of the building with ease. I turn to the bar where Ace is tending, ignoring the taunting coming from the kid's friends.

"Everything going okay?" I holler over the bar and Ace gives me his sly smile, no doubt winning the hearts of many of the ladies in here. With his luscious, built body, tattoos peeking out under his shirt and those awesome blue eyes, my heart stops. He strolls over, wiping his hand on a white towel, and then whips it up over his shoulder where it stays resting.

"Good. Night's hot. You back up there?" He nods to the stage.

"Nope. Done for the night. I'm leaving, just want make sure everything's good." With only an hour left, the guys will lock up and there shouldn't be any more catastrophes in that short of time. Hopefully. Normally I stay, but tonight the pounding music is playing havoc with my brain, the pain slicing through me like a knife. All the thumping is about ready to bring me to my knees. I took pain relievers about four hours ago and they didn't do a damn bit of good.

The hairs on the back of my neck stand up before I see him. How is that even possible? Tug's here. I'm a damn yoyo. Part of me is elated and the other part, not so much. I sweep the area and meet his stare, his eyes locking with mine. The electric current flows between us. I scramble to pull myself together. His brothers follow him as he effortlessly strides toward me, through the throng of people moving out of their path like the parting of the Red Sea.

"Hey, sweet lips." He stops close and tilts his head to the side. It's sexy as hell.

"Hey. I'm leaving. Enjoy the show." I motion with my hand to the girl up on stage, Tug doesn't react. His eyes stay locked on me. Buzz and Breaker's eyes focus on whoever is there, paying no attention to Tug.

"Good. Let's go." He reaches over and grabs my hand, and an instant shock courses through me so intense that

I'm momentarily paralyzed. I get my wits and try to yank my arm but, he doesn't let me go.

"I'm going home. You can do whatever you want." I try for stern, but I fall flat and he knows it. Dammit.

"Come on." Tug nods at Ace and clenches my hand, then leads the way through the crowd. If I wanted to fight I could, but I can't cause a scene. And shit if his grip isn't strong, like he wouldn't take no for an answer anyway. Cali catches up to us right as we pass by Doug, who nods in acceptance.

I jerk my hand, but his grip is firm, not painful but demanding. "Cali's here. He'll make sure I get to my car."

"Nope. I will. Get your stuff." He holds out his hand for my key to unlock the door to my dressing room, but I don't hand it to him. Instead, I unlock the door my damn self. I do not need some guy doing shit for me. He smirks but doesn't say anything as I barrel into the room and gather up my things. This room has become more of an office over the past week instead of a dressing room with papers piled up for lineups and music lists. But I like it.

Tug makes himself comfortable on the couch, leaning back and crossing his boots one over another in front of him, his arms behind his head in the sexiest of ways. "You gonna ask me where I've been?" he asks patiently.

"No."

He answers anyway. "Had club business. Now I'm free for the night."

I look at him through the mirror. His leather rag fits perfectly over his wide chest, the black shirt underneath only enhancing it. His hair isn't laced with product, but looks like his fingers have been through it hundreds of times today, sleeking it back. His deep chocolate eyes are locked on mine and I catch my heart doing this weird thumping that I'm not accustomed to. Immediately, I move away and try to get myself together.

"Tug, I've got a massive headache. I'm going home to lie down." Thank God for it, score me. Never been so happy to have one.

"I'll come with ya." His words come out matter-of-factly, like I what he says goes. *Uh...* no.

I turn fast and my head spins a bit, but I get it together. "You are not coming to my house!" I declare. He is not coming into my space, just not.

"I'll follow you. Make sure you get there okay." The lines around his eyes tell me he's full of shit. This is not going to happen. He can follow, but he will not come into my house. Absolutely not.

"You can follow," I grab my bag, "but that's it." He chuckles, following me out.

Through the entire drive, I keep checking my rearview mirror, watching the lone light following me through the darkness. I've never had a man over at my home before and the thought is very nerve racking. It is my safe haven; the place I can go to get away, and I'm not ready to have anyone in my space. This will be one fight that Tug will not win.

Pulling up to the house, floodlights kick on, illuminating the brick home that I love so much. I open the garage door with the remote. The sound of Tug's bike roars and then cuts off behind me as I park. My eyes are so glued on the man behind me that when I look up, I slam on my brakes, almost driving through the damn wall of the garage. Shit. My pulse flares and I grip the steering wheel. Dammit. Get a grip woman.

My door whips open and Tug is standing there. "Put it in park, Blaze!" he orders and I don't hesitate to follow what he says, shifting the Jeep in park and killing the engine. His hand cups my chin, my face mere inches from his. "You okay?" The absent movement of his thumb over my jaw relaxes me and I suck in a breath. Concern laces his eyes, making me all gooey inside.

"Yeah. Thanks for following me. You should go." My words come out breathy and I hate it, but can't stop it.

He assesses then releases me. "You really don't want me coming in?"

Yes. "No." His hands fall into his pockets and I rise from the Jeep, shutting the door. "I'm going to bed." I proceed to the door of the house.

He steps in my path and his deep concerned eyes trip up my resistance. I want to haul him to me so badly my hand twitches. *No.* "All right." Tug bends down and sweeps his lips across mine, igniting an inferno inside of me. He steps away all too quickly, but doesn't move to his bike. He saunters over to the swing off to the side of the porch. I added the swing when I got the house. I love being able to come outside and listen to the crickets or the occasional car that drives up the street, and just think. Just be. It isn't anything special, only a swing from the home improvement store, white and held by chains from studs in the roof, but I love it. And he should not be sitting there.

"What are you doing?" My hand reflexively goes to

my hip, jutted out in my frustration. I don't want him on my porch. It's too damn close. God, he needs to leave.

He sits in the swing and rocks back and forth like he's done it for years. "I'm gonna rest. That was a long trip here and I'm a little tired. Go on in. I'll go soon." Yeah I just bet you will, his entire body language is screaming, *I'm not going anywhere.* And long trip, my ass. I don't live far from X.

"Fine!" I huff, spinning around and closing the garage door behind me. I race through the house, flipping all the lights on as I walk to my bedroom. I strip my clothes off and jump into the shower, washing the Studio X off of me. After putting on some baggy sweatpants and an oversized hoodie, I go into the kitchen in search of some pain relief. This headache has only gotten worse, for some reason. Probably Tug's fault. Yep, I'll blame it on him. After downing the pills, I enter the living room. Tug still swings methodically without a care in the world. It's been well over an hour, I thought for sure he'd been gone by now.

Stubborn man. Jumping on the couch, I pull my fuzzy blanket over my body and curl up, snagging the remote to the television and flipping through the stations and all the mindless chatter that is on at two in the morning. I settle in, watching some jerk yell at a guy for giving him a parking ticket when his car is parked in the wrong spot. Whatever. Boring.

Movement outside has my heartbeat racing. Is he leaving? I peer out the window. Nope, still rocking. I let out a small sigh of relief.

How could I leave him out there like that? It's not like

he'd hurt me physically. I know he wouldn't. How I know is left to be determined. I just do. Emotionally is a whole different story. Damn that man. I battle with my thoughts for long moments. I throw off the blanket and advance to the front door, swinging it open in a bit of a huff.

Tug turns to me in surprise. "Get in here." I leave the door open, inviting him in, and let him choose if he does. I head to the kitchen in search of a beer for Tug and a water for myself and bring them into the living room. Tug takes his boots off at the door and I stop dead. "What are you doing?"

"Don't wanna get your floor muddy."

Damn considerate man. I sit on the couch and place the drinks on the rectangular glass coffee table in the center of the room. As Tug comes into the space, I expect him to sit in the open recliner as I am on the couch, but he doesn't. He plops his ass right next to me, our legs touching thigh to thigh. I ignore the stream of pleasure coming from his warmth and hand him the beer.

"Thanks, sweet lips." He takes off the cap, drinks, sets the bottle down on the coffee table, and then removes his leather and wallet, placing them next to the bottle. I don't even bother asking him what he's doing because I don't want some smartass response. He's getting comfortable. Damn.

"You still got a headache?" His gentle tone makes my stomach flutter at his thoughtfulness and compassion.

"Yeah." The constant throb hasn't gone away and with Tug in my space, my anxiety is increasing.

Tug sits with his back against the arm of the couch and spreads his legs open wide. I quirk my brow at him and take another drink of my water. "Go grab a couple pillows and come back."

"Why?" My face contorts, confused by the change.

"I'm gonna help you relax." At that moment, a slicing pain rips through behind my eyelids and I reach up, trying to rub it out with my fingers, and give up when it doesn't disappear. If he can help, I'm all for it. I rise and get the throw pillows from the corner of the room and return. My eyes are a bit blurry from rubbing them the entire trip to retrieve the pillows.

"Sit down with your back to me. Put the pillows in front of you and lay your stomach on them," he instructs calmly.

"What?" My mind hurts so badly I can't think right and I'm having a slight bit of difficulty understanding him. He positions me exactly where he wants me, my body falling in line with his automatically, but the pain stopping me from even giving the smallest bit of argument. He sits behind me, my back to his front, but not touching. He places the pillows in front of me and asks me to lean on them with my head resting on the top of them, one leg tucked in the couch the other on the floor. Damn it's comfortable.

Rough hands snake up my back over my hoodie, my body tenses then relaxes into his touch. His thumbs draw tiny circles up my spine, but my thick hoodie is concealing the touch and the pressure of each caress of his fingers. I let out a frustrated moan, wanting more of the touch.

"Take it off," he orders and I freeze. I know exactly what he means and I have nothing on under my shirt, nothing. It's not like he hasn't seen my naked boobs before but this is different, in my home with no one around. This is intimate.

"I'm just going to rub your back, neck and head, sweet lips. I promise not to fondle you." He pauses. "Yet." I shiver at the seriousness of his tone. Breathing out, I trust him at his word and remove the hoodie. I lie back down on the pillows, covering my chest. "Good," he praises and my body tingles.

His touch cascades over my skin and any tension I had from removing my shirt dissipates as I relish in his touch. His thick fingers rub my neck in all the right places. My body turns to Jell-O, wiggly and loose. When his fingers feather into my hair and caress my scalp, I moan as he rubs right where the throb is intense.

He moves to my neck, then back, then neck, then head, his fingers touching all the right spots and my throbbing headache becoming a memory. I get so lost in his touch, my eyes become heavy, and I fade into darkness.

I'm being picked up like I weigh nothing. I'm floating down onto the softness and lips brush mine as something warm envelops me. I snuggle into the heat.

Too warm. Way too warm. My eyelids flutter open. Blue-green walls and drapes. My room. A steel arm is wrapped around my waist as I rest on a muscular chest. Tug's eyes open, the morning light shining in them. Shit.

"Morning, sweet lips." He yawns and his mouth contorts in the sexiest of ways, just doing such a mundane thing. I involuntarily lick my lips. His gaze drifts down my body and I follow. Shit, my tits are completely and totally bare. I abruptly clutch the blanket, covering my breasts, and try to scoot away from him, which he doesn't allow by gripping me tighter.

"What are you doing here? In my bed?" I hold the blanket around me. The words sound a combination of shocked and pissed off, but really I love the vision of him in my bed against my sheets. Does that make me some kind of freak?

"Brought you to bed. Was tired. Went to sleep." His deep, sleep-filled voice bellows and my pussy throbs at the magical sound. I snap myself out of it.

"I didn't say you could sleep in here." I try to get up but the arm around me tightens, holding me down. I swear his arms are stronger than steel, but I don't give up.

"You didn't say I couldn't either," he retorts and he's right. Damn, shit and fuck.

"So, that just means you can jump into any bed that you want?" I come back, exasperated.

"Pretty much." I do not like the way this is going and a rock falls in the pit of my stomach. He could be with anyone he wanted, anytime he wanted. I sigh. I'm only a pit stop along the road. Someone to mark off the list. Screw that.

"Let me up, Tug, and get out." His body freezes at my hard tone, but instead of removing the steel around my waist, he turns. He lies on his side, arm propped on elbow, hand holding his head, and staring down at me.

The arm around my stomach loosens enough that I can lie on my back.

"I'm playing this your way. For now. That time is almost up, sweet lips."

"What in the hell does that even mean, Tug?" I huff. I sure as shit don't speak biker lingo and I'm not playing anything. I'm just trying to get him to go. It's better in the long run.

"Means I'm letting you call these shots. Want you used to me. But soon, babe, we play by my rules." The intensity in his eyes has me believing it too.

I try to get up. This time he lets me and I sit up on the bed, crossing my legs together in front of me. I face him, making sure the sheet covers me. "We play by my rules and there is no us. No sex. No relationship. Nothing. You need to get your stuff and get out now." I scoot off the bed with the blanket and hightail it to the bathroom, shutting and locking the door.

I grumble at the reflection in the mirror. What the hell is wrong with me? I splash water on my face and try to wipe the sleep away.

There are so many reasons why I can't get involved with that man out there so why is my body saying *go back. Screw him. Do it.*

"No," I chastise myself and do my business. I grab a baby pink t-shirt that is strewn over the handle of the shower and make my way to the bedroom, keeping the blanket around me. Tug lies on the bed, stretching his muscles in the most delectable of ways and those tattoos lining his chest and arms are on full display. Damn.

"You need to go, Tug," I say, standing by the closet

door on the opposite side of my bedroom. My words come out so much weaker than before.

He rises from the bed, giving me a fine view of his ass that only has a pair of boxer briefs covering it. The ones that are skin tight and show every ripple when he moves. His wide shoulders are toned with a distinct line down his spine. Tattoos grace his muscled back but I can't tell the design. Overall, he makes my mouth water and sends my pussy into meltdown. He turns, making eye contact with me, and I instantaneously look away. *Shit.*

"I'm going." He turns around, putting his jeans on. *What a shame.* I mean, good, he needs to leave. "But I'll be back and soon." His words bring me to the task at hand.

"Tug. Really. We can't do this," I plead because pure determination pulsates off of him along with persistence. Shit.

After slipping on his shirt, he places both hands on either side of my cheeks. I meet his hot gaze. The promise in them unnerves me. "We can and will do this, Blaze. I promise you that."

He dips down and this time his lips are not soft, they are determined and precise. They mold to mine and take me in a demanding, sensual kiss. I gasp, giving him the opening he needs and he goes deeper, all the while still cupping my cheeks. All I can do is hold on for dear life as his tongue seeks entrance and finds it readily. I grip his wrists at the side of my face and I kiss him back as all the bullshit I keep telling myself washes away into a big puddle on the ground and I step forward.

Long minutes pass and he keeps up the effort and I follow right along. When he releases me, I can't find air. I forgot to breathe. Is that even possible? I gulp in big breaths, my heart pounds, and my entire body is a live wire ready to explode. Wetness and warmth are pooled down below and I want more.

My eyes flutter open to a smiling man that takes my breath away. "Your time just got shorter." He pecks my lips and strolls out of my bedroom. The distinct sound of a door shutting tells me he's left and the rumble of his bike tells me he's gone.

I sit on my bed and place my fingertips on my tender lips.

Shit, what have I done?

"Sit." Princess is in today and asked me to meet her in her office. That was about an hour ago before I got sidelined with questions from the girls. One even asked me to show her a technique on the pole. The things I do, but teaching her was kind of fun. And judging by Princess's face as she stands behind her large wooden desk in her office, she's not very happy about me being late.

Princess's office is kick ass. Deep red covers the walls. Two of the walls have heavy, black drapery that falls down in a swoop, held by little black ropes attached to the wall. A large, black iron cross hangs behind her desk with thorns weaved all around it. Her desk is the focal point of the room and filing cabinets are up against a sidewall. Two chairs sit in front of her desk, one of which I'm currently sitting in.

"Sorry. Drama out there." If she's pissed, she's pissed. There is really no stopping her when she is.

Her eye quirks. "You able to handle it?"

My steely spine engages. "Of course. But that's what took me so long." I cross my legs and wait for her to join me, which she does, plopping into her desk chair with a huff, all anger in her face disappearing.

"Sorry. Everything going on with Casey and Shaina has me up in knots. I can't help them. I want to, but nothing I say helps, only makes it worse." With the strength that Princess can give each one of those women, I find it difficult to think that she's not helping them. She just doesn't recognize it.

"They went through shit. It's gonna take time." A small snake of a shiver crawls throughout me just thinking about what those women went through. In one of Princess's calls, she gave me the rundown and it was not pretty. Tied up by chains, raped, and fondled, none of it any woman should ever go through. I know.

"Yeah. I want to kill the sorry motherfucker, again." Princess's body tenses and her fist slams down on the desk. Guess the calm has left.

I keep myself together as thoughts of why I took off from home creep up, and suppress them to deal with the task at hand. "What did you want to talk about?" I ask changing the subject.

She blows out deep, lacing her fingers together and placing them on the desk. "I want you to come and work here."

My brows furrow together. "Unless I didn't get the memo, I already do."

The left side of her lip shifts up and I'm glad my off-handed remark helps her melt some of her frustration.

"Okay, smartass. No. I want you to come and do the books, organize and be my right hand here at X. I can't do all this shit by myself and I need someone I can trust, especially after Liz fucked me over royally." Her fists clench and I remember the shit that Liz put Princess through. She continues. "That person is you." Her clasped hands move up to her chin and she rests her head on them as she waits for me, waits for my reaction.

I sit shocked. Though I'm happy to help her out with the club while she's gone, I'm not entirely sure that I want this to be my career. This is supposed to be a means to an end. I don't care for stripping. I only started because it paid good money and I needed it badly. I do not like the men ogling me and the thought of some of them jacking off to thoughts of me naked has me wanting to vomit. If I did this, I'd be stuck in this life.

"Stripping. Will I be done with it?" That would be a plus.

Princess's expression is impassive and I can't read anything that is floating through her mind. "I'd like to keep you on one night a week for now." She slaps her hands on the desk with a thud. "You make damn good money in tips and draw me in a shit load of business, I'd be dumb as shit to pack you up and put you in an office and hide you. But..." Her voice trails as I listen. "I know you want more. So, we need to talk money and see if *you* want to quit or continue to strip."

"All right. Before we talk money, what are my responsibilities?" True I want to know how much I'll be paid, but I need to know what's expected of me first to know if the money is right.

"Smart woman." Princess lists all the things that I will be in charge of here at X and most of it I've been doing anyway, with the exception of the books. That I'm not worried about in the least. I could do them in my sleep. That would be the easiest part of this job. When Princess slides a piece of paper across the desk, surprised doesn't cut it. Holy shit. With that amount, it's a no brainer.

"I'll do it. One night a week stripping for two weeks, then I'll reevaluate, but I have to do my sets this week or it will throw off the entire schedule."

Princess smirks. "See, already thinking like a business woman. I like it."

"One more question," I ask as she rises out of her chair.

"Yes?"

"Do I work for you or the club? And who do I answer to?"

Princess comes around to the front of the desk and rests her ass on the corner of it. "*Ahh.* That is a tricky question. Technically you work for me and I report back to the club if there are any problems. Most of the time, I handle the garbage and don't bother my Pops with any of that shit. Now there may be times that I need you at a meeting or something with the guys, but for the most part, it's just me."

Not that I couldn't handle it either way, I'm keeping all my options open. "I can do that."

"Good. You technically begin right now, except for your routines you are on. We'll split up the hours between the two of us so one of us is here most of the time. The guys are accustomed to locking shit up so that's not a problem. You have any questions?"

"Who's gonna take my spot in the lineup?" That will really mess the schedule up and after doing it for a while, I know what a pain in the ass it is when one of the girls calls in sick. Switching that shit on the fly isn't pretty sometimes.

"I'm not sure yet. One of the ol' ladies has expressed some interest in dancing, but I'm not sure about that yet. Seems like a problem waiting to happen. I have a list of several women who want to strip, but they mostly want the cock that comes with the club, so you'll help me with that shit. If they want to be a flat out club momma that's their business, but if they work here, the rest of it is on the side."

"Got it." I've never understood why some women choose to sleep with all the guys and never get tired of it, but it isn't my place to judge. I never want to have that part of the club, I only want to have a life and now I'll be able to do just that. This may work out.

I rise from my chair. "I'll get busy."

"I wanted to ask ya something." Princess's words stop me dead. This can't be good. "What's going on with you and Tug?"

"Nothing. Not a damn thing." I think to this morning, lying so close to him and listening to his heart beat, the scent of leather and sexy man all around me. I shiver. Lies, all damn lies. Damn.

"Keep telling yourself that one. Those Ravage men don't give up that easily." His statement about following my rules flows through my mind. She is definitely right about that one.

"I'm learning that, but it's not happening," I protest, but even to me it's flat.

"Wanna talk about it?"

I know that Princess only wants to help, but right now, I don't know what's going on. My thoughts are in a big blender filled of mixed-up-ness and I really can't formulate the words for it. "Nope, gotta get busy."

"Sure thing, Taryn. Let me know if you need anything." The way that name rolls off of her tongue gags me. It's not a bad name, just not the one I was given and she damn well knows it.

"You got it, Harlow," I tease and she chuckles as I leave her office, lucky she really doesn't know my past.

CHAPTER SIX
Tug

"WATCH THE BIKES," DAGGER ORDERS AS I GET OFF OF MY custom *Wide Glide Harley* perfect for a guy with long legs like me. It's sleek black with shiny chrome. I love this fucking bike. The brothers stroll into the bar where they are meeting Ransom. At least I have Buzz with me. One thing with being a prospect is no job is too small and right now, our eyes are on the bikes. Scanning the area, I realize there are several eyes on us, but none that appear to have the balls to come closer. That could of course change in the blink of an eye.

Pops said the meeting with Ransom shouldn't be long and wanted Buzz and I to ride along, leaving Breaker at the clubhouse. We don't ask, just do. I'll be damn happy though when we start going to church so I can find out everything that is going on. I hate being left in the dark about shit. While I know this is part of it, every fiber of my being wants to protect. It's the years of training and something I can't shut off.

"So, you and Blaze, huh?" Buzz asks, lighting a cigarette, but keeping an eye on everything around us carefully. One thing about Buzz is I trust him with my life, no question. That man is a fucking machine and anyone who doubts it is a dumb fuck. Fighting side-by-side for your life on little sleep and food, can force you to trust someone fully. Buzz, I trust fully and completely.

I haven't seen her for two days, haven't even made it to X. Shit's been crazy in Ravage with Casey and Shaina recovering and GT being at Casey's side. I'm happy GT got his head out of his ass for that one. She's something else. I won't lie and say at one point I didn't want to hit it with her, because I did. Any man with a dick would want to fuck her. But I knew from the very beginning that she only had eyes for GT, everyone else was invisible. I never had a shot and for some ungodly reason, I am cool with that. Now, Blaze, I'm not cool with just being a friend.

Lately, I haven't had time to breathe much less take time to go to X, but I will and soon. Hopefully, tonight.

"Nothing to tell." I shrug, plucking the pack of smokes out of my rag. I've been trying to quit these damn things for the past few months. But I've been smoking since I was a teen and quitting isn't as easy as people think. Not to mention everyone around me lights up and when you have a beer it's nice to have a smoke in your hand. I have to say, I've been doing pretty good in my quest, only smoking about a half a pack a day. I light the stick hanging out of my mouth and breathe in deep, the nicotine flowing into my lungs. I instantly remember why I wanted to quit as a small chest pain attacks. Shit. I shake it off.

"Not like you, brother. Since when do you chase after a woman?" I pause for a minute. My first instinct is to punch him in the jaw for his smartass comment, but then I think. Is that what I'm doing, chasing after her? Nah. I'm sure as shit not a fucking puppy dog. She's a hot piece with a brain. I call it persistence.

"I ain't chasing shit."

FOLLOWING the brothers in our pack, Buzz and I bring up the rear, keeping eyes behind us and to the side and in front, never know who's lurking. Pops and Becs ride front, Dagger, Rhys, Cruz and Zeb behind them, us in back. We were due to the clubhouse about an hour ago to help GT and Casey get moved into their home. The meeting with Ransom took much longer than anyone anticipated and it's eating at me that I have no fucking clue what was said. The guys came out with stoic faces, not giving anything away. These fuckers are hard as shit to read, which is a good thing.

Pulling up to the clubhouse, boxes are lined up by the front door. While we know that GT isn't really moving out, Casey brought a lot of shit with her while she stayed here and apparently, she has more shit that needs to be moved.

Two of the new guys, Derek who is some sort of intellectual genius and Ethan who is fast as shit on his feet are loading things into the awaiting van. Those two have been hang-arounds at the club for the last couple months. Mostly they stay in the background of Ravage and work in the garage. It's my guess though they'll be prospecting soon. They seem to have the itch, but only time will tell. I like them, have no problems with them. Buzz checked them out when they first started coming around and so far they are clean. Derek is Zeb's nephew and he brought them around, even vouched for them which is enough for Pops so it's enough for me. Not saying that all of us aren't keeping our eyes on them, because we are like fucking hawks. But so far they haven't given at least me any indication they aren't here for the right reasons.

After seven trips from here to there, everything is in GT and Casey's place and my ass is dog tired.

I'd thought about going over to X, but it's not happening. At least not without a shower and a little bit of rest. Following Buzz and Breaker into our three-bedroom apartment, the cool air rushes over me. Moving in this heat sucks ass. Thank God for the coolness of beer.

I strip, shower and change, joining the guys out in the living room or what one would call a living room. The room is stark white, and we have two mix matched couches, one red and one blue with some type of pattern on it, and a recliner. The large flat screen is the focal point of the room with a leftover coffee table from the last tenants littered with beer bottles in the middle between the three pieces of furniture. The walls are blank except for the nail holes also left by the previous tenant.

When we rented the place, we were only trying to

find somewhere close to Ravage that had rooms to sleep in and that's exactly what we found. We didn't need anything more considering we are either at the club, garage or runs.

All three of us had different ways of making money before joining up with Ravage and now get a check from the shop, which lately isn't much, but it's enough to get by. It is just another reason for us to become brothers. Paid runs. Or so I've heard. That would be nice to get in on the cut.

"Here." Buzz holds out a beer to me as we sit: me on the blue couch, Buzz on the red and Breaker in the recliner, all kicking our feet up. Buzz flips through the TV as I drink my beer, my muscles relaxing.

Buzz settles on a football game that was probably played weeks ago. Before joining the service, I watched that shit religiously. Now, I can't even tell you who ranks where or who's on what team. None of it was important to me after coming back to the US. A lot of things didn't seem important, really the only things that did before Ravage were my mom and sister. My mom could barely look at me. That shit hurt. My sister was only sixteen or seventeen at the time and she went into post-traumatic stress after it happened. I tried comforting her, but everything I tried made her worse. Everything I fucking did, I did to protect them and when they seemed almost scared of me, it pushed me over the edge.

That's why I joined the Army. Luckily, my father's death was ruled self-defense or who knows what my life would have turned up like.

When I got out, I tried to go home to Mom's for a bit.

My sister had gotten better, but fear was in her eyes. Each time I came in the room, she would shy away from me like I'd hurt her or something. My mother wouldn't talk much. I needed out. That is why I called Buzz.

I'm damn glad I did.

"So, you think the T-Darts are done now? I know the boys wiped out most of them, but you think the ones left will come back?" Breaker asks, cutting off my thoughts. Guess we do know more than 'nothing.'

"Who knows? The fuckers that are left are few. If one of them wants to start it back up and run the show, they know they'll have to deal with Ravage so let 'em." Only a pack of fucking morons would come after us now, knowing we wiped out their leader and most of the crew that was with him. That was all their own damn fault though. They kidnapped Casey and Shaina. We'll find out soon enough if the ones that are left are smart or stupid.

"I think we should blow all their shit up just for the fun of it. I tagged their two buildings and they'd be easy to do." Buzz takes a pull from his beer, not removing his eyes off of the TV while he talks. "Those fuckers messed with my shit. I want them fucking gone."

A few weeks ago, this asshole Paine from the T-Darts started messing with our shit. They had someone cut into our computer system when we were going to blow up a warehouse that was housing Rabbit and his guys. Rabbit killed Diamond, our President at the time, and this was payback, destroying them. Instead, Paine broke into our computer, talked a lot of shit and killed everyone in the warehouse. Paine was fucking nuts. He's also the motherfucker that kidnapped Casey and Shaina, Diamond's daughter. He chained them up to a ceiling and violated them. But he has been eliminated.

"You're gonna have to let that shit go, ya know? The guys took out Paine, you can't bring him back and then kill him again."

"His tech guy is still out there and I know where." he says nonchalantly like the news isn't fucking huge and a break that Ravage has been dying to get their hands on. We all knew that Paine had to have a tech person, but didn't know who it was and Buzz has been itching to find him. Guess he hit the mark.

I cut sharply to Buzz. "What the fuck? You tell the guys?"

"Not yet. Just found him late last night while doing a search, knew Pops was meeting with Ransom and we had to move GT" He turns briefly to me then back to the TV as if this is another day at the office, which in turn it is, but still. "He's young, twenty-three. Apparently a computer genius." He grumbles the words out and it probably killed him to say them. Knowing that this guy is the one who broke into Buzz's full-proof computer soft-ware system has had Buzz in kill mode since it happened. No one shows him up. Ever. "He works for a software company up in Alta designing shit for them."

"How do you know it's him?" Honest question because come on, I have no fucking clue when it comes to computers and shit. Give me a gun and target, I'm there.

"Search after fucking search. Traced IP addresses that led me around the fucking country and back several times. But I didn't give up. He landed in my lap." Buzz's tone is calm and collected, which means he's planning. He's probably been planning for a while now, but this ups the ante.

"Got family?" I ask. Shit, the guys have to know this, like fucking yesterday. We need to scope this guy out and find out everything he knows about Ravage. It doesn't take a tech genius to know that if someone could hack into a video feed, they can tap into books, money, accounts... you name it they can do it.

"Mom and Dad divorced, talks to both of them, sister married with three kids, girlfriend is a secretary. Lives alone in his house. Can't tell yet if he's a T-Dart or just someone they hired. Doesn't matter to me though. I want him eliminated." The last words out of Buzz's mouth were ground out, almost as if he had to physically spit them out.

Buzz left a lot of his emotion in Iraq, hell, maybe even before he got to Iraq. He has it for those he cares about, but the ones that cross him hell hath no fury. We get along well in that area too.

"We need to call Pops." I check the time. 11:37 p.m. "He needs to know now."

"Yeah," he groans and sits up on the couch with his cell. The volume on the TV is cut down, I'm assuming by Breaker as Buzz is dialing.

"It's Buzz. Got some shit on the techy who hacked into my system." I listen to the one-sided conversation, watching Buzz for clues, but he gives nothing away.

"Got family, but lives alone."

"Alta." Nothing.

"Yeah."

"Nine?" Not even a tick of his jaw.

"We'll be there." He switches off the phone and tosses it to the cushion of the couch. "Meeting at nine. All of us there."

"He pissed?" Breaker asks.

"No more than normal." Buzz lies on the couch and puts his feet up. "I'm sure he'll want more information on the guy. I'll give him everything I have electronically, but we'll have to go to Alta and get some shit together."

I figured as much. No big deal. One thing the three of us are good at is staking places out and not getting caught. Even though Breaker was in a different unit than us, he still learned the same principles and it kept all us alive for a long time. "Fine. I'm going over to Blaze's." I get up from the couch and grab my boots.

Buzz and Breaker exchange a simultaneous look. What it is who the fuck knows, who cares.

"Later," Buzz and Breaker say at the same time. When they're not thinking too much, they do that a lot. Answer at the same time. Normally, it's only when they are both relaxed enough to let it happen. Some kind of twin voodoo or something that I ignore.

I leave with only one thing on my mind. Blaze.

PULLING UP TO X, I see cars are parked everywhere, must be a full crowd tonight. I park my bike and stroll in. Travis, one of the bouncers, stands at the door and I give him a chin lift. I breeze into the place, people line up three maybe four deep at the bar and all the tables are taken. It is standing room only. Ace spots me, holds up a beer, and I charge through the people to take it from him.

"Blaze due up?" I ask as he's trying to pour a thousand drinks at once.

"Five minutes she goes on," he says and leaves.

I stride toward the stage, people moving, giving me a wide berth. The table I usually sit in has two guys in business suits sitting there smiling, like they've never seen a tit before in their lives, which sucks for them considering they both have wedding rings on their fingers.

I stand in front of their table; their eyes follow up to meet mine. I cross my arms over my chest. "Move!" I bark with authority.

They gape at each other and scurry to get out of their chairs. I sit down and rest my feet on the other chair. Do I know there are people standing that want to sit? Fuck yeah. Are they sitting next to me? Hell no.

The girl in front of me has decent tits, but she's so fucking thin her bones peek through her skin. I hate that shit. I like curves. Better yet, I like Blaze's curves.

A hand grips my shoulder and I turn quickly, ready to fuck someone up. Princess. I settle. "Gonna let me sit?" she asks, pointing to the chair my feet are on. I slowly remove them one boot at a time. She rolls her eyes and plops her ass in it. "You know you're taking up space and these people pay," she jokes.

Princess is an animal in and of herself. Not only is she the President's daughter, she is also Cruz's girl. Princess is in this life full on. She did time in jail for a crime she didn't commit. Went through shit and came out of it sitting across from me, smiling.

I shrug.

"You here to see Blaze?"

I should say that's a stupid fucking question, but instead of talking, I nod and take a pull from the beer in my hand.

Princess gets closer to me so I can hear her since the music is thumping so loud. "She said yes by the way. She's gonna take over."

"Good." That's real good. I don't want all these fuckers gawking at her. The word *mine* rings in my ears.

The lights go dark, the music blares, and Blaze takes the stage. First, the light only points to blood red, fuck-me heels. Shit. My dick jerks, all attention on her. The light trails up her long legs, hitting the V covered in red lace and silk. Fuck me. The light continues up, illuminating her bare stomach, and then up further still to reveal a red lace and leather halter-top that ties around her neck, her huge tits already almost spilling out. Then the light focuses on her face, perfection. Her hips begin their torturous and erotic sway to the music.

Her eyes meet mine as if she knew exactly where I was in the room, and she winks, giving me a soft smile. I fucking love that I get the real one. This time I wink back and her lips part. Her eyes widen and she falters a step. Good, new thing—catch her off guard.

Blaze adds more hip thrusts in her routine, driving the crowd wild. Out of the corner of my eye, I see a man running. How in the fuck he's doing it in a crush of people I don't know. I rise as the man leaps up on stage, arms extended out, and grabs Blaze around the chest and falls with her to the other side of the stage.

Princess leaps up too, but I'm already on my way over, throwing people out of my way to get to Blaze. Where in the fuck is Cali? Pandemonium breaks out and guys start shoving each other and doing stupid bullshit. A chair flies but all I can do is think about getting to Blaze. After shoving yet another guy out of my fucking way, I find her. The asshole who jumped the stage is on top of her, grinding his hips like he's fucking her. Blaze's knee comes up and knocks the bastard in the nuts before I fully get to her. The asshole keels over, about to roll to his side, when I pick him up by his collar.

Cali comes up and picks Blaze up off the floor. I do a full body scan over every inch of her flesh and there's no blood. "Take her to the dressing room. I'll be there in a minute. Don't let her out," I order Cali, he nods. Princess gets through and rushes up to Blaze to escort them.

I lift the stupid motherfucker up and drag him through the crowd of screaming people, knocking a few over in the process, and out the side door of X. My anger is so ripe, so raw, that it unleashes on the man. He fucking *touched* her. I throw him up against the brick wall, his skull hitting it with a crack.

"What the fuck is your problem?" I yell at the bastard, not really caring, but demanding answers.

His eyes are glassy. The stupid motherfucker is completely wasted, too bad because he won't feel the pain as much as I want him to. My fist connects with his jaw and his face swings to the side. He slumps down the wall. What a pathetic piece of shit. I grab him and hold him up. I give two hard punches to his ribs, knowing I bruised them pretty fucking bad, maybe even broke them. He doubles over in pain. I give one more punch to the eye, his head cracking on the brick once more.

Then I let him slump down to the ground. I reach around to his back pocket and pick out his wallet. I remove his ID and talk low and deep. "Do not ever show your fucking face in this place again. You do, I'm coming to your house and I'll bring my guys. It'll be much more fun."

I throw his wallet at him and it bounces off his chest. I make sure the picture on the ID is him and search for my woman in the club. The flood lights are on in the place and bouncers are escorting all the people out of the club, most of them running to get out. On my way into X, I run into Doug who gives me a chin lift and is trying to calm the other girls. He's cradling one in his arms. Tough fucking job.

At Blaze's door, I turn the handle. It's locked. Cali shrugs. "Is Princess in there with her?"

"Nope, had to go out and take care of shit," he says, shrugging and crossing his arms over his chest.

Shit. I knock on the door and she doesn't say anything. "Blaze, open up." Nothing. I bang hard, shaking the walls around the door. "If I have to get the key from Princess I will." After what seems like an eternity, she opens the door a crack and I step in, closing it behind me.

My hearts stops for a beat. Her eyes are blotchy and red. Fuck. She's been crying. Fear runs in her eyes, but it seems like there is more to it. I don't ask, don't say a word, just go to her and hold her in my arms.

Small shudders come off of her and I continue to hold her tight. Her arms wrap around my waist and she squeezes hard. We stand there for a long time, holding each other.

She pulls away first, releasing my waist, and wiping her eyes with her hand. "I'm okay," she says without any prompting, like an automatic response.

"If you're not, that's okay, Blaze." I don't let go of her and she reaches up to my chest, palms down on my pecs. I love the feel of her hands on my body.

"Really, I'm okay. I want to go home now." The red rims tell me more than I thought. She is done. D-O-N-E Done. With stripping or just for the night, I don't know, but it's there.

"I'll come with you." She nods, shocking the shit out of me, but I don't show it. No fight whatsoever, only flat out acceptance.

"Are you okay to drive?" I ask.

She nods.

"Get your stuff and let's go." I release her reluctantly and she gets all of her things, putting them in her bag mechanically. The light isn't shining in her eyes. More is going on here. What, no fucking clue, but I seriously want to fucking know.

I get her into her Jeep and follow her all the way to her house. No one bothers us in or out of the club and I check the house before I let her come in. Everything is clear.

"I need to shower." She goes to the bathroom door. "I'll be out in a minute." She disappears, her stride slumpy. Every fiber of me is telling me to go and get in with her, but I know I shouldn't, not after what happened. It's too raw and I'm not a total asshole.

I take off my boots then do a double check of the house, doors, windows and blinds. Not that the asshole from tonight would dare come, but this happening tonight puts her living out here by herself in a different perspective for me.

I fill up a glass of water and luckily find some pain relievers in the first cabinet I open. I turn off all the lights on my way to her bedroom. I set the water and pills on the small table by her bed, turn on the lamp, and click off the main light.

I sit on the edge of her bed and wait for her. She comes out wearing gray sweat pants tugged up to her knees and an oversized t-shirt with *I didn't do it* printed on the front. She startles when she sees me, taking a huge gasp. I watch her try to relax herself.

"I guess you're staying?" she says in a question but it's really a statement.

"You are not wrong, honey." Her arms wrap around her body, almost to protect herself. "Do you want me to?" I ask, giving her the choice, not that I would actually leave, but something tells me that she needs this. To have a choice.

She stares at me, her eyes moving back and forth. She's thinking hard and it seems there is an internal battle going on. What it is, I'd love to know.

"Yes," she whispers. "I'm tired." She steps to the other side of the bed.

"Wait!" She jumps. Damn. I'm a fucking ass for barking. "Shit, sorry, babe." I grab the water and the pills.

"Here, take these." She downs the pills without question, proving her trust in me.

She climbs in, snagging the covers over her body. Her being quiet and solemn is not the Blaze I know and I fucking hate it. I remove my shirt, jeans and socks and climb into bed with her. She lies there unmoving when I lie down. Fuck that. I turn her around and rest her head on my chest, her arm on my abs, and intertwine my legs with hers. She doesn't protest.

I turn off the light and kiss the top of her hair. "What are you thinking about so hard?" I ask in the darkness, staring up at the ceiling. Her body tenses. I'm beginning to really hate that shit.

"I'm tired," she answers and I'm sure she is, but I really want to talk about this shit.

"I know you are, sweet lips, but you gotta talk about it."

After a few beats she says, "There's nothing to talk about. A drunk guy bum-rushed me on stage. I'll have a bruise on my shoulder and maybe my leg, but other than that I'm fine." She doesn't seem fine; to me she seems anything but.

"That's all true, babe, but how do you feel about that?"

"I'm pissed. That shit isn't supposed to happen at X. The bouncers are supposed to stop that shit from happening." Now at least we are getting somewhere. "What did you do to him?"

I wait a minute and think about what to say. "I made sure he wouldn't come near you or X ever again." She lifts from my chest, her eyes piercing mine.

"Did you kill him?"

"Do you really want to know the answer to that question?" I ask, knowing she doesn't.

She turns and lies on my chest. "No. I don't want to know."

I chuckle. "No, sweet lips, just taught him a lesson. One he won't forget anytime soon." We lie there in silence and I listen to Blaze's breathing even out. I sweep my hand up and down her back, the movement hopefully soothing her and definitely soothing me. I'm so fucking revved up from seeing her on the floor like that and that motherfucker dry humping her, but having her in my arms helps. She helps.

"Thank you," she whispers so softly I barely catch it.

"Always."

Sleep doesn't come easy for me. I should be calling Buzz, getting a trace on this asshole that jumped Blaze, but I'm not getting up. I'm not leaving this fucking spot until I have to. Having her in my arms is right and I'm going to keep it that way. Somehow I manage to drift off.

MOVEMENT WAKES ME. Blaze tries to get out of my arms that are tight around her. Her back to my front, Blaze's ass cradles my morning wood. I will him to stand down, but well... he has a mind of his own.

"Where are you going?" I ask gruffly.

"Bathroom." Her voice quiet. I let go and she gets out of bed, not scurrying like she's trying to get away, just that she has to pee. As she walks toward the bathroom, she's not putting a lot of weight on her right leg. Fuck.

The clock reads 7:03 a.m. I have to be at the clubhouse around eight thirty and there is no way I'm leaving Blaze alone, not yet. I grab my phone and hit Princess's name.

"Are you all right?" she asks in a sleepy voice.

"Gotta be at the clubhouse. Can you come and stay with Blaze?"

"How is she?" She yawns into the phone.

"Think she bruised her right hip or leg. She's not putting weight on it and I'm sure her shoulder hurts like a bitch."

"I'll be over in twenty." She disconnects without saying goodbye. She is seriously like her brother. He does the same damn shit.

I turn off the phone as Blaze comes out of the bathroom. Even first thing in the morning without a spot of makeup on, she's absolutely beautiful. She comes around the bed and climbs in. This time she doesn't hesitate and pushes against me and I envelop her in my arms.

"How are you today?" I expect her to tell me she's fine because that seemed to be her answer for everything last night.

"Sore. My shoulder and hip," she says instead, shocking me but in a good way.

"How else are you doing?" I prod more.

"I'm all right, Tug. It was bound to happen sooner or later. It could have been worse." She shrugs her shoulder against my chest. "It'll be all right and I'm sure the stage will be heavily guarded now." She's not wrong about that either. I will definitely be talking to Princess about that shit or Pops.

I kiss her temple and her body quakes. I love that I can do that to her. Blaze is not the type of woman that you fuck and leave. She's not the type that you play around on or with. She's the type of woman that poses a challenge. And if you meet that challenge, the reward is so fucking big nothing else matters. I will meet the challenge.

"I've gotta get to the clubhouse. Princess is going to come and stay with you," I say, rubbing small circles on her shoulder with my fingertips.

"I don't need a babysitter, Tug."

"I know that. I just didn't want you alone, so I called Princess." I wait a beat. "Just humor me alright."

She sighs. "All right." Silence fills the air. "Thank you for last night. It was exactly what I needed."

It was what I needed too.

THE VEIN IN POPS' neck throbs but his face remains stoic. Dagger, Cruz, and Rhys haven't said shit since Buzz started showing them his computer and talking all his techy jargon. I'm sure half the shit no one in this damn room but him understands. Breaker keeps quiet, letting his brother talk, which is something else he does a lot, staying in the background and allowing his brother to lead. I haven't chimed in much either since I have no clue about any of this shit.

Word had already spread through Ravage about last night at X before I even got here. I gave the ID to Buzz and asked him to check the guy out for me. No one was happy about what happened to Blaze. The guys may be a bit gruff, but they take care of what is theirs.

Pops picks up his phone, dials, and holds it to his ear without saying a word to us. "Becs. How long till you're here?" His brow furrows.

"Then get your fucking ass in my office now." Pops clicks off the phone as Becs enters the room.

"What's up, boss?" Becs, Ravage's Vice President, enters as if the world is his oyster and nothing is going to get him down.

"Sit. Buzz found the guy that cut into our computer for Paine." Pops runs down the information for Becs and then asks his opinion. They come to an agreement fast.

"Find out if he works for him or if he was contracted out. Also, find out what else he knows and if he has stored that information other places that we need to know about. Either way, he goes. He knows too much about Ravage," Becs says.

"Agreed," Pops replies.

Pops turns to Dagger and Rhys. "You two take Tug and Buzz up to Alta. Get everything you can on this man. Need to know if he stored Ravage shit somewhere. Get all electronics from him and find out if he has a safe or a safety deposit box. Chat with him *nicely* and see what you come up with. Then take care of it." Dagger and Rhys nod in approval. I knew he'd ask Buzz to go because he's a tech genius, me I am a little surprised about. The level of trust Pops just gave me is not taken lightly.

Rhys stands. "We telling GT this shit? Cause right now, he's got his hands full."

"No. Leave him out of this. Let him deal with Angel so he can get his fucking head screwed back on right. Sooner he does, the better off we all are. Cruz, Zeb and Breaker stay here in case of blowback." Pops rubs his hands over his face and through his hair. No doubt all the shit that happened to Shaina and Casey has been weighing him down. No offense, but I wouldn't want that kind of responsibility.

My thoughts drift to Blaze and there is no way in hell I want to leave her right now, but I have no choice. "Can one of the guys keep tabs on Blaze?" I turn and ask Pops.

"Shit," he mutters, threading his fingers through his hair and giving it a tug. "Yeah. I'll have her covered."

I nod, giving him affirmation and a thank you for doing this for me.

"Done. Let's go," Rhys says to us as we rise. "Get your shit. You two will drive the cage and Dagger and I'll follow."

Even knowing this is the best option since Buzz needs all his techy shit, I still don't fucking like it. I hate being cooped up, especially when I could be riding my bike, but it's what the club needs and what I'll do without argument. And somehow, I need to keep my mind off Blaze to get it done right.

"We leave in two hours. Hurry your ass up." Dagger strolls out of the room and we follow.

I move over to Breaker, assuming that he will be the one to watch over Blaze. I don't like it, but I'll deal. "Hey." He lifts his chin. "Shitty time to leave Blaze. Need you to keep an eye out." I let him fill in all the blanks, which he does quickly.

"You got it," he says and he's gone. I need to go get my shit.

"I GOTTA LEAVE FOR A BIT. Club business." My arms go around her body and she loops hers around my waist. Her eyes show a hint of fear, but she blinks rapidly and it vanishes.

"Okay. I'll be fine." She lies flat out and whatever expression I have on my face has her rolling her eyes.

"Are you okay to go to X?" I ask.

"Yes. I won't let this get to me." I search her face for a hint she is lying to me and find nothing. Such a strong fucking woman.

"You stay with Princess, when you're not with her, Pops will have a guy keeping his eye out." Her brows draw close together and before she speaks I do. "It'll help my peace of mind."

Her body sags into me, the fight she had in her gone. I lower my lips to hers and kiss her. Her lips are so soft, and when her tongue touches mine, I hit it hard. I thread my fingers through her hair, turn her and deepen the kiss, so much so that when it breaks we are both breathless. Damn straight.

"I'll be back as soon as I can." I rub my thumb across her jaw and I'm liking this new Blaze.

"I'll be fine. You don't have to worry about me. In fact,

don't even think about me while you're gone." And the new Blaze is gone. Damn. She steps out of my grasp and grabs her things for the shower. "I'm going to shower and then go to X."

She only gets two steps in before I snag her around the waist, yanking her body into my chest. She tenses and whatever was going on in bed this morning has left her or she's hiding it very well. But, her body doesn't lie. Her breaths pick up and her body begins to relax.

"You need to go, you'll be late." I will if I keep this up, shit. I squeeze her and then release. Whatever is going on will have to wait.

I kiss her lips, not hard, but sweet. "Be safe," I whisper to her as she opens her eyes.

"You too."

FOUR DAYS too long if you ask me. I understand the need for information, but this fucker should be dead already. He doesn't do anything but go to the office and come home. Nothing. Boring as shit, this dude. Doesn't even bring his girl here to fuck.

Where he found out about the T-Darts and how he got himself involved with them is beyond me. Buzz has been typing at his computer day and night. Hell if I know what he's doing, but I'm getting fucking itchy to get this shit taken care of and get home.

I've talked or texted Blaze a few times each day and her responses are very short. She's fine, of course, and nothing bad has happened, which is good. If she thinks I'm buying the fine shit anymore after I get back, she's sadly mistaken.

I've checked in with Breaker and he's kept his eye on her as per Pops' request. And luckily, everything's been quiet. I even put a call into Princess, making sure the security is tight at X. Just in case. She said she was already on it. It isn't much from here, but it'll have to do till I get to her.

Buzz didn't have time to run the name on the ID before we left and I don't think the guy that knocked her down is trouble, but I'm not taking chances. The way she curled into me that morning when I left had every protective instinct in my body on full alert. It's why I want this fucking job over with. Fuck.

"Got it." Relief washes over me and the adrenaline kicks in. Buzz has been trying to get past the fucker's security system since we got here. Asshole has it locked up tight. I wonder what we'll find because no one has that sophisticated of an alarm for nothing. He's not home and if the last few days are anything to go by, we have four and a half hours before he steps foot in the house.

We all sit in the cage after our latest find-the-info search. "Thank God," Dagger mumbles. "All right, Rhys and Tug go in the side. We'll go in the front. Pick the door. We want this clean." Dagger turns to Buzz. "Sound good?"

"Perfect. Everything is disabled, including cameras. Even the three back up security systems he has. Something is in that fucking house." This does not sound good, but we're in it so let's do this shit. We climb out of the cage, the warm sun beating down on us. Luckily most of the people that live around here are gone during the day. The only one we had to worry about was the cat woman down the road, but luckily she left this morning and we haven't seen her since.

Getting out my lock pick, I easily open the door. My gut sinks. Why in the hell would a guy who has his house secured like Fort Knox have a simple deadbolt holding the door that anyone who picks locks can get into? My guard is way up now. I draw my gun, holding it out in front of me. The door creaks open and the smell of cinnamon waifs through the air. Stepping through the threshold, we enter the tidy kitchen with white appliances, light wood cabinets, and seemingly nothing out of place.

I notice the cameras as they are not hidden at all but strategically placed on top of the walls near the ceiling, which I'm sure gave every possible angle from wherever they are controlled. Moving through the kitchen with my gun drawn, pointing it down at the ground but ready for a moment's notice, we enter the small living room where Buzz and Dagger stand, also with weapons drawn. They nod and Buzz goes down the hallway. After all of his research, he knew exactly where he was going. I check the rest of the house, making sure it's clear, and join the other three.

Buzz stands in front of a door with a large padlock on the outside of it, along with more deadbolts lining the side of it, three to be exact. What the fuck? Both Buzz and I get busy picking each of the locks and it is not easy. These are more sophisticated. Sweat pours down my face, falling into my eyes and I wipe it with my shirt. After what seems like hours, we unlock each of them and open the door.

Dagger flicks on the light and the four of us carefully enter the room but stop dead a few feet inside to take in the scene around us. It is totally not what I expected, not that I really knew or had a clue what to expect. I was just definitely not this. The room is stark white, reminding me of a hospital with navy blue drapes covering the windows. The only furniture in the room is a wooden desk, placed in the center with a chair in the crook of its opening. On the desk are three computer monitors, and a keyboard lay in front of them. Other than that, nothing else is on the desk.

Buzz wanders further into the room and I follow, noticing a door to the right and nodding to Dagger. Dagger slowly turns the handle of the door, gun pointing inside the dark room, the light filtering in from the computer room providing our only means of illumination. Empty. Totally and completely empty. Strange.

Sitting on the floor next to the desk is a large box about the size of a small refrigerator, the kind that fit in campers or RVs. Wires are poking out everywhere on it, some blue and some yellow. The wires are attached to a small box underneath the desk and then the wires lead up to the monitors.

"What the fuck is this?" I ask Buzz.

"Computer hub and backup." Buzz's gloved fingers type on the keyboard and the monitors shine to life, each one with a small box stating *Enter Your Password*. Buzz brings a small box no bigger than a cigarette case out of his pocket. Lights flash on it as he places it close to the hub. I have no clue what the hell he's doing, but I'm ready to get this shit done with.

A small beeping noise catches my attention, stiffening my spine. I scan around the room for it.

"It's all right, just my box. It's hopefully cracking the password. If I can't get it, we'll come up with plan B. I'm sure this asshole has something set up where the wrong password will lock it or worse, erase it," Buzz says, fiddling with his box.

"Fuck," Dagger murmurs as he and Rhys walk around the room, seeing there is nothing there.

"We're gonna check the rest of the house out," Rhys says, obviously bored out of his mind but totally alert to what is going on around him.

"Shit." Buzz stops us as we follow his gaze to some wire attached to the computer. "Guys, see if there's another hub in the basement, just like this one." He points to the machine, still following the cords. "Don't touch it if you see it."

"What the fuck is it?" Rhys asks, perplexed, and I'm with him there.

"It's just another hub, but I'm sure most of what we want is saved on it and one wrong touch could set off some trap that this asshole has set up. I'm just being overly cautious," Buzz replies.

"How do you know he'd do this shit?" Dagger asks, moving toward the door.

"Cause it's what I would do." Buzz continues typing while speaking.

A short time later, we learn there is another hub

downstairs and Buzz is getting nowhere fast, not to mention the asshole will be coming home in the next couple of hours. Buzz is tiptoeing around that damn machine like it will bite his fucking ass off. I've cased the damn house and found nothing, no paper trail anywhere. All I know is I'm ready for some fucking action already.

"You almost done?" Dagger asks impatiently.

"I'm not getting anywhere with this shit. We need to pack it up and take it with us." Buzz's exasperation comes through loud and clear.

"And how in the fuck do you propose we do that?" Rhys clips, the tension rolling off of him.

"I have an idea." Buzz turns to us, giving us his full attention and we wait. "All right, I thought this might happen. So I put together something, but we gotta hurry." What the hell? Buzz has a fucking contingency plan? I should have known he would and why it shocks me in this situation, I don't know. He always had a plan B in the field.

"All right. In the van, I have magnets that go on the side of it for an appliance company. There are some boxes broken down and packing tape, you'll need to tape them so it looks like you're delivering something. Bring them in here, we'll pack this shit up and carry it gently to the van." Buzz is so calm as he explains everything, it's like he does this shit every day.

"And a bunch of bikers are delivering shit now?" Dagger chuckles, gripping his leather.

"In the van are two plain, blue jumpsuits from the garage and hats. Put that shit on and we'll load this up."

Dagger and Rhys seem very shocked that Buzz went this far in the planning, but play it cool.

"All right, Tug," Dagger says. "You and I are gonna go get the van and wear the jumpsuits. We'll park the cage as close to the house as possible and move fucking fast. I want this done in fifteen minutes and we are out of here."

I nod and ask, "What about the guy? He comes home and sees his shit gone..." My voice trails off, leaving the guys to fill in the blanks.

"I say we do the same thing. One of us stays here, knock him out when he gets here, put him in one of the boxes, and haul his ass out of here," Buzz says.

"Let's do this," Rhys says, a sadistic gleam in his eye.

This isn't an easy task, but somehow we manage to accomplish the first part of it and get all the electronics loaded. Dagger and Rhys decide that Rhys would stay here and greet the asshole when he got home. We'll watch the house and as soon as the car pulls up, drive the van in and Dagger and I will get out in our navy jumpsuits and stroll into the house, pick up the box, and bring it to the van. At least, this is the plan. Right now, we are waiting in the cage, and each one of us is jumpy as shit, ready to get this over with.

"There he is," Buzz says from behind us. He wanted to be next to the computers to protect them. I would have thought he'd want a piece of this asshole right away, but he must be saving it for later. He wants to stay.

Everything goes as planned until we enter the house. The asshole, as we keep calling him even though his name is Joseph Harrison, is standing in the corner of the living room with a gun pointed at Rhys. We raise our guns on him.

"What the fuck, Rhys?" Dagger asks, trying to get a read on the situation.

"Joey here carries a gun on him. I said hi, he put the gun on me, I put my gun on him and here we are." Rhys is calm and cool, his gun steadily trained on Joey, who, on the other hand, seems like he's going to piss and shit his pants at any given second. The hand holding his gun is shaky as shit and his eyes keep bouncing back and forth between all three of us. While I'd like to put a bullet between the asshole's eyes for fucking us over, we need his information before that can happen. And if we can't get in the computer, we need him to do so. But he doesn't need to know that quite yet.

Tensions are thick inside the room, the air hot and uninviting. I'm ready to get gone. "Just come with us. We have a few questions." My tone is even but demanding.

"I'm not going anywhere with you. You'll kill me," Joey stammers and he's not wrong there.

"How long you been watching us?" Rhys asks, Joey's face shifting to him, his eye quirks.

"I'm not telling you anything either and if you try to access my computer, it'll send you on a wild goose chase through cyberspace and you'll never find anything." Joey is almost cocky, he's so damn sure of himself.

"Who you working for?" Dagger questions, not listening to the computer mumbo-jumbo. He's poised like me with his finger on the trigger and ready to shoot.

"If I knew, I wouldn't tell you that either." This guy

either has balls of steel or he's got a plan B; I'm going with the latter.

"So, what do you suppose we do in this situation?" Dagger's voice is laced with pissed-offness.

Joey sneers. "You leave me alone." I want to laugh, but don't. I keep my face stoic because if this asshole thinks we will leave him alone and go on our merry way, he's got another thing coming.

Rhys on the other hand does laugh, but not a funny one. It's the kind that has most people quiver in their boots and practically piss their pants. Joey hears it too as his eyes flicker to him and widen. Then Rhys speaks so low and deep that it is practically a growl. "If you've been really watching us all this time, you should know by now that isn't happening."

Joey's knees shake and the gun in his hand trembles. Sweat beads on his forehead, telling me he's seen enough information about Ravage to know this shit is true. Good and bad. "If you enter the password wrong one time, it will send all the information on a roller-coaster ride through space. If you kill me, I can't enter it and everything will be lost." The confidence in his tone is waning.

"What all do you have?" I ask, thinking that maybe he'll answer. Long shot.

"More than you'll ever know." I shouldn't be surprised, but I am a bit. Who would have thought this straight-laced guy would have balls to tap into all this shit? What exactly, we don't know for sure and that is the problem.

"Alright, put the gun down and come with us," Dagger requests.

"No," he says, his spine stiffening a bit.

Rhys's nostrils flare with anger. It's never good when he gets really pissed off. Rhys is not the type of guy that anyone fucks with, ever, and if my calculations are correct, Joey will be learning that here in the next few seconds.

"How about I fucking shoot you right here on the spot and say fuck it. Or maybe I'll blast off that fucking hand of yours that's holding the gun," Rhys taunts, aiming his gun at Joey's hand. "Or how about I take that fucking gun out of your hand." Rhys steps forward and my eyes stay trained on Joey's trigger finger. Joey jumps, obviously scared of Rhys and with good reason.

"Stay back or I'll shoot," Joey shouts unsteadily. Rhys takes another step forward. Damn that fucker's got balls of steel, fucking love it.

Dagger speaks, "Look, asshole, all we want to know is who hired you to get information on us, and what information you have. Give us that and we'll leave."

"Liar. You'll kill me," Joey clips.

"You're dead either way," Rhys says, laying it out there for him as he inches closer. "And at this point, I'll take great pleasure to make sure it's as painful as fucking possible." Another step. Rhys is only three feet from him.

Joey reaches behind his back with his empty hand. My eyes hone in on the movement. Something flicks to the floor and bounces with a tap. Then Joey jabs himself in the leg with a syringe. Shit.

"Good luck with that, fuckers," Joeys says as he injects whatever is in the syringe into his body before I have time to pull the trigger. His body instantly collapses to the ground as Rhys is there, jerking the syringe out of Joey's body.

"Fuck!" Rhys exclaims and puts his fingers on Joey's pulse point. "His breaths are shallow, but he's still alive. For how long, I have no fucking clue."

"What was that shit?" Dagger steps closer.

"No idea." I move next to him, taking in everything.

"We gotta get him in the box and out of here. Get the syringe and his fucking gun and let's move," Rhys orders and we get busy.

It's not easy carrying dead weight in a box and loading it into the van, but we do it. As soon as we are in the cage, we retell everything that happened inside the house to Buzz and he doesn't seem happy, but it's nothing he can't handle it either.

I open the box while Buzz drives, getting us the hell out of there. I check for Joey's pulse and it's still there, faint but there. We drop off Dagger and Rhys to their bikes and hightail it to Ravage.

CHAPTER SEVEN
Blaze

I SIT ON THE COUCH IN MY LIVING ROOM WITH MY LEGS tucked up underneath my body, and lay my head on the cushion, embracing the softness. I cover my body with my throw blanket, the one with the skulls, and flick on the television. I don't really want to watch it, but it's my day off and I want to relax. I tried a bath, that didn't help. I tried reading and that did nothing. It can't be X that's my problem. These last few nights have been cake. Princess upped security and if a guy wanted to get that close to fling himself on me again, he'd meet one of the four bouncers around the stage. I don't feel anything different when I go to X, but I do keep my eyes open more.

When the guy tackled me off the stage, I was terrified because in that split second something in me thought it was Santos or Frankie. Then I started fighting because I sure as shit am never going back to them. I've been so strong over the years not letting it weigh on my mind. But in that brief moment, I made a mistake. I let Tug see a different side of myself, the one that is vulnerable, and that should not have happened. Even as he held me that night, I didn't care. I let every single wall come down and just was there, with him. I gave everything to him to absorb for me and he did.

I'd be totally lying to myself if I said I didn't miss him, because the sad thing is I do, and that scares the ever-loving shit out of me. I don't want to miss him. I wanted him to be gone, far from me, but since he left a huge part of me aches. How am I supposed to stop my heart from feeling even when my mind is telling me to stay away?

I blink back those thoughts and my mom is there instead.

She was such a good woman, strong confident and self-assured. She worked her ass off to provide for us, sometimes taking on two and three jobs at a time. We didn't have much, but we had each other. Then she got sick. Breast Cancer, but that wasn't what made her really sick. It was the brain and spinal tumors that came with the cancer that ended up taking my mother's life.

When she first found it, she didn't tell me. She was trying to protect me like she always had while I was growing up. Sure, we had to move from place to place, but there was always somewhere and that was what mattered. Until finally, I noticed the weakness in Mom and called her out on it, and she told me. I was crushed but more so because she didn't have the money for treatments.

That is where Santos Markus came into play. A snake filled with venom. Rich and powerful, he took a liking to my mother after coming into the diner where she worked. She fell for him hook, line and sinker, and we had an instant family. Santos has a son, Frank, and the four of us became one. Santos didn't care that Mom was sick and helped pay all of her medical bills to treat her illness. I believed that he truly did love her, at the time. He told her so repeatedly and was affectionate toward her constantly. He'd kiss her before leaving the house every single time and would hold the doors open for her when we went out as a family.

Frank and I never got along. I was fifteen and he was seventeen, not close in age but not far either. The way his eyes crept over my body weirded me out. I tried hard to stay away from him and I achieved it for quite some time.

Everything was going pretty good in our lives. I was going to high school regularly, had my own room, had good food every night, and my mom was happy and getting better. Then the doctors said that tumors had developed in places they couldn't remove without fear of hurting her worse or paralyzing her, for that matter, so they treated her. She was weak, but happy and that was all I cared about. I never had to want for anything. Santos provided well for us and I was grateful for that.

Then one night when I was sixteen, everything changed. My life turned to shit and there wasn't a damn thing I could do about it because if I breathed a word to anyone about what was happening in my room, my mother would die. That threat is what got me to comply and Santos knew it. I love her more than anything in this world and would do anything for her, even suffer and damn that is what I did repeatedly over the years.

When I found my mother's dead body on the floor of her room, I tried everything to make her come back to me, the compressions, breathing into her mouth... Nothing. She was gone. Then self-preservation kicked in and I did the most painful thing I've ever done. I kissed her softly, ran to my room, packed a bag and left. On the car ride, I called the ambulance and cried the entire way to my aunt's house in North Carolina.

I checked for her obituary repeatedly, stopping at libraries along the way. My aunt gave me her car and a GPS that wasn't connected to anything that could be traced. Each day I looked, I both dreaded and hoped that I would see it. I dreaded it because it was confirmation she was gone. And I hoped, because I wanted to make sure that someone got to her and gave her the respect she deserved. When I found it, I broke out in tears right there in the middle of the library. I couldn't stop them even though I tried.

What really killed me was the funeral. I couldn't go. I so wanted to be there to tell my mom goodbye, but couldn't.

The ring from my phone tears me out of my painful thoughts, thankfully, and I pluck it off the coffee table. Princess's name is on the screen. I swipe it to accept the call.

"Hello." Since our *talk* everything at X, minus me

getting tackled, has gone well and I like my new job. Princess may be a badass, but she has a huge heart, though I'd never tell her this because she'd probably throat punch me.

"Hey. I'm going over to see Casey. You want to come?" Her words catch me by surprise. I haven't seen Casey since her kidnapping. GT has kept her under lock and key, which I don't blame him for, but the truth is, I miss her.

I met Casey shortly after taking the job from Princess and something between us just clicked. Our bond really grew when Princess was in jail. Babs, a jealous bitch who wanted to be Princess, and Liz who ran the club while Princess was in jail, set Princess up. They are both dead now and the fact that I say that without hesitation should unnerve me, but it strangely doesn't.

But while Princess was locked up, Casey and I became really great friends. We had each other to lean on and I miss her.

"Love to. How's she doing?" Casey has been through a lot these past few months. She lost her and GT's baby, almost lost GT, then was kidnapped. All Tug told me is that it was bad. I know bad and hope that Casey didn't have to live through what I did. I would never wish that on anyone.

"She's getting better. She talked to Shaina and I think that helped. The last time we spoke, she talked about my brother and it screamed a satisfied woman." She stops then continues. "Not that I need to know shit about what they do in the bedroom."

But she would listen to her because she loved her.

That part isn't said, but I know it's true. The relationship between Princess and Casey is something that I'd love to have. They've known each other since they were kids and grew up side-by-side. I don't have any connection to my childhood and any of my old friends I severed ties with and don't dare find them. I can't risk it. But what I have with Casey and Princess now is good, and I like that, a lot.

I chuckle. "I bet he's good," I tease and Princess sighs. "You going over to her house?"

"Yeah. You want to meet me or want me to pick you up?" she asks.

"I'll drive. I need to change real quick and then I'll come." I get up from the couch and go to my bedroom.

"All right, meet ya in thirty."

"Bye." I end the conversation right before Princess disconnects the phone. I change into a pair of faded blue jeans with holes at the knees. Some would think this is stylish, but I ripped one of the legs on a nail that protruded out of my doorframe when I first bought the place. So, I tore the other so it would match. Now, they are my favorite jeans. I add a blood-red baby T, a black belt with small metal stars all over it, and my sling back sandals. I brush my hair and then set out for Casey's.

The door opens in a whoosh to reveal Casey behind it, grinning, but a hint of sadness hides behind her eyes. "There you are! I was so excited when Harlow told me you were coming!" Casey has always called Princess by her real name, Harlow. In the club, they have club names like Harlow is Princess and now I hear that Casey is Angel. Nice, fits her perfectly.

I hold my arms open as she falls into them and I hug her tight. "I missed you, woman."

"Come in. I've been trying to de-man cave the place and it's a full time job." She laughs and it is awesome to hear that sound out of her.

The house does not look like a man cave to me. The buttery cream walls create a cozy atmosphere along with pictures of Casey and GT, and some of their family among them. Dark brown curtains with buttery cream stripes hang to the sides of the windows but are open to let in the light. The couch and chair are a deep brown matching the curtains and the coffee table is a beautiful dark wood. I breathe in deep and smell the scent of cherry vanilla, calming and very soothing.

"It's not a man cave to me." I enter the room fully and kick off my sandals in the walkway.

"Oh God. You should have seen this place when I moved in. It was a pit. I made GT take me to the bedding store to get a new bed and sheets before I'd sleep here. And the living room, damn I needed a shovel to get through all the pizza boxes and beer bottles." Her tone is serious but with a hint of humor. "Come on in the kitchen. Harlow's there."

The kitchen is quaint. It has the same butter cream walls, with light wood cabinets and a tan, speckled Formica countertop. It's small but very clean. Linoleum lines the floor in some type of blue, triangular pattern. Princess rifles through the refrigerator.

"Hey, bout time your ass gets here." She sets a pitcher of sweet tea on the counter, opening a cabinet to the right of the sink and removing three plastic tumblers.

I set my purse on the small kitchen table off to the side of the room and place my hands in the back pockets of my jeans. I shrug. "I had to change and then I came."

Princess pours the tea into the cups and I have no doubt that it's sweet tea. Here in Georgia, I learned quickly that when you order tea it comes sweet. If you don't want it that way, you have to say unsweetened and you get funny looks, but that's the way of the south.

"Here." Princess passes out drinks to Casey and me.

"Let's go in the living room where it's more comfortable. I'd like to go outside and sit, but we don't have any chairs yet." Casey leads us into the living room. She sits on one end of the couch and Princess on the other, I lounge in the recliner.

The air in the room changes. It isn't uncomfortable, but nobody wants to talk about the elephant in the room. I sure as shit don't want to bring up the fact that Casey was kidnapped a short time ago.

"All right. Let's get this part over with so we can move on. I was kidnapped. It wasn't a good time. He didn't rape me, but he touched me. I was scared shitless but the part that haunts me is Shaina. Much worse was done to her, but that's her story to tell, not mine. I'm seeing a counselor thanks to Doc." Doc is the clubhouse doctor and the only reason I know that is because he's come to X to help a couple of the girls out over the years, mostly when their shitheads of boyfriends thought it would be fun to use them as human punching bags. "I really don't want to go into any details of it, but just know that I'm getting better."

I breathe out. "I'm so sorry that happened to you, Casey." I pour every bit of sincerity in that statement because I mean it deeply. I never want another woman to go through the pain of someone taking from them what they are not willing to give. Some things in life are beyond wrong, that is one of them.

"Thank you. But no more of it." Her butt touches the edge of the couch and she places her cup on the coffee table. Her eyes meet mine, her beautiful blonde hair framing her face, her green eyes intent. "This will be the last time we talk about it. I don't want it to be me or define me. It's over and done. I also don't want you to feel bad for me. I love you for it, but I want to move on."

I study her briefly and though there is pain there, there is also determination and strength. I like it. "I love you too, woman. Not another word from me about it." I pretend to zip my mouth and toss the key in the air.

Satisfaction gleams in her eyes. "Great." She must have already had this conversation with Princess because she doesn't go into it with her and Princess doesn't speak a word about it. "All right, tell me what's going on with you two." She reclines and we sit in silence. My eyes question Princess without words, asking if she told her about the guy at X. I really don't think she has because Casey being Casey would have asked about it flat out. Princess's eyes flick back and forth, telling me no, Casey doesn't know. I don't know whether to be happy about that or feel shitty, like I'm hiding something from her.

Princess starts. She talks about how wonderful things are with her man Cruz and her now son, Cooper. The love in her eyes is so vibrant it shines through her, making her glow. It's awesome to get a glimpse of tough-ass Princess's soft side, the woman that could kick anyone's ass, including her brother, GT, who is bigger than her by the way.

"And Blaze is working for me," she adds at the end.

Confusion laces Casey's expression. "Huh? I don't get it."

"I hired her to do the books and take care of things. We are going to run X together." Pride shines from her words and a lump crawls up my throat.

Casey turns to me. "Are you going to quit stripping?"

"Eventually. Right now I'm doing it once a week and will probably do so for the next week or two, maybe longer. I don't know yet." Princess and I haven't had time to sit and really talk about it again, she has been letting me do my thing. "The money is too damn good to pass up, but stripping is not what I want to do with my life. I just can't give it up quite yet." It may sound petty of me to want to do it just for the money, but that money is way too important to me. I need the safety net.

It never has been my dream to be a stripper, but when I got to my aunt's and explained what happened at home and to my mom, she told me that I needed to hide out. Since her place would be the first place they would look, she gave me cash and a business card. On the front of the card was a large X with an address in Sumner, Georgia. She told me to go there and they would help me, but didn't explain any further. And Princess did.

I wanted to build up my savings, and boy have I. I'm glad numbers are my thing because my egg is well nested.

Having the money on hand will help me in a pinch and I need that.

"Understandable. I never had the balls to do it," Casey says and it shocks me that she even considered it, especially growing up in the club. Her dad was Bam, who was a member of Ravage and has been dead for over four years. I didn't think that Bam would have allowed it, but I could be wrong.

"You wanted to?" I ask incredulously.

"I want to learn how to dance, sexy-like. I love working in the garage, but I always wanted to learn how to move my body." She scans me up and down. "And have a body like that." I sit stunned.

"Seriously?" She nods and words fall out of my mouth like vomit. "You don't want this body. Guys only see you as a piece of meat they want to devour. You don't want that."

"I'm sure that's how they feel in X cause that's what they are coming there for. But outside of there, there are lots of nice guys that would kill to have your brains and fuck them out of you." She giggles.

I chuckle. "I'm sure you're right, but I don't take the time to do that. I work, sleep and that's about it."

"You mean to tell me, you're not getting any?" Princess asks like it's the worst thing in the world and she's going to run out and find me a man to screw immediately.

Not that this is any of their business, but it is girl talk and the only time when my steel shields are pliable. Just not so pliable that my past life seeps through. "I have my vibrator and lots of batteries."

"Fuck me." Princess's eyes widen, her mouth hanging

open a bit. I wonder what the hell is up with that. I mean it's not really that strange to have a vibrator, everyone has one of those. What's the damn problem?

"What?" I sip my tea.

"You're not screwing Tug?" Princess asks and I choke. It lodges in my throat and I cough, a lot, and gasp for breath. Casey comes over and pats my back until I get my breathing in order.

"No," I croak out with finality and certainty. One thing good about him being gone this week, it gave me time to fortify my walls. They are back up and strong. I will not let him get past them again.

"Why not? He's hot." Casey sits down, assured I'm not going to keel over on her floor.

"I don't fuck brothers." Both Princess and Casey burst out laughing so hard that tears run down their faces and they are gasping for breath. I swear their shrieking continues for like five minutes. They pat each other on the legs, their hands flailing as they bark out and I sit here like an idiot because I have no clue what the hell is so damn funny.

Casey takes a breath and speaks through her laughter, "We," she points to herself and Princess, "said the same damn thing and look at us now." Casey's body shakes as she breathes, getting herself under control, as does Princess.

"Yeah," Princess agrees. "And I had that pact since I was old enough to know what it meant. Now," she shrugs, "it's great. Why did you want that to be one of your conditions when I hired you?" In all the years I've been at X,

Princess has never asked me this question. She's avoided it or didn't want the answer. I'm not ready to give the real answer and I never will be, so I go with half-truths.

"When I first met the guys, they were big and scary. So, I made the decision then." Which really is the truth because they were intimidating as shit, like they would chew me up and spit me out. I had just left a man and his son who did exactly that, I didn't want to have that again. But I'm leaving that part out.

"Do you find them scary still?" Princess asks.

I think for a moment. "Rhys scares the shit out of me." That man has a danger about him that no one could touch. It circles around him like a magnetic force. Yikes. When he comes into the club, I do not look in his direction, ever.

"I've known him my whole life and I agree with you on that. But he really is a teddy bear when it comes down to it." Casey's teddy bear analogy is not a way that I would describe Rhys at all. He's definitely more like a predator. A lion or a panther just waiting to strike.

"He is. All of them are scary when they're pissed or when they're protecting what they believe in. But, they each have a loving side. My Pops, I've seen him blow many times and sometimes, I'd never tell him this, it scares the shit out of me. But then I see him with Ma and everything is right in the world. The way he takes care of her shows his heart is huge."

Princess's dad Pops is Ravage's President and took over the position when Diamond was killed; at least that's what she told me happened. Ma is the honorary mother of Ravage. At the very few get-togethers I've been to, I've observed each one of those big, rough men around her and her love for them is huge, and vice versa.

"That may be true, but I don't want a guy. *Any* guy." I don't need a man to make me whole or complete. I can stand on my own two feet without that bullshit. Right?

"Don't you want a man and kids?" Casey asks.

"No." The word is abrupt and precise. I don't want kids, ever. I would never take a chance on the child living the same hell that I went through. While I have thought about it, I dismiss it just as fast. I would die inside if I knew something happened to my child. My mom did the best she could, but there is so much she never knew about. I'll never subject a child to that, ever.

Both Princess and Casey stare at me so I continue. "I don't need a man. I don't want to have children. I just don't."

I would think that if anything, they would understand this and be cool with it, but they just glare at me. Just like Tug does, trying to read my damn mind. I don't back down.

"Tug really is a good guy, Blaze. I wouldn't shit you." Casey defends and I'm positive she's right, considering all the nice things he's done for me. Hell, he beat some guy up and held me when I cried. Unfortunately, she's right. I steel my spine.

"I know you wouldn't. I am just not on the market for anyone right now." My words come out weaker than I intended as a small edge of dread fills me. I'll never have what Princess and Casey have. Never.

"All right, enough of this tap-dancing bullshit," Princess says, staring at me, she's going to tell Casey. I sigh and Casey stares. Better to tell her now than hear it from someone else. The guy attacking me isn't a big deal, it's Tug's reaction to it that is going to call bullshit on everything I just said. I nod and brace myself. "A few nights ago, a guy jumped onto the stage and knocked Blaze off onto her ass. Tug was there and took care of her. The next morning, Tug called me to come and stay with her because he had to leave."

Casey's eyes swing to me. "First, are you okay?"

"I'm fine. I've been up on stage a couple times since." I shrug it off and wait for it...

Then her eyes fill with amusement. "Second, you're a lying sack of shit!" she screams, not in a bad, I'm-going-to-kill-you way but in a funny-ha-ha kind of way. She turns to Princess. "And you let her spew that shit about her not wanting a man, blah blah, blah, when you knew she is seeing Tug?" Princess doesn't say a word. Casey turns to me. "So, you lied about sleeping with him?"

I straighten. "No. I haven't had sex with him, but I have slept in the same bed as him." I pause and wince at the next word which will air out what I don't want them to know. "Twice."

Princess joins Casey's chuckle. "Now that," she points to me, "I didn't know about."

"You really do like him." Casey's eyes turn dreamy. Do I lie? Do I lead them down the same path I want to lead Tug? My heart warms. These women like me and I can't do it. No more lies. It's getting tiring.

"All right, I like him," I blurt out to their happy screams. "But," I add on, "I am not going to be with him. He doesn't get that point yet, but I'll make myself perfectly clear when he gets back."

"Wait. What?" Casey's jaw falls. "Why are you not going to be with him?"

"I don't want a guy right now."

"Why not?" Princess doesn't let up. Damn.

"I just don't. Can we leave it at that?" My tone turns a bit more serious.

Casey and Princess glance at each other and have some wordless conversation going on that I'm sure involves me being a crazy woman, and they are probably right. My heart squeezes.

"Oh, girl," Princess says, "you are in for it now."

"No, I'm not."

"We shall see," is all Princess says with a knowing look on her face. My stomach plummets. With a promise to come to Casey and GT's house warming party, we leave and I'm a ball of nerves.

AT THREE IN THE MORNING, I pull into my driveway and slam on the brakes, stopping dead and jerking myself in the seatbelt. Christ. Tug leans on his bike, legs crossed at the ankles, and arms folded. He is so damn hot, my panties heat to the point of burning right off of me. Shit. All too soon he straightens. I get my senses together and park. I breathe in deep and try to get control of the butterflies that decided to reside in my stomach. It doesn't happen. They must be having one hell of a party because they are flitting all over. Shit. I haven't seen him since that morning he kissed me and left. It's only been a few days but for some reason seems much much longer.

A small tap comes to the windshield and I snap to the sound. Tug grins, no doubt remembering all the times he's had to coax me out of a car. I turn off the Jeep, open the door, and get out, ignoring him.

"Hey."

A strong arm comes around my back and before I mutter a word, I am pressed up against Tug's warm, hot, hard body having no choice but to clutch his chest. Every inch of where he's touching me lights up and all the sudden I'm hot, way hot. So hot, and I want to do something monumentally stupid.

"Hey." His voice is gruff and since I have only heard him on the phone these past few days, I've come to the conclusion that I like his voice in person much better. One of his hands snakes up my back between my shoulder blades, the other down to the small of it. Suddenly, his grip tightens, something I didn't think was possible, but he somehow accomplishes.

His chin is so sexy with his I-haven't-shaved-in-a-few-days stubble. My pulse races and I realize that I'm scared. He's seen me at my most vulnerable and I'm nervous about what will come of it.

"Blaze," he murmurs, his jaw moving in that sexy way as he speaks. My fists tighten on his black t-shirt. "Look at me." His words come out husky, sexy, and wrap around my heart like a vise.

I scan every inch of his face. Even his slightly angled nose is hot. My eyes meet his and all the air seizes in my lungs and my chest constricts to the point of pain. Inside his brown eyes is a tornado of emotions, all thrown together to completely knock me off my game. But the one that shines brightest of them all is lust, full-blown, unadulterated lust. When other guys look at me this way, it does nothing for me, but with Tug, I want to throw myself on top of him and rip every stitch of clothing off his body. Then ride him until my legs stiffen.

I close my eyes, breaking the connection. This is not me pushing a man away; this is me telling him that this can't happen, dammit. Focus.

"You're thinking way too fucking hard, sweet lips. Here, let me help you." His lips touch mine, hot, wet and perfect. Hesitation gone, I fall into the kiss, opening up for him, tasting him, teasing him with my teeth, gently nipping his lip. He growls deep, his fingers thread through my hair and his lips are rough with an aggression that coats my panties in wetness.

His hard length presses into my stomach. God, he's so big. His knee slides between my legs, high enough to rub against my clit, giving it the perfect amount of friction. I hold onto his soft brown hair for dear life, all the while rubbing my pussy on his leg like a cat in heat. Every touch revs me up even higher. My brain shuts off, takes a vacation or shuts down. I don't know, don't care. This is all about my body and what it wants. And right now, that's Tug.

The sweet roll builds so rapidly that air becomes difficult to inhale. Only a little more stimulation and I'll blow. I need it, want it. His knee drops from my core and my eyes flash open. Why in the hell did he stop? I'm so damn close.

"I love the tremble of your body and the flush on your face is sexy as hell. The heat of your pussy burns through my jeans. It's begging for me isn't it?" he asks and I moan, unable to answer as I'm trying to catch my breath. "I bet if I let you rub just a little more, you'd set off." I nod, staring into his eyes and pleading wordlessly.

A wickedly sly seductive smile crosses his lips then he kisses me hard. We move and I follow him, or I should say follow his lips, to wherever he's taking me eyes closed. The garage door goes down, then a door opens and my alarm beeps. His lips disengage and I growl at him. He chuckles. "Punch in the code and then arm it." He doesn't let me go and it takes me a minute to remember how to work the damn electronic thing. I do it as fast as my fingers will allow then turn back to Tug.

His lazy eyes are warm, happy to be exactly where he is, and my heart skips a beat or ten. His lips meet mine and my arms come around his neck, not leaving a centimeter between us.

Somehow, we manage to get to my bedroom and the back of my calves hit the bed, stalling our movement. Tug lays me down, coming with me and breaking the kiss. His eyes devour me. "Tonight, I make you mine." He crashes his lips to mine, sucking the air from my lungs. My mind doesn't catch up and all I can do is feel. And it's wonderful.

His lips leave mine and before I can protest, those wonderful lips are moving down my cheek to my jaw to behind my ear. My entire body shakes in anticipation. "I think I found your spot," he whispers.

"Oh God," I moan as his lips continue their assault. I have just determined that my ear is the most sensitive part on my body, ever. God, it's so good. His lips leave nibbles down my neck, his gruff hands roaming my body. Tug rips my shirt from me so fast I don't even register it until the cold air from the fan touches my skin. His lips trail over my collarbone then down the middle of my chest. My body throbs and aches, needing him to really touch me. His lips turn my body on like it has never been before.

He reaches behind my back and I lift a little, knowing he wants my bra off. May as well help him a little. He unlatches it then removes it from my body. His lips, tongue and hands begin their sensuous torture of my breasts, not leaving one part of my flesh untouched. He sucks my nipple hard into his mouth as he squeezes my other roughly. My body arches, my orgasm right there. Can I come just from having my nipples played with? God, I hope so. My breathing comes out in small pants. His teeth bite on the tip, giving me a sting of pain. I like it and my hips buck on their own accord.

His rough hands glide down my stomach to the button of my jeans. He makes quick work of the obstruction along with my underwear, tearing them off my body. I clutch the blankets of the bed and my legs come together. I rub my thighs together, trying to get a small amount of friction. Just a little more and it'll hit.

"Bad girl, Blaze." He grabs my knees, pulling them wide and exposing my flesh to him. "When you blow, it'll be on my tongue." I quiver at his words and really, really want to come on his tongue. His hands snake up my legs from my knees and he stops. I wait, breathing heavy and about ready to lose my mind.

He stares at me and self-consciousness hits me. What the hell? "What, Tug?" I ask but it comes out so breathy it's a mumble.

"You have the most beautiful pussy lips and I can smell you from here." He smirks and makes a show of sucking in air. He tears his shirt from his body and I gasp, taking in all that is Tug. Fuck me. His chest is so defined it could be chiseled from stone, and his abs? Holy shit. I thought abs like that were only in movies. He smirks knowingly then kneels down between my legs, his hands slipping under my ass. Then he licks. One hard, knowing touch of his tongue from, I swear, my ass all the way up to clit in a full sweep. I groan deep and my hips jump.

"Just like I thought. Sweet. Damn, baby, I'm fucking hungry." Before I can process his words his mouth is on me, as in *on* me. And he does not do tiny flicks of his tongue, no he goes full out. He consumes me. He sucks, nips and nibbles every part of my flesh. My body heats to the point of combustion and I'm so close. The licks become harder and faster then he adds his fingers I don't know if it's one or two, all I know is it is exquisite. My hips buck hard with each thrust of his fingers and suck of my clit. The tension builds up, winding up so tight I'm afraid if I let go I'll explode into a million pieces. His fingers touch the upper walls of my pussy and I scream. The orgasm courses through me, my back arches, fingers scraping his scalp, my entire body implodes in a way I've never felt before in my life.

I'm not sure how long my orgasm lasts, but when I fall to the mattress and am able to open my eyes, his are on me. His tongue licks my pussy, but his fingers have disappeared. God, this is so good. His lips leave me and he kisses the top of my mound. I never thought that was sexy before, but damn, I was wrong about that. He edges up my body, licking and kissing his pathway. Stomach. Each breast. Neck. Behind my ear. Across my jaw. Shit, my body is ready to go again. His lips take mine, searing me. My hands lace through his hair, the one place I love to be on him. Best place ever.

This kiss is different than the ones before. It's hot, hard and totally fierce, but there is also desperation. The distinct sound of a zipper going down fills the room. He stands up, his pants disappearing.

My gaze drifts from his abs to his rock-hard dick.

A moment of fear hits, not because of his size, but the piercing. Shit, his dick is pierced! I bolt up from the bed and he smirks. "Come here." He moves to the side of the bed. I scramble to my knees, run my fingertips over his abs, right down to the tip of his dick. His piercing slices through the head, end to-end, with round silver balls on each side protruding from it. Holy shit.

"You're pierced," I state the obvious and he chuckles.

"Caught that, huh?" Humor laces his voice, but I focus on his hard length.

I squeeze my fingers around him and his body jerks at the touch. With my other hand, I touch the bar, moving it side-to-side and even circling it. His sharp intake of breath tells me he likes this and gives me the edge to keep torturing him. Damn, I bet that hurt though. I wonder what it will feel like inside my body.

"If you're done inspecting me, I need to be inside of you." His words rip through me. He *needs* to be inside of me. Holy shit. This is really happening. "Shit," he mutters, his lips connecting with mine and all my thoughts drift. "Are you on the pill?" he mumbles against my lips. My periods are rough and I need it to regulate them. I've been on them for years.

"Yes," I say through short breaths.

"Thank fucking God," he says and glides his dick to the opening of my pussy. He rubs it up and down my lips, hitting my clit with little taps. I moan as the pleasure builds inside of me. His elbows come to the side of my ears and his hard dick rests on my pussy. I release a moan. "Are you clean?" he asks and I nod yes, unable to form words. "I am too. Always glove up, but with you I just fucking can't. I need to feel all of you."

He arches his hips and the tip of his dick finds my entrance. He glides inside slightly and the barbells enter my opening. Holy shit. Sex has never felt like this before. With each inch of his dick, those bars stretch me in the most delicious ways, touching unfamiliar places in my body. I've never in my life felt this good. God. He presses in the rest of the way and I swear I feel him at my cervix, my breath leaving my body. Our gazes connect.

"Fuck me," he mumbles. "Gotta move, sweet lips." I nod, unable to speak as sweat drips from his brow.

"Oh God," I say repeatedly, over and over, as each

thrust hits a spot inside of me that I didn't know was so damn sensitive. His hips grind from side-to-side, increasing the places his barbells touch. I'm on the shaky edge. He lets loose, pounding, thrusting in and out of me hard, fast and deep.

I close my eyes, absorbing all of the sensations rolling through my body, then it hits. Harder than the last. This one rakes my body over hot coals and sends shards of bright light floating behind my eyelids. When I'm able to come down, euphoria washes over me.

Tug's body is covered in a light sheen of sweat. He's up on his knees, his arms out straight next to me, and with each thrust inside of me, he's doing pushups. Fast ones. His arms ripple and his eyes go liquid, melty and hot.

Then as if in slow motion, his eyes close, his head goes back and his dick throbs inside of me. His face tightens, brows furrow and he grunts hard, his breath stopping. Damn, that's fucking hot. Hot spurts of his cum spill deep inside my body and I almost come again.

He opens his eyes, fire and desire burn me with intent. He leans down, covering my body with his, his dick still inside of me. "Watching you come is the best fucking thing I've ever seen." My heart squeezes. I never thought words like that would make me lose it, but they do.

He kisses me, but this kiss is not hard and frantic like the others. This is sensual and just as damn hot as the others he's given me. Damn, this man is good with his mouth. Tug drags his dick painstakingly slowly out of me. Every movement flares my pussy to life. He pecks me on the lips and rolls. His arm snakes around me and pulls me into his body. I rest on his chest, listening to his heartbeat and enjoying his heat.

My body is so relaxed and sated, something it has never really been. As I listen to the rhythmic thumping in his chest, sleep takes over.

I wake up with a start. My entire body hits something hard. I try to clear out my foggy mind. Tug's hard chest. Shit. I'm not lying next to Tug, no I am lying on top of Tug, full on, all skin-to-skin.

He woke me up twice during the night, saying he needed more and after he touched me, so did I. It was amazing, like nothing I've ever experienced before in my life. His stamina is something I've only read about in books.

Then it hits me like a thousand bricks falling off a tall tower and I'm standing right in the middle of it. I had sex with Tug. Holy shit. I didn't want it to go this far, but when I saw him, I couldn't think. I call it the Tug's Scrambled Brain Effect. Dammit. I need some space, some time to think, and being on his rock hard body is not helping the situation one bit. I try to roll off of him when his arms wrap around my body halting my movement.

"Where are you going?" he asks in a deep, sexy, sleepy voice. My body comes alive, but my brain kicks in. *Need space.* Right.

"Bathroom." He squeezes once then lets go of me. I'm thinking the night's festivities wore him out since he doesn't argue. I scurry like a damn mouse out of the bed, naked, and into the bathroom. I shut and lock the door. I turn my back to it and rest my head against it in defeat. What have I done? *You had sex with him, you moron.* Damn, damn, double damn. This was a total mistake. I got so caught up, I didn't think. Didn't think of the ramifications of this. I stop. What are the ramifications of this? I know a big one, that wasn't just sex. That was something that wove into my heart and no matter what I do, he's there. How did this happen?

I need a breather. I search around the bathroom for something to wear. Clothes are the first step. Shit, no clothes. Why can't I be messier and leave shit laying around? My robe hangs by the shower. I put on the fluffy, blue terry cloth, wrapping it around my body, and tie the belt to cover me up. I do my business and brush my teeth. I wince at my bedhead and try to tame the wild beast with a brush. Yikes.

I need him gone, need to think. I open the door and square my shoulders, then my breath catches. Tug is sitting up, his back resting on my headboard with the blue sheet lying loosely around his lap. The sheet is tenting up in the middle. He obviously has morning wood. My mind drifts to last night. He did things to me I've only dreamt about. He can be slow and sweet or rough and hard. I can't do this right now. I need to think. No more.

"Hey. I'm gonna get dressed and get some breakfast." I enter the closet, pretending to search for clothes. I grab the first thing in front of me, a bright blue t-shirt and rip it off the clothes hanger then turn around. I jump and gasp as Tug is right in front of me, gloriously naked. I keep my eyes on his shoulders. "What are you doing?" I hold my shirt to my chest.

He's silent so I look up into his eyes. They tell me he wants to eat me alive and my body says *yes please*. Too bad my brain is functioning this morning.

"I'm hungry." His lips come down on me in a flash. My stupid body gives, melting right into him. He ushers me to the bed and lays me down, his kiss never retracting. He undoes my robe and it falls away. His weight comes on top of me and I love it. The ripples of his fantastic muscles hit my skin in all the right places. God, yes.

His lips leave mine and my brain tries to kick in, but it doesn't make it that far. "Before you start thinking, this was something. It means something to me and you are not just another fuck. Get it through your head now."

My eyes widen in surprise. How in the hell did he know I thought that way? And by the seriousness on his face, he means it. Shit. Need. To. Think.

He continues, not giving me a reprieve. "I don't know where this will lead, but I want to find out." My breath catches. He leans in and kisses my lips softly. I say nothing. "And after last night, you're mine, sweet lips."

I try to blink the Tug-fog away and process his words. *I'm his?* No. No, no, no, no. This isn't happening. I am not anyone's. I am my own woman.

"You have any questions?" Any questions? He can't be serious.

I give him my most evil glare. "Tug. I belong to no one but myself. You need to get this *mine* stuff out of your head."

"It's too late, sweet lips. As soon as I slid into you, the

deal was done." He kisses me swiftly. "I'll be back." He leaves, striding into the bathroom, his ass tight as hell. *I bet I could bounce a quarter off it.* Shit, Blaze. Get a grip.

I get dressed, throwing on the sweats I wear around the house. I'm not entering a beauty contest here, and I throw my hair up in a messy bun.

My mind races. I do like him or I wouldn't have slept with him. He is definitely persistent. And it's not like I don't know him. We've known each other since he joined Ravage a year ago, not that we were actually together, but still. And we've talked. More than I've talked with really anyone. Hell, even Casey and Princess stick up for the guy and I'm sure Princess's approval doesn't come lightly. Casey told me he's a good listener and I've learned that for myself.

My mind is a big ball of confusion. I think I lose either way. And it's not like he's promising me sunshine and lollipops. Getting to know each other while fucking each other's brains out, I could do that. *Just give in, Blaze.* The problem is there is only one heart in my chest and I don't want it shattered.

I have choices. One, I get with him and he dumps me. Then it's over. I could deal with that. Two, get with him and I have to leave suddenly, my body shivers at that one. Three, block him out totally, which would suck ass considering he was only gone for four days and I missed him like crazy. And I'm not sure he would allow that either.

The bathroom door opens, startling me from my thoughts. When I turn around, my jaw drops. Tug is completely naked with a power inside of him that quakes my knees. He doesn't walk to me, no he prowls to me, picks me up in his arms and kisses me hard. I fall into the kiss without hesitation.

Yeah, I kind of like this guy. Damn it, when the hell did that happen?

"As much as I want to take you back to that bed and fuck your brains out, I've gotta run to the clubhouse." He sets me down and goes to his clothes and puts them on. I can't help but watch each movement with utter awe. "I'll see ya tonight. Yeah?" he asks and I don't answer fast enough so he answers for me. "Yeah. I'll be here tonight."

He kisses me and he's off.

I sit on my bed, drop my head in my hands, and wonder how in *the hell* all of this happened.

"The new girl's here," Princess calls from the doorway of my dressing room-cum-office space. Princess has on jeans and an old vintage Rolling Stones t-shirt. It's one thing I truly love about this job. When I'm not on stage, Princess doesn't give a shit what I wear. Jeans, dresses— she told me to be comfortable, so I am.

I have on lightly faded jeans with a pale blue top that has a slight V in the front, giving me a tad bit of cleavage, but my boobs are pretty well covered.

Princess decided that she was going to let Stage, an ol' lady from some other Ravage charter, dance at X. Princess says that she got her name by dancing and that's where she met Bobbie, her ol' man.

"All right," I answer, moving to the door and slipping on my flat shoes.

Princess breathes out, steps in the room and shuts the door. Her movements stop me and I stare at her in confusion. "She's an ol' lady to the club, which means that she follows a different set of rules than other women. Here though, even though she's an ol' lady for the club, she has to follow my rules. She may give you shit because you're not an ol' lady, so it might be best if I handle her."

I shrug because I really don't give a shit. If Princess wants the newbie more power to her, less I have to deal with, and if she gives me shit, I'll deal with it then. "Fine by me."

Princess appears a bit off but I can't place what it is. "I need to feel this one out. I don't know her all that well."

"That's fine." I brush it off. I've been dealt with worse stuff in my life.

"Let's go." Throngs of people line X as we make our way up to the front, up the stairs, and into Princess's office where a striking brunette stands, waiting for us. Her hair is silky and flowing down below her shoulder blades. Her brown eyes are pretty but they lack sparkle. Her face and body are built to perfection, and the way she's standing with her hip cocked, tells me she knows it.

"Hi, Stage." Princess moves around behind the desk and I sit in the chair next to it as Stage sits in front of us. "This is Blaze. She helps me run the place and is your boss alongside me. Anything she says, I would say."

Princess's words come out as a warning. Stage smiles brightly, but it doesn't reach her eyes. My gut is telling me this isn't good.

"Okay. When do I start?" Stage asks with the utmost confidence.

"Tonight. I want you up for one set so I can see you. Then after that if I approve, next week," Princess says.

"Sounds good. Where do we dress?" Stage is impatient, like this meeting is a waste of her precious time. It rubs me the wrong way.

"I'll have one of the girls show you around." I remain quiet, wondering why she didn't have me do it, but not gonna waste my thoughts on it because in truth, I don't want to.

"Great!" she exclaims, a little too bubbly.

Everything about her screams fake and I try to fight it back. I shouldn't cast judgment, but it's there. Trouble.

"Tonight you'll go on at eight o'clock. Blaze isn't dancing tonight so we rearranged things for you."

Stage's eyes flash to me. "You dance here?"

"I do, for now." I cross my legs and clasp my fingers on my knee. Stage's eyes scrunch in what I think is confusion or disgust, who knows.

"Blaze is helping me run things, so she still dances but is moving away from it."

"And that's where I fit in?" So, Stage has brains. That could be good or bad, don't know which yet, but if I were a betting woman I'd vote for the latter.

Princess doesn't say anything else about it but the amusement is there. "I'll get Luna to show you around, be ready in an hour and a half to go on."

We rise from our chairs and Princess leads Stage out of the room. Well, this is going to be interesting.

THE NIGHT WAS SO busy that I left X in total exhaustion. Every muscle in my body aches and I'm sure it's more from last night's sex romp than the pole. Hell, I didn't even dance tonight. But I did go out on the floor with Princess to watch Stage. She dances well and the crowd liked her so Princess is hiring her. I left before they talked.

When I pull up to my house, an instant pang of disappointment clutches around my heart. Tug isn't here. I begrudgingly take a shower and then snuggle up on the couch, wrapping myself tight in a blanket.

I think about watching a movie or television but neither sound good. Instead, I lie here with my mind running faster than a NASCAR on the track. So fast that I can't make sense of it. I close my eyes and try to calm all the wayward thoughts and focus. Peace doesn't come.

All the happy memories that I have of my mother are watered down with the bad. The bad invades me. My stomach tightens and I fold my knees into my chest, making myself as small as I can.

I'M late and Santos hates it when I am. I didn't mean to be, but Jenny's car stalled on the side of the road and we had to wait for her mom. Santos refuses to get me a car. I asked once and never tried again. When he says something, it is law.

I open the door to the house quietly, the lights are off.

Relief washes over me. Thank God he's asleep. I quietly move to my room, which is on the opposite side of the house from Santos and Mom. I turn the handle as quiet as I can and open the door. I shut it just as quiet and breathe out a deep sigh of relief. I made it.

I set my purse down and flip on the light, then scream. Santos is in my room, coming toward me like a bull seeing red. He doesn't cover my mouth, no, he backhands me hard, my face turning to the side, and tears sting my eyes. My hand comes up as I cup my face, the pain slicing through me.

"Shut your fucking mouth," he growls, clutching my hair and throwing me to the bed. "Thought I fucking told you not to be late. Ever!" he barks out and I've learned not to give him excuses. It doesn't help and only makes it worse. I put my hands in front of me as he throws me on the bed, straddling my pelvis and holding me down.

I'm lucky he has clothes on. I fight. I kick and block, but it doesn't help. I know it doesn't but I can't just give in to the punches. Eventually he wins, he always does. He lands a fist to my eye and pain explodes. I don't have time to think about it though because his other hand comes up and he slaps me hard across the face a second time.

He moves off of me, dragging me with him by the hair. "You want to be a little slut out with your friends all night?" he questions and I don't answer. His fist connects with my ribs and I double over, falling to the ground. I curl into a ball on the floor as his foot lands on my hip. The pain is too much and tears I don't want to fall do.

His hits stop, the sound of a zipper and clothes hitting the floor echo throughout the room. No, no..no... "You want to act like a little slut, I'll treat you like one," he growls, grabs my

hair and lifts me up off the ground, throwing me on the bed.
"Time I teach you a real lesson."

THE DOORBELL RINGS and my nightmarish thoughts vanish. I blink a few times, clearing out the cobwebs of my past, and try to focus on the here and now. The clock on the wall reads three thirty-six in the morning. It must be Tug.

I toss off the blanket, go to the door and glance through the peephole. It's him. My heart that a minute ago was filled with such pain is squeezing for a whole other reason.

I open the door and am greeted with the deepest brown eyes, shining with happiness. My belly flutters. "Hey," I say, stupidly.

"Hi, sweet lips." His arms come around my waist, pulling me into his body. Then he kisses me, washing all the bad memories aside. The door slams, the lock engaging as he continues to devour me with his lips. He pulls away and I gasp for breath, not realizing I haven't taken any in.

When I open my eyes, he is staring at me, a smirk playing on his lips. "Love that fucking look on you, babe." A blush creeps up my cheeks. His thumb comes to my bottom lip and swipes across it, sending shockwaves through me from that simple touch. His eyes burn and his rock hard cock presses against my stomach, sending pulses to my clit.

He smirks and I melt. No thoughts other than the handsome gorgeous man in front of me. "I'm gonna fuck you till you can't move," he says softly and my blood pressure skyrockets into another atmosphere. His lips come crashing down on mine and I'm lost. Lost in him, lost in us, whatever us is... I'm lost.

WE LIE IN BED, me against Tug, my head resting on his chest and our legs entangled. Our breathing is slowly coming down from our frantic interlude that started in the entryway and ended in the bed. I thought I was sore, but as soon as he touched me, I was on fire and ready for him.

I cover us and snuggle into his warmth.

"What's wrong?" he asks, kissing my hair.

I search for something to say, but come up short. I am not blurting out, we *are* together. That would sound totally stupid and like I'm a teenager with her first crush. Not happening. So I lie. "Nothing," I say, softly enough for him to hear.

"Your mind thinking again?" He strokes my arm and I revel in the touch.

"Yes."

"Talk to me."

"Don't you think this is kinda fast?" Even though we've been tiptoeing around it for months, it's really only been a few weeks and there is no way in hell my heart should be squeezing this hard in that short of an amount of time.

"Life's short, gotta grab the good stuff when you can."

His words shock me. Not the words actually, but the weight of them. I take a second to really think. He's right. So very, very right. Because if something happened tomorrow, if I died or if God forbid have to run, I'll have these memories to get me through all of it. I squeeze him tight and allow the happiness to surround us.

CHAPTER EIGHT
Tug

SHIT. FUCK. DAMN. BUZZ SET UP ALL THE EQUIPMENT WE got from Joey's house as soon as we got back in the basement of the clubhouse. He's been trying all day, and part of the night, to crack Joey's codes. We had Doc examine Joey as soon as we got to the clubhouse. Doc ran a shit load of tests and told us the guy was brain dead. The chemical he gave himself was supposed to kill him instantly, but for some reason he hung on.

Ravage ended up putting him out of his misery. After that, Buzz started and hasn't stopped. He gets so close and then something happens to the drive that sends him on what he calls a 'cyberspace chase,' leaving him pissed as shit.

So, technically, we are exactly where we started before going to get Joey except we have a computer that we can't crack.

I've been helping out where I can, mostly keeping Buzz going by feeding his ass because he won't get away from the computers except to pee every once and a while. That motherfucker is determined to break it and I have every bit of confidence that he will.

I sit at the clubhouse bar nursing a beer. The brothers are in having church. Breaker and I just got done cleaning a couple of the brothers' bikes, another one of our many prospecting tasks. I swallow the beer and enjoy the coolness as it slides down my throat.

These last few days have been pretty much the same: garage, Ravage, Blaze, sleep and repeat. I wouldn't change a fucking thing about it. The garage is going well, cars coming in and out. Things with Ravage are calm except for the computer shit. Blaze. Shit, that woman. Every fucking night, I come to her late and she doesn't complain at all. I fuck her until she's bowlegged the next day, and then fall asleep with her in my arms.

Right now, I'd say my life is pretty kick ass.

Buzz ran the info on the asshole that bum rushed Blaze at X. He's thirty-six and has a job at an advertising company. His record is squeaky clean, but when Buzz hacked into the advertising agency's computer, he found the asshole got a promotion that day. So, my guess is the dumbass was celebrating. Congrat-u-fuck-ing-lations.

The guys come piling out of church and I head to the bar, handing out drinks to whoever wants them.

Pops steps out and whistles loud, catching everyone's attention. "Let's ride," Pops announces. Those two words mean it's just a ride, being part of the family, part of the pack. It's not a run or situation we have to take care of. It's a ride and I fucking love that shit.

The ride is freeing. It allows me to stop thinking about everything and just focus on the things around me. The only thing that would make this shit better is to have Blaze on the back of my bike. Fuck yeah. That would be perfect.

WE CUT our engines and my phone rings. The display says *Mom calling*. What the fuck? She hasn't called me in years, something must be wrong. "Yeah."

"Andrew?" my mom says, using my legal name. Technically, I'm Andrew Tugger, but in the service, everyone called me Tug. It stuck.

"Yeah, Mom. What's going on?" I walk with the guys into the courtyard. Some go into the clubhouse, some sit out on the tables. I choose the picnic table and sit on top of it, my boots planted on the seat.

Silence on the other end. "Mom?" I pull my phone away to see the call has not been lost. "Mom," I say, but this time with a bit more authority.

"I'm here." Her voice sounds broken, like she's been crying. Shit. "I wanted to call you and tell you that your sister was in a car accident." She sniffles and my heart seizes in my chest. She may have kept me away all these years, but I'd do anything to protect her from pain.

"How is she?" I question when she doesn't continue.

She lets out a breath that sounds like static on my end

of the line. "She hit her head and has a broken leg. The doctors are waiting for the tests to come back. They're afraid of brain damage." All the air in my lungs leaves my body. Fucking shit.

I yank my hair hard as I get up from the table and pace the courtyard, needing to move. "Where are you?"

"Sumner Medical."

"I'll be there in a few." I hang up the phone and search for Pops who I find at the bar.

"Hey, Pops. My sister was in an accident and it's not good. I gotta roll." If Pops is surprised about me talking about my mother and sister, he doesn't show it. When I started prospecting, we let everything hang out, even our screw-ups. The guys know what I did to my dad. It is not something that I've hid. They also know how my mother and sister feel about it. So, this, could be a shock.

"Hope she's all right, son." He nods, not giving me an ounce of shit. That is why I love that man and want him to be my President.

THIS PLACE IS TOO damn bright. I kept my sunglasses on, trying to block it. People gawk and I don't give a shit. I head to a round woman, her blonde hair tied in a bun. Who knows how old she is, but the bright blue makeup on her eyes is fucking nuts. "Ma'am." Her eyes widen. Fear flitters in them and she gulps. Whatever. "What room is Alexis Tugger in?"

She continues to stare at me like I didn't even ask her

a question. I snap in front of her face and she comes to with a jolt. "Sorry." She looks down to her keyboard. "What was the name?"

Fuck me. "Alexis Tugger." Then I spell out the last name so she gets it right.

"Ah, yes. Here she is. ICU 3820." I take off, using the signs to guide me through this maze of whiteness.

I enter the ICU area and notice my mom sitting in the large waiting room. Her eyes are down so she doesn't spot me approach. My mom is pretty with short dark hair and the same brown eyes as me. Her shoulders shake. She's crying. I remove my glasses and put them in my rag. "Mom?" Her head whips up as the tears fall from her eyes.

"Andrew," she whispers softly, gets up from her chair and wraps her arms around me tight. I do the same as her shakes become harder. I absorb all of her pain and suck every bit of it in.

She pulls away and looks up at me, surely taking in all the changes that have happened since I last saw her. "You get more handsome every time I see you," she says quietly and I grin. There really isn't much you can say to that. "The doctors should be in any time to tell us what's going on. They took her in for more tests and told me to wait in here."

I can't tell her it'll be okay because I can't predict what's going to happen. "We'll wait to see what they say." She waves her hand, motioning me to sit in the chair next to her and I do, stretching my legs out in front of me. These damn things are hard. "Tell me what happened."

"Cops said it was a drunk driver. He sideswiped her

car in the middle of the afternoon." Her face turns to mine. "Who gets drunk in the middle of the afternoon and then drives?"

"A lot of people do, Mom. They arrest the guy?"

"I don't know. I'm sure I'll find out later." Her eyes are filled with unshed tears.

"When you find out, I want to know." More like when I get to the clubhouse I'll be asking Buzz to find out everything he can on this asshole. Mom nods.

"How have you been?" Every word coming out of her mouth is soft as a whisper.

"I'm good." For the first time in a really long time, I'm exactly where I want to be.

"What is this leather about?" She points to my chest, taking in my rag.

"It's a motorcycle club. I'm working on being a member of it." Her eyes grow wide.

"What?" she gasps and I'm sure she really wants to dig in her purse and douse me with the holy water that she's carried since I was a kid.

"It's a club. We ride together. I work at the garage on cars. Got an apartment and a girl. I'm okay, Mom." She has always worried about us. That is why I don't understand why she stayed with my father. She was so protective of us all the time, getting into it with other parents over stupid shit us kids had done. But when it came to her, she let herself be a punching bag. I don't get it and probably never will.

"Is that safe?" There is no way in hell I'd tell her the truth. I'm glad I locked my gun on my bike.

So, I lie. "Yep."

"What about this girl?" Warmth fills me at the mention of my woman.

"Her name is Blaze."

"Blaze, what kind of name is that?"

"She works at X and that's her name." I let Mom put two and two together. I stay quiet until it hits her.

"That titty bar?" She gapes at the fact she said titty, her eyes wide.

"Yeah. You'd like her. She's smart and has a really good head on her shoulders." And she's all mine.

"Andrew. You should not be associating with..." She pauses. "With... *those* kinds of people."

This does not surprise me in the least. "I am those *kind* of people, Mom. Accept it or don't. You don't, I'm gone." It's an ass move, but I haven't talked to her in years, a few more won't hurt.

"I do not believe that for one second," she challenges.

I lean down to her ear. "I did it to protect you, Mom." Her body stills at my words and I'm sure she's remembering that night all those years ago. She loved my father with everything she had and would have died by his hand if I had allowed it.

"Mrs. Tugger?" A man's voice says, stopping my mother from saying anything. Both of us follow the voice. A balding, slim man with glasses and a white coat searches the room.

"Here." My mom answers him. The doctor smiles and comes to us, his eyes flickering between Mom and me. My mom shakes beside me. I wrap my arm around her shoulders and she doesn't resist.

"Your daughter's tests came back good." Mom

slouches against me in obvious relief. "We didn't find any bleeding on her brain and everything came back normal. I expect her to wake up at any time."

Mom comes out of my arms and stands, holding out her hand for the doctor, who reciprocates. "Thank you." I breathe out a sigh of relief as well. It would crush me if my sister died. "Give us a bit to get her settled then you can see her."

"Yes. Thank you." My mother's face lights up and her shoulders slump as if a huge weight has been lifted. She really is beautiful.

"Everything is fine. She'll wake up soon," I reassure her.

"Are you going to come back with me and see her?" I think about it and no, not today. A family reunion shouldn't be done in the ICU.

"Nah, you go on. I gotta take off." Her body deflates and I'm not sure why. She's the one that can't get over what I did. I got over it the minute his dead body was in front of me. This is on her, but I love her.

"Will you come over for dinner?" She's extending an olive branch. Shit.

"Yeah, Mom. Call me when Alexis gets out and I'll come." I give her a soft hug and get the hell out of here.

My lips trail from the corner of her mouth to her jaw to the back of her ear, down her neck, down the middle of her breasts, down to her stomach and suck in at her bellybutton as she shivers. She smells like vanilla ice cream and I want to fucking lick every inch of her. My tongue continues to taste my ice cream all the way up to her tits. I fucking love her tits. They are to die for, large, round, perky with the sexiest light pink nipples. I suck, kiss, and nip with my teeth as she writhes under me, her hands lacing through my hair. Her moans and mews coming louder and faster.

She tightens her grasp and tugs my hair to her. "Kiss me," she says breathlessly. I climb up her body, whipping off my shirt in the process and throw it to the floor. I do as she asks and kiss her hard and deep.

I rest on my arm, trying not to put too much of my weight on her as we continue to kiss and damn she is good at it. She explores my body, each bite of her nails has my dick jumping to attention. She runs them up the side of my abs. Fuck.

I unbutton her jeans and move my fingers down to her bare pussy, every inch of her soft skin meeting me as I go. Before I can get them off, she bends down and yanks her pants off, rolling me on my side. She lies down, her arms coming around my neck, her eyes glassy and hot. I kiss her, my hand moving to the lips of her pussy, rubbing the little nub on the outside. I place a finger inside her heat and it takes all I've got in me not to fling off my jeans and plow into her, but I refrain... barely. I want her to want me so badly that I'm all she thinks about. Then I'll fuck her.

Her back arches, pushing her boobs into the air and she breaks the kiss. I take this opportunity to kiss down her neck, between her tits down her stomach. I move up to her face and kiss her leisurely. We duel with our tongues as I continue pumping in and out of her heat. She's wet, hot, and her pussy tries to suck me in deeper.

I curl my finger up in a come hither motion and she explodes, trying to buck her hips but I hold her down. Her face is beautiful as it contorts into the sexiest fucking vision, one that gets better every damn time I'm inside of her. I kiss her neck and jaw as she falls back down, soothing her fall. I continue pumping into her, keeping her attention.

"God, yes," she moans loud. She finds my lips and kisses me hard, her arms around my neck, holding me to her. One of her hands leaves my neck and wanders ever so slowly down my body, leaving trails of fire down my flesh. She unbuckles my belt and undoes my jeans.

"You ready, sweet lips?" I tease on grin.

"Yes," she answers breathlessly. I strip my pants and climb on top of her, my knees and elbows holding most of my weight. Holding my dick, I rub it up and down her pussy, getting it nice and wet. Her eyes roll in the back of her head in pleasure.

I place my dick at her entrance and advance centimeter by centimeter. With my piercings, she has to be really wet or it could hurt, though we have yet to have that problem. Her eyes stay closed and I wish I could know what she is thinking. "Sweet lips, open your eyes." She complies and I stare into their shiny depths. They are filled with excitement, lust and desire. I inch further in her and she bites her lower lip. Then further in and her body tries to arch, but I hold her down. I go deep inside of her, her pussy clamping me hard. I still and thrust hard, straining my calf muscles. She gasps and groans at the same time. Her fingers dig into my arms and I love the bite of pain.

"Move," she barks out impatiently. First instinct is to make her wait, but I'm done playing. I need to fuck her. In and out, each thrust better than the last. She keeps her eyes on me and I'm glad. I want her to know it's me fucking her. Know that no matter what she says, she's mine. Each thrust massages my dick in a way I haven't felt before and when the tip touches her cervix, Blaze cries out to God. The piercing hits nerve after nerve, and I lose it. Control gone.

My thrusts become harder, faster and my orgasm approaches. My hips circle, needing Blaze to be there when I fall over the edge. Her breaths pick up and her nails dig harder. She screams her release, clamping my dick. Then mine hits as I continue to thrust. I close my eyes, the release taking me over.

When I open them, Blaze's beautiful smile lights up the room. I could so fall in love with this woman. I bend down, kiss her lips, and slowly remove my dick. I fall to the side of the bed, bringing her body with me. Her head rests on my chest, arm over my abs and leg over my thigh. It seems to be our position since we usually end up this way even in sleep.

"Damn, baby." I try to catch my breath.

"I think I saw stars," she says quietly and I grin. Damn right, she fucking did. I kiss the top of her hair. I turn off the bedside lamp and we lie in the darkness, not saying a word. We don't need to say a word because the silence is comfortable between us. Just being together is enough.

"What did you do today?" she asks, yawning on my chest. Guess silent time is over.

"I went and saw my mom." I squeeze her and wrap both arms around her.

"I thought you said you haven't talked to her in a while. Did something happen?"

"My sister was in a car accident. Mom needed a shoulder so I went." Her body tenses so I continue. "She's fine, all the tests came back good, but she does have a broken leg."

"You'll have to go and see her." A heavy stone forms in the pit of my stomach. I want to and I will. I just don't know the reaction.

"She invited me to dinner when Alexis gets out."

"What happened that you don't talk to your mom anymore?"

I suck in deep and close my eyes, not wanting to tell her but it's time. "I killed my father." Blaze stills in my arms, her body becoming tight in a jolt. "My father used to beat the shit out of my mom. One night, he was beating her and it wasn't going to stop. I took a lamp from their bedroom table and hit him in the head with it."

"I'm so sorry," she whispers.

"It had to be done. He wasn't going to stop and if I didn't do something, he would have killed her." Much rather have him dead than my mom.

"But, it was an accident. And isn't your mom even slightly grateful, though?" she asks and I've wondered the same thing at times.

"Mom loved him. So I don't think she ever forgave me

for doing what I did. I tried to explain once, but she shut down and talking to her wasn't any use."

"That's horrible." Blaze stares up at me, horror and sadness all over her beautiful face.

"It's life. You deal with the shit that life throws you. This is what my life threw me, so I deal." I shrug it off. I can't say that it doesn't haunt me sometimes, but I can't ever let it invade my life.

"Then she's trying to reach out to you. You should take it." Her voice is soft and full of hurt. She turns, lying on my chest. Her breathing picks up and expels out deep. I squeeze tight.

"What you are thinking about, sweet lips?" I ask and she stills.

"I don't want to talk about it," she mumbles quietly. I want to haul her ass up to my face and demand she tell me, but that wouldn't get me anywhere with Blaze. She'd for sure close up then.

"No problem. Let's get some sleep." My mind trails off to different scenarios that could be spinning through her mind, none of them good. Eventually I drift off.

CHAPTER NINE
Blaze

I sit in front of the mirror in my dressing room and apply my heavy eye makeup. Strong dark colors on the lids give a dramatic and sultriness to my blue silver eyes. I don't know my father, but I'd guess he has the same eyes. My mother had green ones. I line the rims of my eyes with dark eyeliner, paying special attention to the corners and flaring them out a bit. I add blush and bronzer to my face, neck, and shoulders. I start the task of mascara, which normally takes me about three coats to get my lashes soft and fluttery. I swipe berry lip-gloss across my lips, rubbing them together and opening them with a *pop*.

As I look in the mirror, a whole other woman stares back at me, one that doesn't have a lifelong history of shit to deal with. A person that can just be. A person that can be happy with Tug. A light tap comes to the door and I get up and unlock the door, opening it a crack.

"Ms. Blaze, you have three minutes," Cali says through the crack. Since taking on the one night a week dancing thing, it's working out well. Tonight is one of those nights. I've already been on stage twice and only have one more dance to go before I am done for the night.

"Thanks." I close the door and adjust my costume. I would say clothes, but there isn't much to them. Tonight, I chose a football theme. My Falcons gear I call it. Red, black and white line my top in a football jersey I'm positive wouldn't be legal on the field. It ties in the front and cuts up my back, so basically it's a halter-top that covers my boobs. My sparkling black and red sequence boy shorts are cut up high on my ass cheeks. Underneath them is a black lace thong. I strap on my four-inch heels and check the bottoms for the rubber pads. I don't want to fall on my ass.

After everything checks out, I give my long, brown hair another fluff and amble out to the stage. Standing at the edge, I breathe in deep. *You can do this.* I mentally prepare myself for going out there, still trying to push away memories of being thrown off the stage. Once my music comes on I step out and the music takes me away.

ON MY WAY into the dressing room, there is a flurry of action. Princess isn't here tonight. That leaves me. I change my clothes and use to the backstage bathroom. I sit on the toilet and hear sniffling. My eyes shoot up. Is one of the girls crying? What the fuck? I do my business and go to the sink. Under the stall, someone in bright red heels stands, turned sideways, and not on the toilet. She must be standing. What the hell?

I wash my hands, taking an inordinate amount of time doing so. The woman in the bathroom still doesn't come out. I turn the water off, dry my hands then open the main door, but I don't go through it, just shut it. I stand off to the side and wait.

Not five seconds later, the new girl comes out, wiping her nose and sniffling. Her eyes have no redness or puffiness from crying. White powder lines her upper lip. Fuck me. She's doing fucking drugs. Shit. Shit. Shit.

"You doing all right?" I say from the door. Stage jumps and swirls around, her eyes wide. She clutches her chest like I just gave her a heart attack or something.

"You scared me," she breathes out hard. Not only does she have white powder under her right nostril, she also has it on the small side of her nose. Dumbass.

"You got some on your nose." I brush my own nose to demonstrate where it is. She wipes her nose abruptly and turns to the mirror, checking her reflection. "You know the rule. Princess went through all of it after your first dance. You're out. Get your shit and leave."

She turns to me and snarls, "You can't fucking fire me, you bitch. Who the fuck do you think you are?"

I cross my arms over my chest. "I'm in charge, therefore I have the authority to fire you. And when I tell Princess what I saw, she'll back me a hundred percent."

She steps a bit closer. "I don't know who the fuck you think are, but I'm an ol' lady in this club. I will not take orders from a piece of shit club momma like you." Oh, she just didn't say that. Did she just say that?

My face tightens. I am beyond pissed-the-fuck-off. I ignore the club momma jab because a reactions is what she wants. I damn sure am not going to give it to her. "Here, you are a stripper. You break the rules you're out. If you'd prefer to get the final word from Princess, that's no problem. But you are not going on that stage."

Stage's face contorts somewhere between anger and disbelief. She steps closer and I keep my eyes and ears alert. "You fucking bitch," she spits out and little drops of spittle come with it. Gross. I want to wipe it off, but I stand my ground. Her hand swings toward my face and I step back quickly, enough not to get slammed.

"Well, if the drugs didn't do it, taking a swing at me di," I smart off as she comes toward me. "Leave me the hell alone."

"And if I fucking don't," she huffs, coming closer.

"You know what. I'm going to let Princess handle this. You are so not worth it." I move to the door, turning around so I am facing her. I could fight her, but I really fucking don't want to.

"You, bitch!" Damn she really needs to brighten up her vocabulary. She charges toward me. I sidestep and she runs smack into the door, slamming her face into it. Seriously, how much coke did she snort?

I twist her arm and clutch it behind her back. I bend her wrist until she screams in pain. I learned it in one of my self-defense classes a few years ago. Thank God. She groans and tries to kick, but I bend it further to get her to submit. Somehow, I open the door to the bathroom where Cali is standing.

"Get Doug to escort her off the premises. I don't want her here again." Cali takes Stage, gripping her arms behind her, and I follow after.

I call Princess who answers on the third ring. I tell her exactly what happened and she says she'll deal with it. Man, Stage is something else. I just knew she'd be trouble.

I run the floor, check the girls, and an hour before closing take off for the night. I need to get out of here. After the incident with Stage, I was so damn pumped it's like every bit of adrenaline was coursing through my veins. Now I'm crashing from it.

I'm also ready to be with Tug. Things with him this past week have been amazing. I didn't have a choice but to fall head over heels for the biker. I can be mad at myself all I want but it isn't going to change anything. He's a great guy. He even took me to the movies the other day. The movie sucked and we ended up leaving early, but it's the thought that counts. I know he's busy with Ravage and I'm busy at X. Somehow it just works.

I jump into my Jeep, and Cali shoves off as I pull out of the parking lot, home my destination. Something moving on the windshield catches my eye. A small piece of yellow paper folded into a square blows in the breeze. Probably someone selling something. About once a month, we get people putting flyers on top of our cars selling anything from carwashes to miracle drugs that cure fat. I throw them away. This one can wait until I get home; I'm sure as shit not stopping in the middle of a dark road to get it.

There is no Tug when I get home and a pang of disappointment hits my heart, but I know he'll be here later. After entering the garage, I click the opener and close it. I get out of the Jeep, heaving my bag along with me, and snatch the paper from the windshield. I enter the house, press the code into the alarm, and give the door a tug. I kick off my shoes and my feet relax once they are out of their confines.

I open the yellow paper, wondering if it's for food or for something else. I stop dead in my tracks. The words are in cursive but so clearly written, my veins turn to ice.

WE'VE MISSED YOU PAIGE. ~S & F

FUCK. Fuck. Fuck! I throw the paper down on the table as if it was poison and it leaked onto me. My brain stops as I let my body absorb the shock. They're here. They found me. How in the fuck did they find me? I rush to my bedroom, flicking on the light. Nothing is out of place. I dart to my closet, yanking the hangers out of the way, digging behind the racks of clothes. I have to find it. Clothes fall off of the hangers and I leave them scattered on the floor.

I dig and dig until I find my mother's old hat box my

mother. It was the only thing I took from home, and that was because it was the only thing of hers that I could grab. I tear open the light green circular lid. I haven't had to carry this in so long. I haven't had to use it ever, but I have practiced at a shooting range not too far from my house, though I am a bit rusty. My black and silver .9mm sits inside with its clip fully loaded next to it and a box of high power bullets. I bought it as soon as Princess gave me my ID and put my mom's box to use. Thank God for that ID. Here in Georgia, there are no laws about registering guns, only a simple background check, which was on a very squeaky clean Taryn McKnight. All I had to do was go in and tell them what I wanted and then I strolled right out of the store with it.

I grip the handle of the gun and I place the clip into its chamber, hearing the click. I ready it but leave the safety on and tuck it in the back of my jeans. I rush around the house making sure that all the windows and doors are locked. I check the basement as well. I will need to do something about those windows. They're locked but don't look as sturdy as the ones upstairs.

I take the stairs two at a time and enter the kitchen. I need a damn drink, but I can't. I need to stay clear and think. I'm going to have to leave. I'm going to need to pick up my shit and get the hell out of town, and find a way to get another identity. Shit. Fuck! I want to scream. I can't just leave Tug. *But you always knew it could happen.* That voice inside me needs to shut the hell up. This is serious. I have to go.

What in the hell am I going to do now? Princess. I

need her help. She can get me another ID and I can disappear. I can do it. Start all over. I'm strong enough for that. Right? Shit. Tears well up in my eyes. It will kill me to leave Tug, to sleep without him, not hear his voice again. Dammit. I fucking hate them!

I have to pack. I can wipe out my savings and have it all liquid so I can find another place somewhere. *You don't want to start all over.* Shut up! No, I don't, but they are leaving me no fucking choice. I rest my elbows on the countertop and place my head in my hands. Why is this happening to me? What in the hell did I do to deserve this? I know one thing is for sure, I will not go with them. I will fight until I am dead, but I will not go anywhere with them. Ever.

A knock comes to the door and I jump. My hearts thumps so hard I fear it will burst out of my chest. Shit. It's Tug. In all my trying to figure out what I'm going to do next, I forgot about him coming over. Shit. Shit. Shit. I breathe in deep. I can have one more night with him and then I'm gone. One more night to feel him. I can do that. They won't come and get me if Tug is here. Right?

I unlock the door and there stands sexy ass Tug, his shoulder leaning against the doorjamb, so very hot. I can't believe I have to give this up. "Hey, sweet lips." He strolls in and I smell him as he passes, trying to etch it in my brain.

"Hey," I say, my voice showing a small bit of a tremor, and close the door.

I turn around and meet angry, scary eyes, ones I've never seen before. My breath catches in my throat.

"Mind telling me what the hell you're doing with a gun?" Shit! I forgot it was there. Dammit.

I think quickly. "I have it for protection." Lame. My shoulders sag.

"Why do you need a gun?" I freeze. Why does he have to be so perceptive? Why can he get into my brain?

"I just do." I head to the kitchen, but he secures me to his body in a tight grip, his eyes fierce. I shiver at the coldness in them.

"Tell me what's going on." I say nothing. "Dammit, Blaze, tell me!" he orders and in a voice that scares the ever-loving shit out of me. I breathe in deep.

I go for vague. "My past has caught up with me. I'm calling Princess in the morning to get an ID and I have to leave Sumner." That was so not vague, not one little bit. What the hell is wrong with me?

"You're leaving?" I shake my head yes and fight back the tears. He squeezes my arms then releases, but he keeps me right in front of him, not relinquishing his grasp. "Tell me what the fuck is going on!" I suck in deep.

"It's the past. Let's enjoy tonight before I leave."

His brown eyes turn black with fury. He spins around abruptly and it takes everything in me not to jump. "God dammit, Blaze. Tell me what the fuck has you running. And running from *me?* I won't let you leave. I don't give a shit if I have to lock you up at the club. I'll do it. You are not fucking leaving," he bellows, and my heart warms at him wanting me to stay. He gets face-to-face with me and I stare into his molten eyes. "Tell me now!" he demands and the warmth turns to ice.

My entire body starts to shake hard. Pain slices

through me like a sharp knife. Pain that he's mad at me, and pain about what I'm going to tell him. I close my eyes and step away from him. I pick up the yellow piece of paper from the floor, hold it out for him to take. His eyes glance on the paper then at me.

"Who the fuck is Paige?" he barks out.

I can do this. "I'm Paige. Paige McMillion." His eyes grow wide.

"I thought your name was Taryn?" His brows furrow together in confusion.

"When I got here, Princess gave me a new identity. I've been running for the past four years." I try to judge what he's thinking but his face has gone blank.

"What are you running from?" That's the biggest loaded question anyone could ask me. I cannot believe I am doing this.

"Let's sit down." I sit on the couch and he follows. I grab a pillow from the floor and hold it in my lap like a shield, kicking my feet up under my butt. The butt of the gun digs in my back so I pull it out and set it on the table. Tug eyes it then me as he sits down on the other end of the couch.

I turn from him and stare at the wall.

Long moments pass before I speak. "My mother fell in love with a man," I whisper quietly, barely audible. This is the first time ever I have spoken about it and hopefully the last. I'm so scared to know what he's going to think of me when I finish. "My mom was really sick and needed treatments that we couldn't afford but the man she fell for could. They got together and Mom got her treatments." I stop, not wanting to continue with the story. It's way too black and I want out of it. I'd rather be up on stage with every man touching me than to tell this story.

Tug waits patiently, giving me time. I love that he doesn't pressure me in this moment. I couldn't take it. "Him and his son." I stop, the words not wanting to escape my lips, and they tremble. Tug scoots closer to me on the couch and his hand comes out to mine. I don't bat him away. I need this, need him. "I was young," I murmur, "way too young." I pause and try to fight the tears.

I close my eyes and say what's been squeezing my heart for years, what's changed me as a person, what's haunted me just the same. "They used to come in my room at night and have sex with me." I let out a huge breath. A lone tear trickles down my cheek and I instantly wipe it away. I will not fucking cry.

"What?" Tug says, snapping me out of thoughts. The air in the room changes, giving me a chill. I turn to him, his eyes bold with fury, but it's not directed at me.

"You heard me, Tug, please don't make me say it again." He engulfs me in his arms and leans back on the couch. He puts me between his legs, my back resting on his chest, his arms around me. It is exactly what I need, the safety and comfort of Tug.

"How old were you?" he asks gruffly.

"Sixteen," I whisper. His body goes ridged. His arms tremble and flex around me. I rub his arm, trying to calm him, but it doesn't appear to help. "My mother never knew. I was told that if I didn't keep my mouth shut, they would cut the money off to her treatments and she would die. So, for years I kept my mouth shut."

"Years?" Tug fumes.

"Yes. I never told a soul until now." His arms stiffen. "I found my mother dead in her room." Tears spring to my eyes. "She was lying there cold, her lips pale, blue. I tried, Tug. I did. I gave her mouth-to-mouth and pumped her chest. I tried to save her..." I trail off, trying to get my hiccupping cries in check, but to no avail. "I knew I couldn't. And so, I left her, Tug. Just left her..." I sob and allow all the tears to fall.

I didn't think I could get any closer to Tug, but it happens. I relish in the warmth as my tears spill on his shirt. "You left her how?" His voice is calm and patient.

"The two that came in my room had a lot of money and a lot of connections. I did not. I packed a bag with some clothes and a few things then drove to North Carolina. My mom had a sister that she hadn't talked to in a while. She never told me the entire story, but it's not relevant." I sniffle. "She was the only person I thought of that wasn't from home and would probably help me. I showed up on her doorstep and shocked the hell out of her. She was nice and led me here to Sumner."

Tug's arms tighten as sobs take over.

"You did it to protect yourself," Tug says deeply. I know I did, but it doesn't make the pain of leaving her go away. He comfortingly holds me, allowing me the time to get everything out.

After what seems like eternity, the sobs cease. He releases me and I get a tissue off the corner of the coffee table, wiping my face and snot. Embarrassed doesn't cut it. "I'm an asshole, Tug. What kind of a daughter leaves the one person she loves more than anything on this planet? What kind of woman does that make me?" My last question ends on a bit of a screech as my words get louder and louder. Each time I ask one I point to myself hard in my chest, punctuating each word.

"A survivor." Authority pulses off of Tug, but I don't believe it for a second.

"Coward," I fire back not skipping a beat.

Tug turns me to him, his face showing no disdain or hate. Warmth and compassion flood in his eyes, almost causing me to lose it, but I hold tight. "It took a hell of a lot of balls for you leave your mother and that house. It is what your mother would have wanted you to do, especially if she had known what was happening to you. Do you think for one moment that she would have wanted you around those two assholes?"

Fresh tears spring from my eyes, roll down my cheek, and fall to the floor. I blink, trying to get them out because Tug's face is blurry. "No," I whisper softly.

"You think these guys are coming back for you?" His question grabs my attention and I pull out another tissue, cleaning up my face.

"That's what the note is. They've found me and they'll force me to go with them." Tears leak down my cheeks.

Tug pulls my chin up with his thumb and finger so I have no choice but to look right in his eyes. "I will not let them get to you. Do you hear me?" I don't move. "I will protect you, keep you safe. I need names. I can have Buzz run a trace on them and find out where they are and get all the information I can on them."

Fear slices through me. "No!" I yell loudly, panicked, and pull back.

"Yes. This will give us a heads up from them," Tug demands.

No. "It'll be best if I disappear. I don't need to be bringing this shit to Ravage's doorstep, Xs or yours."

He holds me. "You are not leaving. You are staying here and if those motherfuckers come here, I'll fucking gut them." A cold shiver goes through my body and it's strange because it's not exactly fear but I believe him. "Tell me names and what he did for a living."

He releases me and I sit back a bit, sucking in deep. "I don't know what they do. Santos Markus and Frank Markus were gone a lot at meetings. We had tons of money and anything that Mom or I wanted was ours by the end of the day. We had servants in our seven-bedroom house and a chauffeur that would drive us around." I didn't want to say the next part, but it needs to come out. "I think it was either drugs or mob. I don't know for sure on either."

"Shit," he mutters.

"See what I mean? You don't need this trouble."

"Get it through your fucking head right now, woman. You are not leaving. You are mine and I protect what is mine. Got me?" I nod slowly. "We need to talk to Pops, get him the information. And before you say it, I know you don't want to, but it's what's happening," he finishes.

"Don't you get it? Everyone will hate me, having some assholes come in and screw with their shit because of me!" I bark out.

"You don't think that's already going to happen. They know where and who you work for and probably know where you live now, which means that we all have our asses in the fryer. Giving Pops the heads up that this shit is knocking on his door whether you are here or not is the right thing to do." I think about Tug's words and he's right. It is already here, already a problem. I have to tell them. I swallow big.

"Fine."

CHAPTER TEN
Tug

Blaze is a big ball of nerves. I tried fucking it out of her but even that didn't help. I put her on the back of my bike and rode to the clubhouse, tense as a stick. Even with all this shit going on, having her arms wrapped around me, her hot pussy against my ass and head on my shoulder, is my absolute favorite thing in the fucking world.

After she fell asleep last night, I got out of bed. I had to. I couldn't lie there and not get out the anger that consumed every cell of my body. I want to destroy these motherfuckers for what they did to Blaze. No wonder she was so freaked about getting with me. She was ready to bolt at a moment's notice. No way in hell I'd let that shit happen.

I glide my hand up and down her back, trying to

soothe her as the trembles wrack her body. It doesn't help.

"You ready?" Pops asks, coming out of his office.

"You ready?" I whisper in her ear. "Relax," I murmur.

"Yeah." Blaze tries to answer but there is a catch in her throat. She clears it and says, "Yes."

"We'll need Buzz, too," I say to Pops, his eyes growing heavy.

"Buzz later. Right now you two, let's go in," Pops says sternly.

We enter his office; the desk sits at the end with a computer on top and papers cluttering the surface. Two chairs are situated in front of the desk and we sit. I make sure my chair is right next to Blaze, and rest her hand on my thigh.

Pops laces his fingers and puts them behind his neck, leaning in his chair with a small creak. "Blaze, Tug tells me you got some trouble."

"Yes." Her voice is strong but the very small tremor is not lost to me.

"Tell me."

Blaze speaks and I do my best to keep my anger in check. I had all night to process this shit, but that didn't help, especially having to hear it all over again. I try really hard not to squeeze her hand too hard.

Pops' face turns hard as stone as she adds more and more to the story. He leans up in his chair and listens intently to every single word she says.

Then she finishes with a *that's about it*. Like it's no big deal.

"Got yourself in a mess, huh?" Blaze nods, but no

tears shed from her eyes. Strong fucking woman. "You should have told us this from the very beginning," he reprimands, kindly. "I'll get Buzz to find out everything he can on those two. I need any and all information you know about them. You are not leaving." Blaze's deep gasp echoes through the room. "No, we don't run, Blaze. You do that you'll run the rest of your life." Blaze shakes her head to contradict what Pops is saying but he doesn't listen. "Tug is your shadow." I lift my chin in acknowledgement, wanting to thank him, but keeping my mouth shut. Blaze does not.

"No," she says, her spine visibly stiffening.

"Yes." Pops charges leaving no room for Blaze to argue and she concedes, her shoulders slumping.

"I don't want the whole club to know," Blaze says in a rush, she must think she's going to be dismissed soon.

"Everyone will know. It's not something I can hide from the brothers and their families. If these two come, we all have to be prepared for it." A lone tear rolls down her cheek. I give her hand a squeeze, hopefully, letting her take my strength. Her other hand comes up and bats the tear like it's some annoying gnat that she just wants to get rid of.

"Fine," is all she says, but she says it looking right into Pops' eyes. She doesn't release from me though.

"You sure you think they're into drugs?" Pops asks her.

"I have no idea. They kept all business out of the house. My mom didn't know anything either. All I know is there was a surplus of money and Santos didn't have a nine to five job."

"Give me something else, Blaze. Why do you think it's drugs?" She stares Pops down, the wheels turning.

"My mother told me once she overheard him on the phone talking about *product* so I assumed it was drugs."

Pops' eyes swing to mine. *Product* can mean thousands of things: drugs, cars, money, guns, or even people. There is no limit and this leaves us little to go on. "I'll have Buzz look. Step on out so I can talk to Tug a minute."

"It's okay. Just wait for me out there," I reassure her when she stills. She nods.

Blaze stands from the chair. "Thank you," she mutters and leaves the room, closing the door behind her.

"Fuck," Pops grunts, rubbing his hand through his salt and pepper hair, clearly frustrated. "We do not need this shit at our doorstep." I say nothing. "Fuck." He stands from the chair then breathes in deep "All right. You're on Blaze until I get some information. Which will hopefully be right fucking now." He picks up his cell and dials.

"Buzz. Need you to investigate two people. Santos Markus and Frank Markus. I need everything you can get on them."

I sit and listen to the one-sided conversation. Pops' face contorts to all different emotions, but anger is over-riding everything.

"No, this is more important." Buzz must be trying to tell him that hacking into that computer is more important.

"Yes, I'm sure. Get me the info then you can go back to it."

"I need it like yesterday."

Pops swipes the phone off and tosses it on his desk. "I'd put her on lockdown, but I don't know for sure who we're dealing with, so I'll wait. But it may come to that shit." He shakes his head absently. "Go. I'll be in touch."

I nod, moving out the door, not able to say anything to make this situation better.

I trudge out to the clubhouse and Blaze is sitting at one of the small tables. I join her, fear and anger pulsing off of her. "You wanna go home or hang out here?" I ask her, not caring what she picks just glad that she is my job for the next couple of days, even if that means some asshole is after her.

"Home." Her lips form an O as she says the word. My dick hardens at the thoughts of where that mouth could go. Then my mind snaps to what she told me. Fuck. I will my dick down. Yeah, right.

"Let's go." I grab her arm gently. I need a ride to clear my thoughts. We'll take the long way *home*.

EVEN THOUGH SHE chose to come to her house, by the crashing of pots and pans in the kitchen, I'm guessing she doesn't like Pops' decision. Too fucking bad. I rest my hip on the kitchen counter, cross my arms and wait. Blaze is putting pans on the stove, filling one with water. She pulls noodles out of the cabinet and sets them beside the sink. Each time she puts a lid on or opens a drawer, she slams it shut with all her might.

"You wanna tear up your kitchen?" I joke, having no

doubt it was hard for her retelling everything to Pops and trying to lighten the mood.

She whips around, eyes shooting up like she didn't know I am standing a few feet away. "I'm not tearing anything up. I'm making some food. I'm hungry." She turns to the stove, dismissing me.

"You want to talk about it?"

She opens a drawer and the sound of metal clinking together echoes through the kitchen. She yanks out a spoon and bumps the drawer closed with her hip. "No." Her voice is much quieter this time but her spine is still straight as a board.

I take long strides up to the stove and stand behind her. Once she removes the spoon out of the pot, I grab her hips and turn her around. Her eyes fill with shock. I hold her tight, needing her as close to me as she can get.

Blaze's body stays stiff, but no words come from those plump lips. After what feels like hours, but were only minutes, her arms wrap around me and she turns to the side, burrowing into my chest. She does not move. I softly stroke her back and her body melts into mine.

I'm reluctant to let her go when she tries, but do. Her eyes meet mine and I want to wipe away every bit of pain that is etched in them. Destroy it. I cup her cheeks, holding her nose-to-nose with me, lightly brushing my lips over hers and wanting more. But now is not the time to take it.

"I know you think it's best for you to leave, but, babe, I fully stand behind Pops. We'll be ready if it comes to that." She nods. "I'm gonna go in the living room for a while," I say softly, meeting her eyes. As much as I do not want to let her go, I do. I take my phone out of my rag and set my rag on the end of the couch, my phone in hand. I took off my boots at the door, so I am left in just jeans and a black t-shirt, pretty much all I wear.

I text Buzz.

ME: Any info on the fuckers?

BUZZ: Some, working, will update in a bit

I SIGH, putting the phone down. I sit on the couch and lie back, putting my feet up. My arm drapes over my eyes and flashes of a young Blaze float through my brain. Her being terrified. Her thinking there is no way out. Her crying because she couldn't go to anyone. Her trying to protect her mom. Anger bubbles in my veins hotter this time than before as my brain is continually processing the hell that she went through, over and over again. And it was hell. It also explains a lot about her.

The fact that she likes to be home alone, and at X, how she keeps herself inside her dressing room. The fact that she swore off the Ravage guys right away. She probably saw us as big domineering assholes, same as the men who attacked her repeatedly. The fact that she doesn't date, accept for me, now. The fact that she barely comes to any parties or get-togethers. Her ramrod stiff spine and how she can take on the world. And in a way she has.

Fuck.

"Tug?" I remove my arm from my face and sit up. She carries in two plates, setting one down on the coffee table in front of me. "I thought you might be hungry. It's nothing fancy, just spaghetti, but it's something." She shrugs her shoulder like it's no big deal.

"Thank you. I appreciate that." I pick up the plate, lean back on the couch and eat. Damn, that's good. Blaze sits in the recliner and eats hers, grabs the remote and turns the television on and flips through the channels.

"I won't make you watch a Lifetime movie or anything," she says absently, and I have no clue what the fuck Lifetime is.

"A what?" My fork stills.

"It's a station that plays romantic and tragic movies that most of the time, make you cry. You've never heard of it?"

"*Uh*... no," I answer with finality. "And I'm not gonna start."

Her eyes meet mine and she points to the TV with the remote. "This good?"

I glance back at the TV and monster truck racing is on. "Hell yeah. You wanna watch this?"

"Oh, yeah. I want to take my Jeep out sometime and try it. Not the racing part but the going through the mud and stuff."

I whip to her, my mouth hanging open in shock. "No shit?"

"Nope." She turns her attention to the TV. We sit in

silence while we finish eating. I make a mental note to make that come true for her.

I set my polished off plate on the table. "Thank you, Blaze."

"No problem." She gets up from the chair and picks up my plate. She takes her fine ass into the kitchen and I watch it sway. Fuck. After a brief time, she comes back.

"Come here. Lie with me." She comes without hesitation. She may be angry at the decision for her to stay, but not at me. I crush against the cushions of the couch and pat the area in front of me.

She lies down next to me, my arms wrapping around her waist. She fits perfectly.

Her body is tense. "Relax," I tell her softly. The stiffness in her body gets a tad bit lighter. Neither of us moves for long moments. She finally relaxes.

"I'm sorry," she whispers, burrowing into my body.

"You have nothing to be sorry for, sweet lips. What happened to you wasn't your fault." Her body stiffens in my arms, but I keep going. "Those assholes took something from you that you weren't willing to give. It's not your fault."

She sits silent for long minutes the television continuing to play in the background. "I just wanted my mom better."

The aching guilt behind her words comes out loud and clear. Damn. "I know you did. And she wanted to protect you."

Wetness drips on my arm. I hold her tighter to my body. "She did. And I was horrible for just leaving her. I didn't even go to her funeral."

"You were a wonderful daughter to her. You had no choice. You had to leave."

Her body shakes as sobs rake through her. I turn her in my arms and rest her head on my chest while she cries. I doubt she ever really mourned her mother. She was running for her life at the time.

I rub up and down her side, trying to soothe her, but glad she is getting it out. The t-shirt on my chest is soaked but I don't give a shit.

Long minutes later, her tears dry up and her breathing returns to normal.

"Why are they coming after you now?" I ask softly, being careful with her.

"My guess is they've been searching for me since I left and since my aunt is in North Carolina, they were probably looking around there. I got lucky that it took them this long."

"And that's why you want to run again?"

Her eyes spark in disagreement. "If I could go, they won't catch me."

"I won't let them get you, Blaze. I'll do anything to protect you," I say with all the power I possess, and I believe that to my core.

She lets out a breath. "I'll die before I go back to them. I will not go through that ever again."

I believe her words with every fiber inside of me and the thought makes me angrier, but I mask it.

"Sorry," she whispers. I maneuver her on top of me, my eyes meeting hers.

"You have nothing to be sorry for, sweet lips." Her mouth slightly parts and fire blazes behind her eyes.

I brush my lips across her soft ones.

"I know I have a lot of shit going on in my head, but the fact that you know my past now is like a huge weight off of my shoulders. I didn't want you to know, but I did want you to know."

"I'm glad you told me, baby."

CHAPTER ELEVEN
Blaze

His strong arms come around me and he kisses my temple, my hands going to his muscled chest. "Get dressed. We gotta get to the clubhouse. Buzz has an update and Pops wants me there."

My eyes widen. "Can I hear?"

His eyes tell me the answer, but he says it anyway. "Not yet. Let me know what it is first. One thing you gotta know is, club business is club business." I start to say *but it's about me!* But he doesn't give me time. "I know it's about you but I won't tell you anything that deals with the club and you need to be okay with that. There will be days when we are together, and I'm in a piss-poor mood but I won't be able to talk about it. Or there will be days when I'm wired and happy and again, can't tell you." He lifts my chin gently. His chocolate brown eyes melt me.

"It's better this way, Blaze. I know it's hard, but you have to trust me. Trust me to take care of you."

Trust. The people I've trusted since Mom are Princess, even though I didn't tell her my past but she helped me no questions asked, and Casey. Putting my trust in him and the club, that's a hard measure. I whisper, "I'll try." Because that is all I can do right now.

He touches my lips with his. "Thanks, sweet lips. Get dressed." My heart flutters.

SITTING at the bar in the clubhouse, I feel so damn out of place. Men and women come though repeatedly. The guys give me chin lifts and the women give me scowls, but I've had experience with that. Wood paneling lines the walls, with pictures of the brothers and a massive, carved emblem that says Ravage and a huge skull with fire coming out of the top, exactly like the brothers' patches. There are some banners from charity events they have done and a huge corkboard with lots of papers tacked to it. The bar I'm sitting at is old and worn with lots of nicks and scratches.

The air smells like musty smoke, which explains all the ashtrays everywhere. Two couches and chairs sit in the far corner; smaller tables and chairs line the large floor. The area off to the side is occupied predominantly by a pool table and a large dartboard is on the wall next to it.

"Well, look who we have here." I jump and turn to the voice, wanting to roll my eyes, but don't.

"Hi, Dagger." I give a soft wave.

"What's a pretty thing like you doing here all alone? I think you need some company." He smirks in a handsome way and sits on the stool next to me. Luckily, the stools are far enough apart that he isn't invading my space. "What something to drink?"

"I'd take a soda if you got one. Diet, please," I ask politely.

"Sure thing." He turns to the room. "Breaker!" he yells loudly, my eardrums ring and that's saying something considering I deal with loud music all the time. Breaker comes out of the swinging doors and lifts his chin. "Get this beautiful lady a diet soda," he orders, "and me a beer." Breaker nods and disappears.

I want to ask if Breaker's job is to serve the brothers but bite my tongue. Breaker opens my soda and puts it on the bar. "Thank you," I say, but he dips his chin with no words. Dagger says nothing to him.

"He's a quiet one, huh?" I smile.

"Pretty much. So why you here?" This question shocks me because I figured Pops would have told everyone about what's going on already, but I guess not and I'm not going to be the one to do it.

"Waiting on Tug." His brow rises as he lifts his bottle to his lips.

"You and Tugger, huh?" I avoid his question and giggle a bit at the name.

"Tugger?" I ask, taking a drink from my soda.

"That's his last name, darlin'" Confusion hits. I always thought Tug was his club name.

"Really?" I question, damn I thought I knew a lot about him.

"Yep."

"Thought you had club names cause I'm pretty sure your real name isn't Dagger." I pause. "Wait, is it?" I hate this confusion.

Dagger lets out a belly laugh, causing everyone in the clubhouse to focus on him. Didn't know I'm that funny.

"Dagger's not my name on my driver's license, but it is my name, the only one that I go by anyway." I nod. I'm learning here. "So what's up with you and Tug? Cause, baby, I've seen you dance and if he's getting that, I may have to beat the shit out of him just for fun."

Heat creeps up my neck and onto my face. Shit, blushing? Seriously, woman, get a grip. "He's a good guy," I answer, wondering if Tug hasn't said anything to the club about us yet. Surely, he has.

"And she avoids it," Dagger continues. Damn man. "You don't have to tell me. But since you're here, did you finally decide to be a club momma and are ready for some action?" He wiggles his brows up and down, his beard-covered mouth stretched in a grin. This time I do roll my eyes. No way in hell.

"You wish, Dagger. I strip, that's it." I pick up the can of soda and put it to my lips.

"Baby, you are sexy as fuck." Seriously. This is how all the guys at X look at me. *Ugh.*

"Thanks," I say wryly. How in the hell is this going to go? All of Tug's friends have seen me strip. How do I act when they've all seen me? I shake myself out of my stupid thoughts.

"I'm just fucking with ya, sugar," he says. His bandana covers the top of his long blonde hair. He appears rough and mean, but from the way he's talking, I can tell he has a joking and kind side also. "Really, what brings you to the club?"

I breathe out deep. "Tug's handling some things for me and he's talking to Pops." Partial truth. I really didn't want everyone to know what happened to me in Colorado, but I know they all will. I'll bide my time.

"Tug there, he's a good guy. I won't say that to his face or nothing, but he is. Loyal, trustworthy, and I'm glad he has my back." My jaw falls open and I'm sure my eyes are as wide as saucers. "He never bitches or complains and always gets shit done fast. He's one of the good ones."

Did he really just say that? Big bad Dagger paid Tug a compliment. Shock doesn't even cut it and I soak in every word that comes out of his mouth because I believe him whole-heartedly.

"I'll have to agree with you on that." I try to pick my mouth up off the floor.

"I gotta split, the ol' lady wants me home, not that I ever listen to her, but she said she had food and a man's gotta eat." He shrugs, getting off the barstool and patting his stomach. "You take care of yourself."

"So, you're telling me you're hitting on me when you have an ol' lady at home?" I mean, seriously aren't there rules on that shit?

A full out smile shines, exposing years of cigarette

build-up, not gross, but not clean either. "Yep," is all he says and he disappears.

It feels like it's been hours since Tug went to talk to Pops and I'm pretty sure it has been. My eyes get droopy and I rest, cross my arms on the bar and lay my head down. Somehow, I fall fast asleep.

"Sweet lips," is whispered in my ear and I slowly open my eyes, getting a view of the clubhouse. I turn to the voice. Tug stands next to me giving me soft strokes on my back going up and down. "Hey. We can go home now."

The fogginess disappears. "Wait, I wanna know what's going on," I say in a rush as he grabs my arm and I stand to my feet a bit shakily. I need to remind myself never to fall asleep on a barstool again, not only do my legs ache but my neck does too. I ignore it.

"I'll tell you when we get to your place."

"I'd like to know now," I demand as Buzz and Pops come around the corner.

"And I said I'll tell you when we get you home." My temper flairs, who in the hell does he think he is? This is about me.

Pops steps in. "Blaze go home and he'll talk." His tone comes out with all kinds of parental authority and I know I can't deny his command.

"Let's go," I say softly.

Riding on the back of Tug's bike is like heaven filled with lots of chocolate. Being plastered up against him ignites every part of my body. And not only that, it's the freedom, like nothing can stop us. On here, it's like I have no problems, nothing bogging me down. It's bliss and I love being with him on his bike. I haven't told him that yet, but I'm pretty sure he can tell as I stroke his abs and get as close as possible to him.

Once he parks the bike, we enter the house and he sits me on the couch. This can't be good. Whenever it's a couch-sitting conversation its bad news. Like the time my mom made me sit on the couch so she could tell me my fish died. Couch Trauma. I wait for it and try not to grit my teeth.

"Those two are bad news." I already knew that one. His eyes meet mine and he clutches my hand, holding it. The touch helps me relax. "Buzz broke into their computer hub and one of the computers shows countless searches for Paige McMillion." I suck in a breath. "I like Blaze better," he tries to reassure me, but it doesn't happen. Tremors come and I try to breathe them out. "Right now those two are confirmed in Colorado. We have a charter up there and Pops set that up. They are there for sure."

"But…" I try to interrupt but he places one finger on my lips and continues.

"That being said, we think one or more of his guys are down here to take you back." I suck in deep. "We don't know who that is. No clue. So, we are running all the video from X to see if we can get a shot of him placing the note on your windshield, and running anyone who comes into X. So, for right now, you're with me."

"So, really the only thing you learned is that those two are in Colorado?" I question, not trying to sound like a bitch but frustrated as shit.

"That's the only part you need to know." He sets me on his lap like I weigh nothing, our faces inches apart.

Anger bubbles up and I squirm to move out of his tight grasp, both his strong arms wrapped around me. Dammit. "Stop!" he orders.

"Stop? Are you serious right now, Tug? This is my life and I need to get far away from here so they can't find me." He does not loosen his grip and I continue to struggle.

"Stop!" he barks out in a voice that I've only heard one other time. I stop struggling and turn to him. His brows knit together, creating an angry V in the middle of his forehead. After I stop, the V disappears and I realize I don't like the V at all. "I told you. I will tell you what I can, but you are not involved with the other shit. What I told you is all you get." His tone turns to the one I recognize and I like it much better.

"I don't like that part." I bite out, clenching my teeth, but say no more.

"I understand, sweet lips, but it's the same with all the women. Talk to Princess and Casey about it." I let out a deep breath.

"Fine. Can I get up now?" I cross my arms over my chest.

"No." His words stun me, but when he kisses me, all thoughts leave. This kiss is hard and rough. I sink deep into it, forgetting.

WE JUST GOT HOME from Casey and GT's housewarming party and I've decided that I'm not talking to Tug anymore. Well at least for tonight. Tug decided to tell me at the party that Pops told all the brothers today. All. Of. Them. Everything. He couldn't have told me on the phone before I got to the party. No, he decides to do it there and around men that now know the hell I lived through.

Casey and Princess didn't let on that they knew anything, but it's only a matter of time now. And I'm sure they'll be pissed that I never told them directly but tonight was not the night to tell them.

Cali ended up bringing me to Casey and GT's house because I was doing the books at X. Tug said he'd come and get me, but I told him no. Cali dropped me off, his eyes on me like a hawk until I got into the house. Then for Tug to tell me that shit a few minutes after I come in the door, it pissed me off.

I enter the bedroom and slam the door behind me. Maybe he'll get the hint and stay away from me tonight. I tear off my clothes and put on my goofy kitty faces pajama pants and a blue tank top. I climb into bed, scoot over to the far edge, and turn toward the wall, pulling the covers over me. Not an inch of my body is exposed except for my head.

I lie there and lie there. Time ticks methodically by and Tug doesn't come. His absence only gives me more time to think and what I'm thinking, I do not like. Maybe I did overreact a tad. I knew Pops was going to tell the brothers, I just didn't know when. But I still didn't want them all to know. It's embarrassing. I didn't want my entire life story plastered out there for everyone to witness. It's degrading. I should just crawl in a hole and never come out.

This whole thing is more on me. Dammit. I took it out on Tug and really shouldn't have. God, I hate when I'm a flipping idiot. *Grr...* I throw the covers off and hop out of bed. Tug sits in the living room, feet up, and beer in hand watching some sport thing on the TV. I stop and take him in, his strong jaw with a day's worth of scruff and his long hair that I love running my fingers through. He is a very handsome man and I'm a moron.

I sit next to him on the couch, picking his feet up and putting them on my lap. He doesn't say anything, just keeps his focus on the game like I'm not even here.

After a few minutes pass and he still doesn't talk to me, I lose it. "I'm sorry, all right?"

"Done being a bitch." I give him my most evil glare and it has no affect on him. All I get is a brow lift. Dammit. "Good. Come here." I climb up his body and lay my head on his chest, my back to the cushion of the couch.

"Why don't people know we're together?" I ask quietly.

"Why don't Princess and Casey know?" he fires back and he's got me. They know that we're hanging out and I'm sure they think we're sleeping together, but that is about the extent of it.

"Point taken," I mumble into his chest.

"You ready to really let the cat out of the bag and not just let people guess?" I hate it when he's right. Dagger guessed and guessed right, but I didn't tell him. I'm sure if I had time alone with Princess and Casey, they would figure it out. This will make us real. Official. Warmth grows in my belly and reaches my heart.

"Yeah," I whisper.

Tug squeezes me and kisses the top of my hair. His lips upturn as he lingers there.

CHAPTER TWELVE
Tug

I can't believe this fucking shit. I sweep the broom, trying to pick up all the broken glass by the bar. Cops came into the clubhouse with a search warrant a few hours ago and tore this place to pieces.

Everything has been fairly calm these past two weeks. No one has bothered Blaze or made any attempt to. We have ears on those two motherfuckers in Colorado. And Buzz is still trying to crack the computer from Joey's house, which luckily he took to our apartment or else it would have been trashed. We also told everyone that we are together and it wasn't the big deal that Blaze thought it would be.

Pops and Ma are having a family-only party with brothers, Prospects, and their women. We decided this was a good time to tell everyone. Blaze and I enter the clubhouse together, hand-in-hand, and all eyes swing to us.

The first voice we hear is Princess. "Hot damn. It's about fucking time!" She hugs Blaze tight. "Didn't I tell you?" she questions Blaze. I raise my brow and she shrugs but doesn't respond.

Casey approaches from behind Princess, her eyes lit in happiness. Princess moves out of the way and Casey, I still have a hard time remembering to call her Angel, hugs the both of us at the same time. "I'm so damn happy." Casey smiles.

"What the fuck is this shit?" Dagger roars from behind them, his tone angry but eyes shining.

"What shit?" I ask him.

Dagger steps closer. "She's supposed to be mine first." My jaw ticks but I get it under control. He turns to Blaze. "Thought you were off limits?"

Blaze turns to me, smiles, and says to Dagger, "I still am."

Dagger shakes his head. "Fucking shit."

He steps away and we get words from the other brothers and their women.

THAT WAS IT.

"Fucking shit!" Dagger yells from the doorway and that's like the seventh one of those. Each person that comes through the door says it, each one making poor Blaze jump and her eyes swing to the door. Each time, she takes a deep breath and calms herself then goes back to what she's doing. The cops did not take into account our personal belongings at all in this raid. Our couches are slashed, the foam littering the floor. Tables are broken as if we were hiding something in the wood. The bottles of liquor were smashed to the ground, hence all the sweeping.

The bedrooms are a disaster, too. Everything is cut and slashed the fuck up. Officer James Lakin led the team in and told them to not leave one inch untouched. And they did as told, hardcore.

Every one of the guys and some of their ol' ladies, including Blaze, are helping out in the cleaning effort and it is taking all of us. We already filled the dumpster with shit and will need to have another hauled in tomorrow.

Before we touched anything, Pops called the club's lawyer, Burnzie, who told us to take pictures of everything, so we did. I'm not sure what that will accomplish, but time will tell. And since it's the cops, we will need to go a legal route instead of handling this our way. Right.

The anger in the clubhouse is so strong I'm surprised the roof doesn't blow off the place. When Rhys got here, he decided to take the already broken tables and throw them in a huff out into the courtyard. Whatever. It is easier to put it in the dumpster out there. At least it took the edge off his rage.

"Let's take a break," I say to Blaze who nods. She's been unbelievably quiet through this whole thing, but remained calm, cool, and collected, except for the shouting.

Blaze sits on my lap as there are only a few chairs that are not busted up.

"You doing all right?" I ask into her ear.

"Yeah. I can't believe they did this. This can't be a

normal search." She's fucking right. There is more here and we need to find out what it is.

"I don't know what's going on." Un-fucking-fortunately.

"I can't believe they destroyed everything. I mean, you can't repair any of it." A small tremor enters her voice. I wrap my arms around her and hold her. She's right and I have nothing to say.

Everyone is somber, coming down from their intense anger from earlier. The guys are in church and damn I wish I could be in there to know what the fuck is going on. So, we sit out here and wait to go home.

The doors to church open and all eyes swing in that direction. Becs comes up to Buzz, Breaker, and I. "Go home and get some sleep. There's nothing else we can do tonight." He clasps my shoulder and squeezes it then releases. "Tomorrow we stop at Randell's."

"You ready to go?" Blaze only nods, her eyes already drooping shut. "Come on, baby, let me get you home."

"WHY THE FUCK did cops come and raid the place?" Dagger holds Randell against the wall, his hand to his throat, cutting off his air supply. Randell gasps, trying to get oxygen and tries to get out of Dagger's grip. Good luck with that shit. Dagger, Rhys, Becs and I came here to hopefully get some answers.

It didn't exactly bode well that when we came in he

was nursing a beer with several bottles littering the floor around him.

"I don't know," he says, trying to breathe.

"Get on your fucking phone right now and find out. I want to know what the fuck is going on," Dagger barks with a tone that most would call terrifying.

"Okay," he gasps as Dagger releases him. Randell bends over, heaving, trying to get his oxygen flowing again.

"Now," Rhys barks from behind Dagger, his arms crossed and feet apart, not giving Randell an inch. Rhys is one badass motherfucker. Definitely one you don't want to meet in a dark alley. Glad he's on my team.

Randell straightens and walks to the living room, all of our eyes on him. He picks up his cell from the coffee table, and I have no clue how the hell he could even find it, there is so much shit in this house. He swipes some buttons then holds it up to his ear and we listen to the one-sided conversation.

"Smith."

"Randell."

"Stenger told me that ya'll raided the Ravage Clubhouse. You find anything?" Randell rubs the back of his neck, not meeting any of our gazes.

"Shit. What were you looking for?" If nothing else, Randell is a pretty good actor. He sounds professional and all business.

His eyes dart to us. "Really? And they didn't have any?"

"*Huh*," he says, noncommittally.

"All right. I'll be in tomorrow to get updated on everything."

"Thanks." He flips the phone shut.

His eyes sweep across us. "They had a woman come in and say that she went to a Ravage party and you were selling drugs. The judge ordered the warrant on her affidavit."

"Fuck me," Dagger bursts out and I totally agree with him there.

"What's her name?" Becs asks.

"Sandra Buckett."

"Fuck," Rhys bites out, but doesn't say anymore.

Dagger pats Randell on the shoulder. "Good job. We'll be in touch."

At our bikes, we gather around. "I know the bitch," Rhys says clipped. "I fucked her lots then she started that whole *be my boyfriend* bullshit so I got rid of her. I know where she lives, let's go."

The apartment building is three floors and in pretty good shape. We follow Rhys, park our bikes, and climb up some stairs and come to a stop at a door. "You guys wait outside the door. I'll leave it open a bit."

We nod and he knocks. The door opens up in a whoosh. "Rhys," a breathy woman says, her voice lustful.

"Hey, baby. I heard you went to the cops?"

"They told me I had to," she pleads on another breathy note.

"*Who* told you?"

"The cops," she replies. The door closes almost shut, and sounds of arguing stream through. After a few minutes pass, the noises turn a little erotic, and a half an hour later, Rhys comes out of the apartment adjusting his jeans and we all head downstairs.

"That was quick," Dagger says, lifting his leg and putting it over his bike.

"Fuck off. I knew you assholes were waiting. Next time, I'll take my fucking time," Rhys barks and Dagger chuckles.

Rhys turns to me. "Stay on her." He points to a green Taurus. "That's her car. Follow it and make sure she goes to the station. If she doesn't, I'll come back and make sure this is taken care of." And I knew how that would be. Hope this woman is smarter than she sounds.

"On it," I say as the roar of bikes take off, me following to sit behind a large bush at the entrance of the apartment complex. Out of sight, but still in the know of all the comings and goings.

I light a cigarette and wait. Four hours and twenty Goddamn minutes later, the bitch finally leaves her place. I follow cautiously, staying out of sight. She pulls into the police station and steps out of the car. Her long blonde hair falls down to her ass, encased in shorts so short her cheeks hang out. Her skin-tight top shows off huge tits and her heels are so tall I'd think she'd break a fucking leg. She marches into the station and I park on the other side of the entrance and kill the engine.

An hour and fourteen minutes later, she still hasn't come out. I hit Rhys's number on my phone. "What?" he answers abruptly.

"She went in and hasn't come out."

He scoffs, "She just called from jail. She recanted her story and they arrested her. For something, I didn't listen.

She wanted me to bail her ass out and I told her I would come soon."

This surprises me. Rhys is not known for his caring side. "Are you?"

Rhys chuckles. "Fuck no. I called Randell and the cops ain't got shit on us. Sandra is collateral damage. Even if she tries to tell the cops something now, they won't believe a fucking thing that comes out of her mouth."

"Be at the clubhouse in a few."

"WHY DO you think they haven't given me another note or made themselves known?" Blaze asks me, lazily lying on my chest, her hand resting on my abs and legs entangled in mine. Sex is always off the charts with Blaze and each damn time it gets better. I'm not sure how that is even possible. I met her at X tonight and we barely got into the house before I had her on the living room wall. Then we made it to the bedroom.

"I'm not sure." After righting the clubhouse and setting it up with some chairs and shit from storage, there has been an eerie silence. Nothing from the cops, who found nothing. Nothing from the two assholes that want Blaze. Nothing from Buzz, who is still trying to crack that damn computer and I'm pretty sure it's a lost cause. Nothing for the four days. The tapes that Buzz got from the night that the note was left showed a person in dark pants and a hoodie covering their head. The person's back was to the camera so there was no clear shot.

One thing I've realized is, I like Blaze on the floor with Cali instead of up on the stage. She's still been getting on once a week and that one day I grit my fucking teeth. I hate that all those motherfuckers watch my girl. I want to tear every one of their eyeballs out and shove them down their throats. And even though it sucks ass to be there on those nights, I try my damnedest to in case of trouble. She was only supposed to dance for two weeks, but decided to continue a bit longer. While Blaze is at work, I do my business for the club and Pops has put me on jobs close to home so I can get there and get back before she gets off.

For once in my life, everything feels right.

I GROAN as the phone rings its annoying self on the bedside table. Blaze is curled up against me, her head resting on the crook between my arm and shoulder, as beautiful as ever. The clock reads 7:39 a.m. Shit. I reach for the phone, knocking off some of the junk I took out of my pockets the night before and it skitters to the ground.

The display says *Dagger*. Fuck. It's only been a week since the clubhouse was trashed and calls at this time usually mean my ass is getting up for the day. I swipe the phone and put it to my ear, my voice gruff. "Yeah."

"Get your ass up," Dagger orders, leaving absolutely no room to argue. "Get your ass to the clubhouse by eight thirty. Princess is coming to hang out with Blaze." He disconnects, giving no further instructions. What the fuck?

Reluctantly, I roll out of bed, being careful not to wake my girl. I jump in the shower and then dress. Sitting on the bed next to her, I brush my knuckles over her face and she stirs. How this wakes her up and not me moving off her, I'll never know.

"What's going on?" she asks after opening her heavy eyes.

"Gotta run to the clubhouse. Princess is coming to hang out with you." I continue stroking her face gently, loving the softness.

"Okay," she whispers. I place a kiss on her plump lips and she snuggles into the blankets. Before I leave the room, she's asleep.

I pull up to the clubhouse, and it's clear by all the bikes that all the brothers are here along with Buzz and Breaker. I make it in with about five minutes to spare.

"'Bout time your ass got here." Dagger comes up to me, coffee mug in his hand, and clasps me on the shoulder with the other. Everyone is in the room. Pops, Rhys, Cruz, GT, Becs, Zeb and the others. There are three chairs in the center of the room. Buzz and Breaker are each sitting in one, leaving one chair open. "Your spot's the empty one. Go," he orders as I walk through the guys and sit in the chair.

Buzz and Breaker's expressions are blank. Breaker may not have been in our unit, but we perfected blank during our time in the service. Never show weakness. No matter what.

"We are here because the three of you want to become one of us. You want to be part of our brother-hood," Pops' words shock me. Holy shit. Is this what I think it is? Excitement bubbles, but I keep my face stiff as stone and eyes on Pops as he talks.

"You may be thinking that there is some kind of sacred ritual that all members of Ravage have done, like say, drink blood from a goat." He chuckles gruffly. "But that is not the case. In Ravage, we vote. Now, it must be a one hundred percent unanimous vote for a prospect to become a member. If even one brother doesn't think you have what it takes to wear our patch, you will not wear it."

Pops widens his arms, showing us all the brothers standing with him forming a semi-circle. The brothers have their arms crossed over their chests and blank expressions on their faces. Dagger is the one guy that has truly had my back this entire time, but he is unreadable as well.

God, I'm nervous, but no way in hell do I let it show. My stony expression stays fully in place. What if Buzz got in and not Breaker? Shit. Why couldn't I have thought of this shit before? Now is not the time.

"Buzz come here," Pops orders and Buzz rises beside me and strides up to Pops.

"Welcome to the club." Pops' stoic face turns to a full out grin as whoops and hollers from the brothers fill the room. Becs holds out a Ravage rag and his hand. Buzz takes off the Prospect one and puts the other leather on his body. Buzz receives congratulations and joins the brothers behind Pops.

"Tug come here," Pops orders. I inhale deep and rise

from my chair. I keep my eyes locked on Pops, whose face is masked. He is all business now. With each step, nerves come in rippling waves, but I don't allow them through. I didn't realize really how important this is to me until now. I want it. I need it. I crave it.

Pops stares at me, years of this life showing on his face. Gazes from the others burn into me from all around the room. If I had the capacity to sweat in this situation, I would. It's a damn good thing that I'm not, especially in this life I am choosing to live.

Pops' face begins to loosen. "Welcome to the club." His lips curve up and I follow suit as relief and contentment fill me. The noise from the room is deafening and I soak every bit of it in. GT steps forward and hands me my rag, putting his hand out for the other. The significance of this is not lost to me by any means. Back when he and Casey got together, he had it in that thick skull of his that I had my eye on her. I didn't tell him different at the time. We fought in the cage and it was the best move ever. In that moment, I gained his respect. We were good. Him handing me my rag means true and honorable acceptance and none of that other bullshit.

I slowly take off my Prospect rag and place it in his hand. He holds open the Ravage one, and I turn, slipping my arms into the leather, a smirk playing on my lips. Breaker sits in the chair and I hope like hell that he gets his, too. I turn to GT, who pushes me into the group of Brothers. Loud shouts and pats on the back ensue.

I find myself next to Dagger, who bumps my shoulder. Pride surges. He taught me everything I know about Ravage. He is now officially my brother.

The voices quiet as soon as Pops speaks. "Breaker, come here." My stomach tightens, only because Breaker is the quieter of the two brothers. He keeps to himself much more, but does as he's told. If he doesn't patch, I don't know what Buzz would do. Their bond is strong. As is this bond we made with the Brothers.

Breaker rises from the chair, his face blank, and approaches Pops. What is really seconds feels like hours. Then he speaks. "Welcome to the club." I breathe out a sigh of relief. Breaker is one-arm hugging Pops. More whoops, and hollers follow, and this time Cruz hands Breaker his rag. He's thrown into the fray and we all congratulate him.

Pops turns to all of us, raises a hand and everyone silences. "Church, ten minutes." We nod and the roar of congratulations is gripping. There are so many hands patting me that I can't tell who is who, but go with it. Happy, try fucking elated.

We enter the room where church is held. I've never been in here as this place is only meant for members. A large rectangular oak table sits in the middle of the room with several chairs around it. Pops sits at the head of the table with Becs to his left and Dagger to his right. Cruz, GT, Rhys, and Zeb fill up the table. Buzz, Breaker and I grab chairs from the wall, and the brothers make room for us. I have to admit, this is fucking awesome.

The same wood paneling from out in the clubhouse lines the walls and a huge Ravage MC symbol, a skull with fire coming out of the top, is centered on the wall behind Pops. The other wall has a huge sign carved out of wood that says *Ravage Motorcycle Club*. Pictures line the other wall, from parties to mug shots. The wall with the doors is empty.

Once Pops slams the gavel, he first welcomes us then gets down to business. And shit if the business is not what I want to hear. Apparently, the two assholes that hurt Blaze are into some of the same shit we are. We are not directly connected, but are connected through one of our suppliers. Therefore, anything done would need to be precise and not fall back on Ravage. If the assholes leave Blaze alone, we leave them alone. If not, we step in. Pops put the word out the first day he learned of the connection. Their response was they were going to leave her alone. I don't buy it.

There is even talk about Princess and how she needs to do better background checks on those she hires at X, as to not bring this shit to the club. I grit my teeth through that part because I fucking want my Blaze here. But do understand where this is going and it is voted that Pops talks to her. Lucky him.

After church is adjourned, I'm elated to be a part of it. Pops asks Buzz, Breaker and I to stay. After the room is clear, he gets up and ambles down to us, resting his hip on the table. His eyes scan us, and he must like what he sees as he starts to talk.

"Anything you hear in this room goes no further than you. All these men in this room trust you to do this. You have problems with something that happens in this room, you *do not*," his voice gets louder, "discuss this with anyone outside of the people in this room. You don't go home and bitch to your woman, your mom, or your preacher. You got a problem, you come to us. You have questions, you come to us." His eyes pin each of us as he says these last words. "You come to us."

We nod.

"All right, let's get some lunch and then it's time to party."

DRUNK. Yeah. Pretty fucking drunk, but not wasted and my wits are pretty much there. Well kind of. Shot after shot were sent my way, along with beers, and I took them all. It takes a lot to get me out of control and thank God for that shit or I'd be making a fool of myself by now, kind of like Breaker, lying on the couch almost passed out.

Ol' ladies, club mommas, hang-arounds are all here to celebrate. I tried calling Blaze, but she didn't answer. So, I called Princess and she said they were doing some girly shit. I told her to bring Blaze to the clubhouse, but she hasn't come yet.

The club is pretty full and I'm sure outside the court-yard is littered with people too. I've had more club mommas than I can count coming up to me trying to get a piece, but I've turned them all away. I only want one piece and if I keep this shit up, I won't get to her tonight. Fuck.

Women litter the side of the room which was cleared out for a dance floor, giving us all quite a show. None make my dick hard. I may be a guy, but when you have a taste of something as hot as Blaze, that's all you need.

I jolt when a touch comes to my shoulder. Princess.

"Hey, Tug. I've got a present for you." My brows shoot up. Not only is she Cruz's woman, she's also the club princess and I don't want shit to do with that.

"Wait. Where's Blaze?" She doesn't answer.

"Come on." She's holding out her hand, but I don't take it. I do rise and follow her to the corner of the club. I notice a huge pole has been installed from floor to ceiling.

A lone chair sits in front of it and Princess exaggerates a sweeping motion with her arms for me to sit. I do and turn to the room, everyone is gathering behind me, even some of the shitfaced women stop dancing and come my way.

"Now, since you are a brother, I thought we'd initiate you," Princess teases. "My way. So, this is for you." The lights go out in the clubhouse, but only for a second. Some lights come on and a strobe light from somewhere starts sending red, blue, green, and yellows through the space.

Standing in front of the pole as the music begins, eyes glued to me, is Blaze. My mouth drops as I scan her body. Sexy, black-leather, bikini top that laces behind her neck, short little matching leather shorts that I'm sure if she turns will show me some cheek, and she is covered from neck to waist in blood-red fishnet. Her hair is wild and her face is fucking perfect.

A soft smile plays on her lips as she reaches up and grabs the pole. She dips her body down low, her ass almost touching the floor but her heels stop her. She shakes and swirls her ass as she goes up the pole. My dick hardens to the point of physical pain against the confines of my zipper.

Her strong arms grip the pole and she drapes one of her legs around it at the knee and falls so she is upside down. She puts her arms out straight to the floor and the fishnet falls from her body, and she gives me a small wink. Holy shit.

She then does some sort of maneuver that brings her feet flipping to the floor. She sways her hips to the music as she comes closer. She leans down and places a kiss on my lips, way too fucking short for my liking, but then steps away and bends at the hips, giving me a beautiful view of her ass. This stops me from rising.

Her fingers slip into her small shorts as she wiggles them down, ever so very slowly, giving me an even better view of her perfect ass. Whistles and catcalls come as the shorts hit her thighs. I snap. No one sees her but me, dammit.

I rise from the chair, clutch her waist, turn her around, and yank her shorts up. With my hands on her ass, I lift, her feet wrap around my back. I fucking kiss her and walk. I don't know where the fuck I'm going, but it could be the bathroom for all I fucking care. Princess yells, "Move out of the way!" and somehow I follow her, my eyes open while I'm kissing my girl.

"In here," Princess says. "I'm told this is yours so I cleaned it. Enjoy." She opens the door and before the last syllables of enjoy are said, I slam the door with my foot and Blaze is pressed up against it. My eyes close as we kiss, full on demanding, battling for control kiss. I set her down briefly and snatch the shorts off her body then devour her mouth.

Her nails dig into my shoulders as they make their way up to my hair and thread through, scraping my scalp. I fucking love it. I unbutton my jeans in a rush and push them down, along with my underwear. Reaching between us, I realize I forgot her thong, fuck it. I wrench it out of the way and glide into her. Fuck me. Her wet heat is like satiny silk as it squeezes my dick, pulling me further in.

Her tongue slides deep in my mouth. I thrust up frantically, the little control I have when she's around snaps like a rubber band. With both hands on her ass, I use the door to help me hold her up. I thrust faster and squeeze my ass to get more power.

She breaks the kiss to moan, mewl, and scream as I pound into her, the door shaking behind us. Her pussy grips my dick like a massage. She screams her release and after three more thrusts, I come, grunting into her neck.

"Shit, babe," I groan, nuzzling her neck. My wobbly legs and jeans around my ankles don't bode well for me carrying her to the bed. "Gotta put you down. You okay?" She nods, her face having that I've been fucked real good glow. Damn, that's sexy.

I turn to the side and place her down on the floor, her legs a bit wobbly. Once I steady her, I tear off my boots and jeans. "Bed," I demand.

I strip off my shirt and turn around. Blaze lies on the bed, hair splayed out on the tan blanket, her thong still to the side of her pussy. Her tits almost fall out of the bikini top. One of Blaze's legs is bent at the knee while she lies flat on her back, arm out. She is a fucking wet dream. *My fucking wet dream.*

I crawl up the bed and strip Blaze's thong off her body. Then unlace her killer fuck-me heels. I kiss up her body and roll her to the side, she doesn't complain and helps me roll her. I untie the leather from her body, throwing it to the floor.

I lie next to her and hold her to my body. "I'm not done with you yet." I crash my lips down on hers. Best fucking day ever.

CHAPTER THIRTEEN
Blaze

I wake up in a groggy haze. Light peers through a window and my eyes finally get the strength to open. My arm is wrapped around my sexy man's middle, my head on his chest, and our legs tangled together. We seem to like this position. He is a Greek God and I can't believe I didn't want to give him a chance. I can't imagine my life without him.

I tear my gaze away and take in the room: wood-paneled walls, bare except for a few empty shelves, a dresser on one wall, and another on a different wall. A door is open wide to what appears to be a bathroom, which is good because I need to make it there soon.

Last night was amazing. Tug was out of control and I have to say I loved every minute of it. He can do it sweet and he can do it hot. I'm happy either way. Riding him was the highlight of my night. It definitely tested the strength in my legs.

When Princess came over yesterday and told me about the plan, which she only knew about because Cruz asked her to get some girls together for the party, I didn't say yes at first. It's hard enough getting up on stage at X, and doing it in the clubhouse for Tug unsettled me. I know he hates it that I still strip, but those nights I rake in some serious cash and I'm not ready to give that up yet. Especially with Santos and Frank still out there somewhere.

Princess didn't tell me that he was becoming a member. Supposedly, Cruz told her to do something special for Tug with a wink. Princess, being a smart woman, assumed it was for this reason and she was right.

Princess being Princess of course had me come around. When I hid before the lights went dead, I almost had a panic attack but I breathed through it. I went on stage and did my thing, but doing it at the clubhouse felt more personal, intimate. But the fact that it was for Tug got me through. I kept my eyes focused on him the entire time, not letting the noises in the background distract me.

The lust in his face when he saw me tied me up in knots in a way I didn't expect. I get gawked at all the time, and when I do, I notice it's nothing compared to the way Tug looks at me. He looks at me like I am the most precious, sexiest thing he's ever seen, and I love that.

I'm not sure how he did it last night, but we continued the sex-a-thon throughout the night, exploring and taking our time. The sounds of the party outside blasted through the door, but we paid no attention to any of it.

My bladder calls.

I slip from Tug, who doesn't move a muscle, and out of bed. I do my business in the bathroom. There's a shower but no shampoo so I'll wait till I get home. I definitely need one. The remnants of Tug's cum is on my chest. I wiped it off as best I could last night, but some is still there.

Since I knew the plan, I packed a small bag with clothes for me, and toothbrushes for both of us along with toothpaste. I open the bag and brush my teeth thoroughly. Wash my face with water and a small bit of hand soap and wipe it off on a small towel on the hanger.

Strong arms wrap around my waist and I crash into a naked warm body. I smell him. Tug rests his chin on my shoulder. "Why'd you get up?" His voice is groggy and sexy, sending chills up my spine, my body wanting more.

"Had to pee and brush my teeth." I turn around in his arms, gripping the strong muscled tattooed wonders and holding on with a death grip.

"What do you have planned for today?" He bends down, giving me a chaste kiss on the lips.

"I need to go to X. Princess and I need to do the lineup for next week, and I have books to catch up on." I pull myself as close to him as possible.

"I've got some shit to do today. You stay with Princess and when you're done, call me. If I can't come and get you one of the guys will." My heart fills. I love how protective he is of me and I know it's not because Pops told him to watch out for me. It's because he really wants to. I know he cares about me, love no. It's too soon for love. Right?

"Sounds good."

"But first." He dips down in a kiss that steals my breath. All too quickly, he ends the kiss, leaving me panting. "We have something to do." He lays me down and shows me his something. I love every second of it.

I SIT in my dressing room, going through numbers. It's been four nights since Tug and I had our sex-a-thon at the clubhouse. The memories of that night will never leave me. It's definitely one for the record books.

A knock sounds on my door. This happens regularly now and I like that the girls feel they can come to me. I set down the numbers I'm crunching on getting a new pole installed.

"Come in." I stopped locking my door a while ago because the girls come in too often and I didn't want to keep getting up and down.

I turn to a huge bouquet of perfect white roses carried in a vase by Brittney, one of the dancers. My stomach plummets and my thoughts drift for a split second.

MY BODY WANTS to wake up, but my mind does not. If I stay asleep, I don't have to face the day. I don't have to lie to my mother and tell her that I fell again or some other excuse. Mom thinks I'm an utter klutz, but she's been so sick that she wouldn't pick up on the lie anyway.

I roll over in my bed, my entire body aches from the rough touch of Santos and Frank last night. Despair fills every crevice of my body.

My hand encounters something sharp and I pull it back. A small drop of blood falls from my finger and I place it in my mouth, sucking the blood away. Next to me lays a white rose. I pick it up and smell it. Even though it pricked me, I've never gotten a flower this gorgeous before. Something good.

After getting ready for the day and making my breakfast, I sit at the kitchen island thanking God that no one is around. I eat in silence, loving it. I bring the rose to my nose and breathe in its beautiful floral scent.

A hand grips my shoulder and I jump, turning around. Santos. Oh God. My smile fades and his grows wider. He bends down to my ear and I shiver in disgust. "I see you like your present, little one." I stiffen.

I wish I could say that was the last rose they left on my pillow.

"THESE ARE FOR YOU," Brittney says, bubbly, setting them on the table next to me and probably thinking these are the best gift a woman could receive. My stomach rolls at the sight of them. Shit. Shit. Shit. Every drop of blood leaves my face and my stomach takes that opportunity to twist in knots. "Are you okay?" Brittney asks and somehow I put my focus on her.

"Fine. Go ahead." I can tell that she knows something's wrong, but she does leave, turning back several times to watch me. As soon as the door clicks, my attention is back to the roses just waiting for them to do something. What? I have no idea, maybe shoot and kill me. I know it's not rational but I'm not rational right now.

A cream-colored envelope catches my eye and as much as I don't want to, I can't stop my feet from gliding toward the flowers.

When I open the card, my breath seizes.

THERE IS a bomb inside X. If you don't want it to blow and kill everyone, then bring your sexy little ass outside by 9:45, alone or else.

Boom! ~S

THE CLOCK SAYS 9:17. Oh. My. God. Oh. My God. Sickness snakes up my throat. A bomb. A fucking bomb. What do I do? There is no way in hell that I am going with him. I won't. But all these people are here. They have families at home. Shit, Princess is upstairs in her office. I snap into action.

I text Princess.

MY OFFICE NOW—EMERGENCY

THEN I CALL TUG. He answers on the second ring. "Hey, sweet lips." He sounds so happy.

"Tug. I got flowers from Santos." I relay the message

on the card as best I can. "What do I do?" I scream into the phone, not knowing which way to go. He covers up the phone. It's muffled but I vaguely hear him retelling someone in the background.

Princess bursts through the door and I give her the card. She reads it fast and her eyes turn dead cold in an instant.

"I'm talking to Tug," I say and she nods, picking up her phone I'm guessing to call Cruz.

I grow impatient. "Tug!" I say tersely into the phone.

His hand moves away from the mouthpiece. "Hang on, baby." Princess is relaying the message on her end to someone and time is ticking fast. A few seconds is like an eternity.

"This is what I want you to do," he says calmly. "I want you to get all the people in X by doors and you have to do it fast. All together, you are going to rush out of that place and run as far as you can. You hear me?" I did but am so stunned I can't talk. "Blaze!" he yells, snapping me out of it.

"I got it."

"Good. We're on our way but there is no way we'll make it to you in time. We're not at the clubhouse. We will be there as soon as possible." Anger radiates from his voice, but also concern.

"Okay." I can't hide the terror.

"I'm calling the cops. You, Princess, and the bouncers get everyone out of there now."

"Okay."

"You can do this," he says and disconnects. My adrenaline kicks in and I welcome it. I need all the help I can get.

Princess stands cool and calm, which helps me do the same. "You know the plan?"

"Yeah. I'll take the side door, you take the back with Cali. I'll get Doug to take the other side door and Ace will take the front. I'll pull the fire alarm by the side door. That's your cue to go. You tell Doug and Cali got it?"

"Yes. Let's do this." The confidence in Princess's orders flows over me.

The next few minutes are pandemonium. We try not to scare anyone, but when the overhead lights go on and you are asked over the loud speaker to find a door and stand by it, it kind of freaks people out. So, there is screaming and tears and I'm trying to keep it all together. Since this is all my fault, the weight of it is heavy.

Standing at the back door with all the dancers, I try to keep them calm. Ten minutes isn't that long but it feels like forever, waiting for the alarm to go off. "Every-one," I yell, getting their attention, "as soon as it blares, you get out this door and you run all the way down to Larry's Parlor if you can." Larry's is a local hangout that serves food round the clock and is about a block from X.

"Dry your tears and get ready. You hear me?" The women nod.

That's when the fire alarm rings loud. The door is thrown open and all the girls run in the direction I told them. I turn to the room before I leave and make sure everyone's out and they are. With Cali on my heels—which thank goodness I wore flats tonight—we dart through the dark night. Princess's group is running the same direction as us and I run directly to her.

"All out?" I ask, chest heaving when we get to Larry's. Some of the patrons and women are on their cells. Not sure if they are calling the cops or their significant others for rides to get the hell out of here. I can't blame them.

"Yep. I'm calling Doug and Ace." She dials her phone and finds that everyone is out. We turn and watch X. Waiting. Five minutes pass. Ten minutes pass. Police cars and a big truck with bomb squad written on the side of it enter the lot and Princess waves at them. They come to her in a rush and she tells them about the note and getting everyone out. The bomb guys suit up in some heavy shit just as the sound of bikes come roaring down the road.

Tug, Buzz, Breaker, GT, Cruz, Rhys and Dagger ride up, parking their bikes. Tug comes directly to me, engulfing me in his arms and lifting me up. I reciprocate and squeeze him, never so happy to see anyone in my life. He sets me down on the ground and searches my face.

"Are you okay?" he asks and I nod. I'm not really okay, not by a long shot. These assholes want to drown me out. I turn as Buzz, Breaker, GT, Rhys and Dagger take off all around the place, no doubt seeking Santos and Frank, which I'm sure are long, long gone by now.

He holds me and I breathe him in smelling leather from his rag, which he told me was not a vest but a rag. I call it that now, not making that mistake again.

The sound of a car moving behind X has us swinging our gazes in that direction. Luna is backing out of the lot, fear etched in her face. *Boom. Boom.* Luna's car blows up right before my eyes. Girls scream and my knees weaken. *Boom. Boom.* One after another, down the lined rows where they are parked. *Boom. Boom.* Each one going up in a big ball of fire, with debris flying everywhere and the smoke almost reaching us. *Boom. Boom.* Eight, and then nothing. No more.

Cries from the girls whose cars blew echo in the night. Weird, my car seems to be the only one that didn't get blown in that row.

Boom!

Before my very eyes, from something much stronger than what was used for the other cars, my Jeep explodes. No it doesn't explode it detonates to a point that when the smoke clears the only thing left is the frame and wheels. Holy shit. Did that just happen?

Tug's grip tightens on me, but I can't take my eyes away from the explosion. The cops do their thing, but I don't pay much attention to it. Instead, I stare at my Jeep and the other cars, now, big piles of metal.

"Luna." I can't hide the gigantic lump in my throat. Tug squeezes. A hand touches my arm and I turn to Princess. "Are you okay?" she asks. I nod at her absently, but physically, I am still alive so it's the best answer I can give. "Luna." I shake my head unable to form words and try to get my shit together.

Tug's phone rings and he answers it. "Yeah."

"No shit?"

"Where?"

"Gotta get the girls safe."

"Got it."

He turns to Cruz, doing some sort of mental talking

thing that only gets a chin lift exchange. I wish I knew what the hell is going on here. Shit!

"We are going to have to stay to talk to the cops. Be short and sweet with your answers. If they ask who the flowers were from, tell them you don't know. The card only had a letter S on it," Tug commands.

He has lost his ever-loving mind. "Seriously," I say, low so no one can hear. "You want me to say that? A woman was killed!" My voice raises, but looking around at the faces turned my way, I tone it down.

"We are handling this in house, our way," Tug says and it sends chills down my spine.

"What does that mean?" I ask stupidly.

"Club business, babe. But I'll take care of you," He vows.

He wants me to lie? Well, it's not really a lie. If I tell them the only letter was an S that is not lying. Now, if they ask me if I know someone by that letter that won't be true, but I think I can swing it. I've been lying for a long time, one more won't hurt. But Luna. Dammit. While I think it'll be better to let the cops handle it, I trust Tug and go along with him.

"All right." Let's get this over with.

After hours of questions and watching the cars burn until the fire department comes and investigators show up, I'm beat. The good news is X had no bombs inside the building. Bad news is Luna and the cars. Luckily, the girls all have insurance as do I so that will help in replacing them. But Luna is gone. Tug brought me to the club-house, saying he had to meet with the guys and it's safe for me here.

I lie down in bed, replaying what happened tonight and realizing that we did a damn good job getting all the people out of there and safe. I turn off the lights and pass out.

Screaming... Fire... Burning... Luna...

"Blaze," is screamed at me and I try to open my eyes but can't. "Blaze." There it is again. I will my eyes to open. Tug is in front of me with concern in his eyes.

"What's wrong?" I ask, groggy from sleep.

"You were screaming. Are you okay?" He scans me up and down. I must meet his approval as his eyes return to mine.

"I was?" I thought it was a dream.

"Yes. Loud, all the guys jumped." He turns and all the brothers are standing in the room staring at me and I'm thanking my lucky stars that I put on a damn shirt before lying down. No underwear though. Shit. I scramble for the sheet.

"Sorry. I'm fine." I rub the grogginess away as the guys file out of the room. Tug eyes me, not knowing whether to believe me or not. I don't blame him because truly I'm anything but fine.

"I've gotta go out for a while. Becs and Zeb are staying here with you and Princess while you sleep. You're safe here."

"Where are you going?" I really do not want him to leave. I want him here with me. It's selfish but right now, I don't give a shit.

"I have business and it's important. If it wasn't, I wouldn't go, you know that." He cups my cheek and I lean into his touch, closing my eyes. "I'll be back soon. Get some sleep."

Tug leans in and kisses me soft and sweet, then kisses my forehead. Before I can blink, he's gone. I lie down and toss and turn this way and that. I can't get comfortable or the night's events are prolonging my sleep. A soft knock comes from the door and I sit up.

"Yeah?"

The door opens and my pulse picks up. Princess steps through and I relax. "Hey, girl. I can't sleep and Ma has Cooper so I thought I'd come bug you." Thank God. I do not want to be alone.

"Come on in." Relief washes over me for the company. She falls on the bed in the spot where Tug usually sleeps and turns to her side so she's facing me.

"You doing all right?" Princess's eyes are concerned and soft, nothing like the take-charge hardness she normally exudes.

"Not really," I answer honestly. "Everything that happened was my fault. That's a lot of weight to carry around, losing Luna."

"You are not the one doing this. Those assholes are. Don't carry that shit. You do not put what happened to Luna on your shoulders."

I stare at her like she's grown horns because she obviously has. "How can you say that? I brought them here. They wouldn't be here if not for me." My words are soft and a small yawn escapes my lips.

"I think you were meant to come here," she says, also quieter now, her eyes beginning to droop.

"I'm not sure of anything at the moment." I yawn.

"Can I ask you something?" Even tired, the question gives me a jolt.

"Sure."

"Why did you come to Sumner in the first place? I know I never asked, but that was because you looked like a scared cat when you showed up." My eyes widen. I did not. "Don't look like that. You did. That's why I didn't balk."

"I... When I left home, I went to my aunt's. She gave me a card with X on the front and your address on the back. She told me to go there and they would help me. So I did."

Princess pops up on an elbow. "Really? What is her name?"

"Sylvia Downing."

Princess sucks in a deep breath and plops back down on the pillow. Her eyes focus on the ceiling. "Holy shit." I never thought of the connection or reason for my aunt sending me here. I was too messed up in the head to even think about it. Now, I want to know.

"What? How do you know her?"

Her head turns to me. "Sylvia is Ma's best friend, well Sylvie to me."

I pop up from the bed and sit cross-legged. "What?" I can't believe this. There is no way.

"Yeah. Sylvie lived here and met Ma. They became close then she moved out to North Carolina. My Ma was crushed, but they still keep in contact."

Oh my God. Seriously? "I know nothing about her. My mom didn't talk to her, but when everything went down, she was the only place I thought to go. I had her address from my mom's address book. Why did she leave?"

"I don't know all the details, but Sylvie and her guy Rocko wanted to leave, they packed up and were gone. Ma wasn't happy, but she didn't say anything." She shrugs.

"Do you think that's the reason my mom and her didn't talk? Because she got hooked up with the club?" I sure as hell hope not.

"Ma told me once that Sylvie had family but didn't talk to them because of a falling out. But that's all she said." Princess's eyes droop. "You'll have to ask her. She'll shit that you're Sylvie's niece."

"So, she gave me X's card because she knew you'd help me, no questions asked?" Princess is way too smart to just 'help' anyone.

"There were questions that I wanted to ask, but didn't. You were scared, had it written all over your face. I figured in time you'd tell me what was going on. I mean shit, Blaze, I knew you were running. I just didn't know why."

"This is just hard for me to wrap my head around," I confess, lying back down.

"Everything happens for a reason. We love you, Blaze. Everyone. We'll do everything we can to make sure they can't get you."

"How did you find out everything?" I ask curious.

"Cruz. He told me what he could." She pauses and gives me the *eye*. "Don't you know that you can talk to me about anything?"

I let out a huge sigh. "I wanted to forget, but when it

comes to bite you in the ass, you have no choice but to talk."

"Come to me and talk from now on," she says and I try my best to smile, but it comes out half-assed.

"What are we going to do about Luna?" Not only was she killed, she was killed on X property. This can't be good.

"Don't know yet. Let's worry about that tomorrow. I know she has family that will do her justice and all the other shit we'll just deal with." I admire Princess so much. Her head is screwed on so well that nothing gets to her, or at least she covers it well.

I decide to change the subject. "What happened with Stage?"

"Beat the shit out of her."

"You did what?" Surely, I heard her wrong. Right? She didn't beat up another ol' lady of the club.

"She got lippy with me. I punched her. She came after me and I took her down. Simple," Princess says as if it's no big deal.

"Damn, woman."

She waves her arm. "No big deal. Shit happens." Princess yawns. "I gotta crash," she says, and instantly falls asleep.

Soon after, my mind twists and turns with everything that I've learned and seen these past few hours, and I finally fall asleep, too.

CHAPTER FOURTEEN
THE CLUBHOUSE

Becs and Zeb sit at the bar nursing their beer. Two club mommas lie on the couches on the far side of the room, fast asleep. Zeb and Becs discuss the dealings of the night and try to come up with a plan to get rid of Santos and Frank once and for all, but they have yet to come up with something that would really work.

A small metal cylinder rolls on the floor, landing in the middle of the room, and their eyes turn to it.

"What the fuck?" Becs growls.

"Fucking grenade! Get the fuck down!" Zeb yells and everything goes blurry as they crash to the ground, paralyzed.

A few moments later, Santos, Frank and their goons strut into the clubhouse like they own the place. Santos believes that his expensive pressed suit, light green shirt and tie cost more than the whole damn building he's in. Santos is not impressed with the space one bit.

"Pitiful," Santos declares.

Santos nods to Zeb and Becs, who are down on the floor unable to move. They hear the intruders but everything is muffled and seems far away to them. Santos has always loved concussion grenades. They do the trick, immobilizing threats for a short period of time. Enough to keep them restrained. One goon moves from behind Santos, holds up a taser, aims and fires, hitting Zeb in the stomach. The shock causes him to shake and go still.

Santos knows it's really not necessary for the stun but better safe than sorry. And it's fun as shit seeing them flop on the ground like dead fish.

Goon number two takes out his taser, shooting it off and hitting Becs in the shoulder. Becs passes out. The goons use duct tape to restrain their arms and legs and place a piece over their mouths.

"Take care of those two," Santos says, motioning to the two women lying on the couch. They sit with wide eyes as if stunned into shock. Dumbass women.

Another goon holds out a stun gun, pressing it into one of the women's sides. "Nighty night," he says creepily. Then he turns to the other woman, pressing the gun into her back as she tries to turn. Lights out for her also. The goon tapes the women up.

"All right, quietly, start checking everything, open every door. Soon as you see Paige I want to know." Five of Santos's goons, including his son Frank, move through the clubhouse, guns in hand. Santos saunters behind the bar, nonchalantly pouring himself a shot of whiskey.

He tosses it as goon five comes up. "Got her." Santos moves from the bar and follows the goon down the hallway. The goon grabs the handle and turns it very gently. The door swings open and a woman rolls to her side, opening her eyes.

"Mother fucker!" Princess yells, gripping her gun that she never goes anywhere without. All the while, she kicks Blaze hard enough to wake her. Princess lets off a shot just as something hits her directly in the chest. Her body convulses then goes limp, her gun falling to the floor with a thud. One of the goons tapes her up.

"No!" Blaze screams, moving from the bed backward toward the open door of the bathroom.

Santos doesn't waste any time as he approaches her, grabbing her around her waist. Her smell permeates the air, making him rock hard. Santos hasn't had a fighter like her in years and can't wait to get back inside of her. And he will.

"Let go. I'm not going with you!" Blaze screams, trying to wiggle out of his grasp, bile rising from her stomach to her throat. She swallows repeatedly, trying to get it down and succeeds but keeps fighting. She'd rather die than be anywhere near this man.

Frank steps in the room and comes close to Blaze, her heart falling to the floor. "Look who we have here. Damn, I can't wait to get reacquainted with you, *sis*." His fingers touch Blaze's face as she continues to fight Santos's grasp. "But for now. Lights out." He places a stun gun to Blaze's arm as Santos lets go of her. She falls hard to the ground, the smell of burnt flesh filling the room from the contact.

"Let's get the fuck out of here," Santos orders. "Get

over here." He points to one of the goons. "Carry her and get her in the car. Now," Santos demands, plucking a pair of jeans off the floor.

The goon picks up Blaze's limp body and carries her past Princess, Becs, Zeb and the two women still lying on the couch. He places Blaze in the car and Santos sits next to her. Frank sits in the passenger seat and goon three drives. The other goons get into the car behind them.

In the garage, Derek, one of the hang-arounds, wipes his hands on a cloth getting the grease off from the truck he's fixing the carburetor on. He doesn't sleep much these days and working on trucks is his way of coping. Losing his baby sister in a horrible way when he could have prevented it, eats at him every moment of the day. He should have helped her, but he was too late. Derek has been around Ravage for a couple of months and is very interested in joining the club.

He hears a loud noise in the night sky and peers out the small window of the garage door. It was the clubhouse door slamming shut. Men he's never seen before are getting into two black shiny cars. One man is carrying Blaze, the hot woman from X, Tug's girl. Her head hangs down, bobbing around painfully. Shit.

Derek grabs the keys to the Explorer sitting in the lot and quietly sneaks out to the car. He watches the cars leave, turns the ignition, and drives out of Ravage on the car's tail. He lifts his cell out of his pocket and calls Pops.

CHAPTER FIFTEEN
Tug

BY THE TIME I GOT OUT TO THE CABIN WHERE THE GUYS took the asshole that blew up the cars, he is tied to a chair, bloody, and one of his shoulders is contorted in some strange way. GT is wearing brass knuckles, punching the guy in the chest and stomach, more than likely breaking a few ribs.

I move over to Pops. "Find out anything?"

"Only that he was paid to set the bombs. Other than that, nothing yet. We're gonna let Rhys have a turn for a bit." He turns to me. "You want some shots?"

"Fuck yeah," I say, not turning to him but keeping my eyes on the grunting man in front of me. GT hasn't even broken a sweat.

"You want these?" GT turns, holding out the brass knuckles, a grim line on his face.

I step forward. "Yeah." I nod, moving in front of the guy.

"Before I break your jaw, want to tell me where the hell Santos and Frank are?" The man has dark hair, is dressed in jeans and a white t-shirt that is covered in blood. He's about my age and dumber than a box of rocks.

"I told you everything I know. Some guy came to me, told me what I needed to do and I did it," he sputters out and most of the words sound breathy and painful to say. "Gave me cash. That's all I know."

Pops nods, indicating that's the same story he's been giving. Fuck. He's a go between. Shit! I unleash my anger on the guy, throwing fist after fist at him. With each punch, a small amount of relief comes over me, but not nearly enough.

By the time I stop, his head is hanging down to his chest, his chin touching it. Blood comes out in several spots and his breathing has turned into wheezing. Good.

I step back when a hand comes to my shoulder. Pops. "Let Rhys have a bit with him."

The man somehow raises his head but his eyes are closed. Moans of pain escape his lips as Rhys steps forward. He unties one of the guy's hands and brings his arm out to the side. He jerks it violently, the guy screaming in what has to be excruciating pain. A crack of bone echoes the air, and if I were any other man I'd probably flinch at the sound, but I don't.

I stand to the side, my arms crossed in front of my chest.

Pops' phone rings. "Yeah." He takes a step back, listening.

"Stop!" he orders the room, and Rhys instantly does. Everyone's eyes swing to Pops as he listens on the phone.

"You stay on them. You hear me. Do not lose them." Pops' face contorts to anger and the vein on the side of his face begins to tick.

My eyes widen as Pops' eyes come to mine. "They got Blaze."

"What. The. Fuck!" I yell, ripping my fingers through my hair. How in the hell did this happen?

I grasp the gun out of the back of my jeans, put it to the guy strapped to the chair's head and pull the trigger. His body falls limp.

"Where? We have to go," I say to Pops who is listening on the other end of the phone.

"Load up. They are on Hausller moving north." His attention goes back to the phone as we get on our bikes. "Text me directions if they change course or if they stop. But whatever you do, do not lose them." Pops growls, hanging up the phone. "Cruz, go to the clubhouse and find out what the fuck is going on there. The rest of us, let's go."

We load up.

CHAPTER SIXTEEN
Blaze

My back and neck ache. My arms feel like they've been touched by a live wire, they burn so bad. I can't move, even though I'm trying with all my might. My thoughts drift and one thing stands out... Santos. Oh my God. Shit. I have to get out of here. I have to. No one will be able to find me if they get me too far from Ravage. Shit!

I try repeatedly to open my eyes, and this time I'm able to just a crack. Santos sits next to me and Frank is in the front seat. My body won't move when I know I'm telling it to. Dammit.

Santos sneers over at me. I close my eyes quickly, but I'm too late to fake. "Paige. My darling, Paige." Pins and needles poke my skin as his arm wrenches me over to him, but I don't cry or scream. It does no good and they get off on that more.

"Thought you could hide from us? Even going to some white trash, biker gang to protect you?" His grip on my arm tightens to the point of utter pain, definitely leaving bruises. "Dumb bitch. You should have known we'd find you," he growls, his eyes crease together in a face that I have always feared, but so much is radiating through me.

"I'll admit you did do a pretty good job, considering it took me four and a half fucking years to hunt you down. But I've got guys everywhere, ones that even watched through the fucking window while you fucked that piece of shit biker." I try not to flinch at the mention of Tug. I'd give anything to be in his arms. "Saw video of you dancing and believe me, you'll be doing a lot of that shit where we're going."

He releases me and pushes me toward the window of the door. Thank God, he's not touching me.

"Been following you for about six months now." He continues to speak, his son turns around in the front and I want to puke at the way he ogles me. I'm only in a t-shirt, giving him a good view. The bile rises and I hold it down. I need to think. I peer out the window, taking my eyes from the guys, trying to place where we are. I think we are in Crawville, about fifteen miles outside of Sumner, so not too far away... yet.

I don't let his words affect me, but he doesn't stop as he knows I'm listening to every single one. Unfortunately, he knew me quite well from when I lived with him. He's smart and doesn't forget.

"I knew setting a trap at your work would get all your biker boys in a tizzy." He chuckles in a creepy way as fear rips through me. "That's why I hired some man off the street. He knows nothing of us. All he was paid to do was attach the boxes with the bombs and hit the switch. I knew those men of yours would be around and find him."

I can feel his eyes on me and scoot as close to the door as I can get, not wanting to breathe the same air as him. "That's what happened, huh? Your man left you to deal with the asshole. It was prime time for me to come in. I was going to send someone, but I didn't want it fucked up. Sometimes that happens and this needed to be smooth."

He turns to his son. "How much longer?" His voice is dripping with authority and like the ever-doting son, Frank answers.

"Ten. Fifteen minutes. Plane is fueled and waiting for us." Plane. Oh shit. No. No... I can't let them get me on the plane. If they do, I'll never be found. I can't endure this. I just can't. Shit. I try to think, but he keeps talking and I want to throat punch him to shut up, but I never would, the punishment would be too severe.

"See, we are going to take you to Italy. You will love it there if I decide to let you out of our home, which is highly unlikely. You'll be lucky if you make it out of the bedroom." His smirk is wickedly ugly. He's dead serious. Shit.

The door handle is very close. If they slowed the car a little bit, I can open it and fling myself out of the car, preferably somewhere where there are lots of people. I pray it's not a childproof lock that won't let me out.

Santos throws something at me, hitting me in the side. My jeans. Thank God. "Put them on," he orders and I do as I'm told. "Can't have you traipsing around the airport naked. But don't worry, once we get to our home, you will never be in clothes."

My body is sore, but I manage to get the jeans on. My faculties are coming back to me, and I'm not the same little girl he remembers. I will fight with everything inside of me. I just hope that he doesn't shock me with that thing again.

The car speeds along and Santos decides to remain quiet, a new thing for him. He was always a talker, never shutting up, used to drive me crazy when I lived with him. His silence is more unnerving than the words that come out of his mouth, shit.

The bright lights of the airport come into sight. It is do or die time. Literally.

The car slows down at what I would assume is a security checkpoint. A building is set off in the distance and I instantly know my plan. I'll open the door, run with everything I have, and get to safety. I can do this. I *must* do this.

"Don't say a fucking word. You hear me," Santos growls and I know he'll be watching me like a hawk. I'm only going to get one chance to get away.

The car stops and the goon rolls down his window as the officer at the gate surveys the car. Then his gaze goes to Santos behind the goon, that's my chance. I throw open the door. Something grips the back of my shirt, but using all my power, I somehow get free. I run. Run like I've never run before. My bare feet burn, running on the harsh pavement, but I don't care. I keep going.

Shouts and screams come from behind me, as the sound of bikes and gunshots fill my ears. I don't stop but burning in my shoulder slices through me. I reach and feel wetness on my shoulder. I swipe the spot and come back with bright, red blood. *I've been shot.* They shot me, shit. I run zigzagged as I go. I saw once on the internet that a moving target is much harder to hit. I have to get away.

CHAPTER SEVENTEEN
Tug

WE ROAR THROUGH THE NIGHT WITH POPS IN THE LEAD AS he keeps checking for texts from Derek. He leads us directly to the airport and my stomach lurches. Fuck, if they get her on that damn plane, I'll probably never find her. Shit!

I ride as fast as I can. Two black cars are stopped at the checkpoint for the airport. A woman, Blaze I can tell immediately from the long brunette hair that I love so much, jumps out of the car and starts running fast. Grabbing my gun, I shoot as the men all file out of the car after her. My brothers begin to fire. An asshole is chasing Blaze and I take off toward him. More fire but I don't look. I have to get to her.

Another shot and Blaze clutches her right shoulder. Shit, he fucking shot her. I race after the guy, weaving through my brothers and the assholes. Blaze's step falters as the guy who shot her catches her, using her as a human shield. My eyes focus on the silver gun pointing at my woman's temple. My stomach drops, but I keep my stone face in place.

Blaze's eyes meet mine, pleading for help. I park the bike, gun pointed at the two of them. More gunfire explodes behind me, but I don't dare turn, just trust that my brothers have my back.

"This bitch is mine. Been mine for fucking years. You think I'm gonna let you have her?" The younger man barks out in a fluster. He's so damn uptight with his tailored pants and white business shirt. His hair comes into his eyes and he twists his neck to remove it. I think I have a shot but then he moves. Shit. This must be the son, Frank.

GT comes up to the side of me. "Others?" I ask.

"Taken out, all of them." He holds his gun up too. My eyes flash behind the asshole and Pops has somehow got behind him. How the hell did he do that? I need to keep this ass's attention.

"That woman is mine, I hate to tell you." Tears form in Blaze's eyes and it fires my anger more. I will destroy this son of a bitch.

"You wish. She may have fucked you but she belongs to me. I was her first and will be her fucking last," he growls, his arm wraps around Blaze's middle, holding her tight. One of her arms is limp, the other is being held by his hand.

After a few blinks, Blaze's eyes change. Fire flares inside of them and I know she is going to make a move. Pops is creeping up, but it's going to happen now. Before I can blink, Blaze lifts her foot, bending at the knee, and kicks the asshole behind her in his knee. The asshole wobbles in pain and Blaze somehow releases her good arm, and punches him in the nose. The asshole turns at the blow. With Blaze out of the way, I take the shot, blowing his hand that is still holding the gun completely off his body.

Blaze turns and runs to me, and I catch her in mid-leap. GT and Pops move toward Frank. I keep my eye on him but shield Blaze. She trembles in my arms and I remember the shot. "Babe, let me see your shoulder." She squeezes then turns, blood trickling from her body.

I yank off my shirt, pressing it to the wound. After wiping away the blood, I see it's a flesh wound, but I'm not taking any chances.

GT and Pops wrap the asshole up with duct tape, take him to the car that Derek is driving, and throw him in. Pops leans down to Derek. He then rushes to Dagger, GT and Rhys, talking in hushed voices.

"I need an ambulance!" I yell. He nods, hitting buttons on his phone. My girl's eyes are open but her breathing is a bit too shallow for my liking.

"So I leave you alone and you get kidnapped? What's up with that?" I try to joke with her and keep her mind off of the pain that I'm sure she is in. I was shot in the thigh during my service and it hurt like a mother bitch.

"I wasn't going to let him take me," she says softly. I think more out of fear than pain. Police cars and ambulances arrive on the scene. Derek's car, Dagger, GT and Rhys are gone. Cops stop and draw their weapons, all the guys putting their guns down and raising their hands in surrender.

I carry Blaze to the ambulance before it has fully stopped. The paramedic opens the door, unfolding a stretcher to the ground. "She's been shot in the shoulder. I think it's a flesh wound, but I need you to make sure."

"Lay her down." I don't want to release her but do because I know they will help her. Her hand comes out and lightly squeezes me.

"I'll be okay," she whispers.

I clutch her hand, pull it to my lips, and kiss the top of it. I never want to see her like this ever again. "I know, sweet lips."

"Looks like you're right, but let's get her to the hospital and checked out," the paramedic says, poking and prodding her. "You riding?"

"Yes," I answer as a police officer comes up to the side of me.

"Andrew Tugger?" he questions and I turn to him, wondering how in the hell he knows my name.

"Yeah," I answer, not letting go of Blaze.

"Step away and come with me," he orders, his hand resting on the butt of his gun that is still in the holster.

"I need to go to the hospital with my girlfriend," I argue, which I know isn't the best thing to do with a cop, but I don't give a shit.

"Fine, but I will have an officer follow you," he says, surprising me. I thought for sure he'd give me shit.

"Fine." I turn to the medics. "Let's go."

"Mr. Tugger?" a woman wearing blue scrubs with kittens on them calls from the waiting room door. I rise quickly. When we arrived at the hospital, they carted Blaze away, not letting me go with her. The cop that followed me tried to ask me a bunch of questions, but I just asked for my lawyer. When he said I wasn't a suspect and that it was only for information, I told him to contact my lawyer. He gave up and left. Pops, Buzz, and Breaker trickled in. Buzz stayed while Pops and Breaker went to the clubhouse to check on shit. They didn't go into detail with me on what happened, but I'm sure I'll get that news later.

"That's me." I wipe my sweaty hands on my jeans.

"Mrs. Tugger has a flesh wound. It grazed her shoulder. She is going to be just fine." Yes, I lied and said she is my wife. They wouldn't give me information otherwise, and it won't be the last time I lie.

"Can I go see her?" I don't give a shit if she hears the desperation in my voice.

"Yes, follow me." I turn to Buzz, giving him a chin lift and follow the woman.

Several long white corridors later, we enter a room and Blaze is lying, eyes closed, on a white bed. The nurse turns to me. "It'll take a bit for her to get her bearings. She was given some pain meds that will make her a bit dizzy and tired. If you want to sit with her, there's a chair over there." She points across the room and my eyes follow. Without hesitation, I sit in the chair by her bed.

I reach for her hand and hold it. Fuck. I don't do scared. I don't do fear. But damn, it's coming off me in waves and has been ever since I learned she was taken and saw her get shot. That's when I knew, really knew she's the woman for me. I lean down, kissing her hand. I close my eyes.

Hours pass. My head is lying on the bed, eyes closed, and sleep takes me under.

"Tug," is whispered softly. I open my eyes and turn to the voice.

Blaze. She is focused on me. "Hey, sweet lips. How are you doing?"

"Tired," she says, trying to keep her eyes open.

"Quiet and rest. It's all over, Blaze. All finished. You're free," I say, and her eyes fill with tears.

I TOOK Blaze home that next day with instructions for her to rest. Currently, she is lying in bed sound asleep, and I have something or someone that I need to get to.

The doorbell rings. Blaze doesn't stir. I sigh and go to the door, where Princess stands with an unreadable face.

"Thanks for coming. I didn't want her to wake up and no one be here." Princess only nods but doesn't say a word. She comes into the house and sets her bag on the floor.

"I can't believe I got fucking tasered," she growls, her eyes growing fierce and mouth in a tight line.

"It happens to the best of us." I wrap my arm around her shoulder. "Everyone's fine, that's what you gotta remember."

"I'm still pissed I got knocked out." She maneuvers away, obviously not in the mood to be coddled.

"She's asleep and I'll be back as soon as I can."

"Go get that motherfucker." She smirks and I leave, shutting the door behind me.

IT'S like déjà vu walking into the cabin. We were all just here. Only difference is this time, the asshole is stripped naked and hanging from the ceiling, spread eagle with his arms and legs tied to the beams. His head is bent down, almost hanging off his neck. Marks and cuts mar his body.

"Did you leave any for me?" I ask, catching Dagger, Rhys, Becs, Breaker and Zeb's attention. They turn to me.

"He's not dead, if that's what ya mean. His heart's still beating but he's not conscious," Dagger says, pulling off his black gloves one finger at a time.

"Shit," I grumble. Nothing I do now will mean shit. I grab the gun from my jeans, aim it at this asshole's head and shoot. His body jerks then goes back into the same position as before.

"Well, that was anti-climactic." Becs lights a cigarette, inhaling deep.

"It's fucking over." I sigh, putting my gun in my pants.

"Brother, it's just getting started. We pissed a lot of people off by offing these dicks." I think back to the discussion earlier. These assholes ran product for our mutual supplier. Well, shit. Becs is fucking right.

CHAPTER EIGHTEEN
Blaze

COMING TO X FOR THE FIRST TIME IN A WEEK IS A BIT surreal. Princess had it closed a few days after the bomb scare. She's been handling everything and I'm ready to get back to business. Last week, Tug made me rest, every damn day. I was bored out of my mind and by day four, I wanted to scream, but when Tug gave me a don't-fuck-with-me look, I rested.

I have a small wound on my shoulder that is pretty much completely healed. After I woke up from all the drugs they pumped in my body, I was scared. No, terrified was more like it. Tug tried to calm me, but I didn't think that Santos and Frank were dead. I knew for sure they were coming to take me with them. Hello, freaky panic attack.

Then the cops came to question me and brought me pictures. I recognized goons one through five and Santos, but didn't spot Frank and my anxiety rose to the point of shaking. Tug was next to me, holding my hand, and he must have felt my panic. He leaned over to my ear and told me, "He's gone." It was so quiet no one could hear but me.

After the cops left, Tug told me to trust him that it was all taken care of and I do. He told me that I am safe and he won't let anything touch me again. I believe him. It was then that I also realized that I didn't just like Tug; I loved him. Holy shit. Freaked me out quite a bit. I still haven't told him and don't plan to for a while.

Tug pretty much moved in with me, though. Slowly but surely, more and more of his things have ended up at my house. I cleaned out a drawer for him and I know in my heart that there will be more drawers eventually. It isn't official, him living with me, but it may as well be. He has a key, and comes and goes as he pleases. I can't even remember the last time he went to his apartment.

"Hey, there you are," Princess says, her eyes coming up from the papers on her desk.

"Hey." I step into the room and sit in the chair in front of her.

"How are you?" Princess questions.

"Good. Really good." And I am. This is the best I've felt in a long time. I've got a good man, job, friends who are my family. It's wonderful.

"Well, I'm glad you're back. These numbers are kicking my ass." She throws her pen down on top of the papers and runs her fingers through her hair.

I smirk. "I'll do them. Have them done in no time." I shrug.

"I'm sure you will." She rests her elbows on the desk. "What's up?"

"I'm done dancing," I rush out. I didn't know how she'd feel about it, especially since I fired Stage and we lost poor Luna, she's still two dancers down. With all the other shit happening, she said she wanted to wait till I got back and for the dust to settle.

"Well, I'm not going to say I'm happy because I sure as shit am not. You bring in some serious cash. But..." She drew out the word but. "I know it's the right decision for you. And that's what matters."

"Thanks." I'll miss the money that's for damn sure, but it's time to be done with it. I want to move on with my life and let it lead to wherever it's going.

Princess snatches a wad of papers off her desk. They are turned every which way and are a huge mess. She hands them out to me. "Here." I take them. "Do whatever it is you do." She waves her hand as she says it.

Contentment fills me. "You got it."

EPILOGUE
Tug

EVEN THOUGH THAT SANDRA chick recanted her story, when the cops came to the airport for Blaze, they pulled the guys there in for questioning. They each lawyered up right away, but what we learned is they were asking questions about Rocky, also known as Officer Macafee. Rocky is the son of a bitch cop who prospected for the club so he could feed information to them. He also turned out to be the asshole that raped Princess in jail when she was locked up. Princess found out who he was and it ended up with a very painful death for Rocky.

Even though his body was never found, the cops knew the last place he was, was at our club. They searched a long time ago, which was a much nicer, cleaner search, for evidence to his whereabouts, but came up empty-handed.

In all, we really learned that the Sandra shit was just a

reason to come and fuck up our place in retaliation. While really, they wanted information about Rocky's disappearance. Not gonna get it. Burnzie's handling it.

They have yet to question Dagger, Cruz, GT or Rhys. Since I lawyered up in the hospital, they've left me alone. So, all has been quiet this past week.

We also haven't heard shit from Santos and Frank's crew up in Colorado. That one we are keeping a very close eye on.

One thing that is not quiet is Blaze. She screams my name at least once a night, every night. I make damn sure of it. That damn woman is something else. She's so fucking strong and smart. I'm not sure how in the hell I lucked out in this area but I'm fucking taking it.

I told Buzz and Breaker that I'm moving in with her today. They were fine with it and I figured they would be. That is why I borrowed the big cage from Ravage to haul my shit. It's not a lot, but I can't carry it on my bike.

When I make it to Blaze's house, she's standing in the doorway wearing snug fit jeans and a t-shirt with a big mouth on it. Beautiful. Absolutely beautiful. And the fact that she stopped showing everyone what's mine, got her a lot of fucking orgasms.

I get out and round the cage. "Hey, babe."

"Hey. You get everything?" she asks, her hand over her eyes to block the sun. Her eyes squinty.

"Yep. I gotta haul all the shit in." I step in front of her, and kiss her, hard and wet.

I release her lips and Blaze's eyes are closed. "Open your eyes," I whisper against her lips. Her eyes slowly open. "Always knew you'd have the sweetest lips around."

A smile spreads across her plump lips. "You know I love you." Her body stills. I kept that shit to myself for a while. So long, but it's time.

"You do?" she questions, as if it's the last thing in the world she would expect from me.

"Yeah, sweet lips." I bend and give her a light kiss.

"I love you, too," she whispers so faint that I barely hear her, but I fucking did. I crash my lips against hers and show her just how much I love her.

"ARE YOU READY FOR THIS?" Blaze asks me after taking off her lid and handing it to me. Fuck no, I'm not. I haven't been to my childhood home in years and coming back wasn't top on my priority list. But when Mom called and asked Blaze and I to come to dinner, I couldn't say no. My sister is recovering and everything is going as expected. She has a casted leg and has to use crutches for the next couple of weeks, but that was all the damage. The asshole that hit her has a court date in a few weeks. But Buzz, Cruz, Rhys, and I paid him a visit. I really don't think he'll ever drive drunk again. If he does, he's a fucking moron, and I'll kill the bastard.

"We'll see." Blaze grabs my hand after I get off my bike, giving it a squeeze.

"It'll be fine," she says, standing on her tiptoes and placing a chaste kiss on my lips. I growl. I fucking love when she does that shit.

"You're here!" my mother's voice calls from the house.

Both Blaze and I turn to her. Mom's face is smiling and if I'm not mistaken, a tear is glistening in the corner of her eye.

"Hi, Mom. This is Blaze."

Mom's eyes light up at the sight of Blaze. Not gonna lie, thought she'd give her and I a bunch of shit because of her stripping, even though she's done with it. Not that she knows that. Mom's eyes light up and it's a step in the right direction. "Hi, Blaze, welcome."

"Hi, Mrs. Tugger. It's nice to finally meet you," Blaze says politely. Everything in the house is exactly the same. Same brown carpet and tan walls. Same scraggly furniture. Same everything.

"Andrew!" my sister yells. She's sitting in the armchair in the living room, her leg propped up, and I make my way over to her.

"Hey, Alexis. How are ya feeling?" Her eyes are the same as mine and her hair is a shade lighter. Her small frame makes her look so fragile, exactly like all those years ago. I'd do anything for her then and I'd do anything now. She seems better and not just from the accident. She seems better with me.

Alexis's beautiful smile greets me and I bend on one knee, coming face to face with her. "So much better." She pauses and wrings her hands. "I'm so sorry," she mutters so softly it comes out in a mumble of words. That vise around my heart loosens a bit and relief flows through my body.

"Why?" I ask, needing something more. It's been years.

Alexis looks down and shakes her head. "When it

happened, there was so much blood and it was everywhere. I dreamt of it every night and couldn't stop. Mom was a basket case. I got on meds and we both took it all out on you. I'm so sorry."

The words make me feel a little better, but it still hurts. I won't put that on her. I grab her chin lightly and turn her eyes to mine. "Good to have you back, rug rat." Her frown turns to a small grin in an instant.

"Rug rat, my ass." She chuckles.

"I want you to meet my girl, Blaze." I rise and hold out my hand to my girl, and she comes without question.

"Hi, Alexis. Nice to meet you," Blaze says.

Alexis's eyes widen. "You sure are pretty. What the hell are you doing with him?" And just like that, Alexis and I are good. Relief. Happiness.

Blaze laughs loud and I glare at my sister. Not in the I-will-kill-you way, but the big-brother-getting-his-sister-back way. "You'd better watch it," I warn, getting more chuckles from my sister.

"Come and eat!" my mother calls from the kitchen.

My sister wiggles to the end of her chair. "Can you hand me the crutches?" Fuck that. I pick her up under her knees and behind her back. "What are you doing?" she screeches in my ear, but I ignore it. I sit her down in the chair and push it up to the table. "You didn't have to carry me," she grumbles.

"Shut it," I clip. The table is square. I sit with Blaze and Mom on my sides and Alexis in front of me. Mom passes the food around and we eat in uncomfortable silence. I can't take this shit. "Mom, are you still pissed at me?" I ask flat out, receiving a gasp from Alexis and wide eyes from Mom. Blaze's hand finds my thigh and she squeezes, and I rest mine on top of hers, feeling her comfort.

Mom sets her napkin down. "Well, I was going to wait until dinner was over, but this is as good of time as any." She closes her eyes like she's gathering what she wants to say. I wait quietly. "I'm sorry, Andrew. It's taken me many years, but I now understand why you did what you did. You said once that I would have stayed with your father and let him..." She stops and coughs. "You're right. I would have. I loved your father and always thought it was a rough patch. I am miserably sad that he is gone." What the fuck? Blaze squeezes my thigh. I appreciate her reassurance. "I am sorry that I took my pain out on you." A tear rolls down her cheek. "I wish I could go back and do things differently, but I can't. I can only work on the future."

I rise from my chair and pull Mom out of hers, wrapping my arms around her tight. Contentment rolls over me. I have everything I've ever wanted. I have my girl, my mom, my sister, and my club.

TWO WEEKS LATER

I'M SLOWLY GETTING into the club life. It's really no different than before, just now we go on rides as a family and do charity events. This past event we did raised over eleven thousand dollars for autism awareness. Princess even suggested we put one together for breast cancer. I cried over that one. We have it in the works.

The one thing that wasn't fun at all was riding in Luna's funeral. That was hard. Most of us went and stayed in the background, paying our respects, but giving her family space. I will never forget the look on her face before the car exploded. It haunts my dreams and those nights aren't good ones.

Tug has been wonderful. After going to see his mom and sister, who are wonderful people, he is lighter, like some of his heavy weight was removed from him. I don't bring it up, but we have gone over for dinner twice more. It will take a while for it all to meld together, but they are on a great road.

Lying in bed each night with him and waking up every day with him is phenomenal. I never knew what I was missing, and now I wouldn't change it for the world.

Today there is a huge party at the club. Princess, Casey, Ma, and I worked our asses off, getting all the new furniture ordered since the cops busted everything and it wasn't repairable. Some things we found in storage, but we did more. We worked tirelessly getting it ready and tonight is a party celebrating.

I've been talking to Princess and Casey about everything to do with Ravage. While I knew about the women's place in the club from Tug and books, it was nice to hear how the other ladies handle it. One thing that was brought up during our conversations was their *Property of* rags.

I was dead set against it. I am no one's property, ever. Santos and Frank thought I was and I vowed never to allow that again. After several hours of explanation and a pissed off Princess, I got it. I understood it. The *Property of* rag is special and significant. It is like marriage, biker style. Princess also told me about the time she entered a party without her rag and a brother from another chapter thought she was free game. It scared the ever-loving shit out of me. It is also why, at a party, I stay close to either Tug, Cruz, GT, Casey, or Princess. I know they would never let anything happen to me and thank God, I haven't been put in that situation.

About a week ago, I had a sit down with Ma. She pulled out pictures of her and my aunt and told me lots of stories. I loved every one of them. Ma also told me that my mom didn't like Sylvie getting with a biker and that is what led to the rift between them. After hearing that, a rock formed in my gut that my mom wouldn't be happy for me that I found Tug. But after long thought and talking to Tug, I realized she would be really happy for me. She loved me and would want me to be happy, like I am with Tug.

Ma had tears in her eyes at times when talking about my aunt. I suggested she give her a call and see if she can come to Sumner. Ma and I agreed on that one.

I add mascara to my eyes then a little blush to my cheeks. The woman staring back at me is happy. I'm happy. I never thought it would be possible for me, but it is. Everything in my life is great. Without having my past cloud me, I've opened up to so much more.

"Hey, babe. You ready to go?" Tug calls from the doorway of the bathroom. God, he's hot. Jeans, black t-shirt, leather across his tight chest, and his hair messed up and sexy as hell. And he's all mine.

I set the brush down. "Yep. Gotta get my shoes on." I give him a soft peck. His steel arm wraps around me and he crashes his lips to mine. He deepens the kiss, taking every bit of breath out of my lungs.

He pulls away. "Now, that's how you kiss your man." He wipes his lips, now covered in my gloss. Sexy. He releases me on wobbly legs.

Damn, man. I sit on the bed, putting on my black, spiked-heels with the gold toe.

"Babe." I look to my man and everything stops. Tug stands there, holding a leather rag with Ravage's emblem. On the bottom of it, it reads 'Property of Tug.' Holy fucking shit. I gasp in a breath, not realizing I forgot to breathe. "You gonna put it on?"

I stand on shaky legs and move to Tug. True, we live together and are happy, but this is huge. He is making a real commitment to me. Holy shit!

His eyes blaze with fire and love. A lone tear falls from my eye, but I let it go, instead of swiping it away.

"Yeah, baby." My voice is so much quieter than how elated I am on the inside. Tug holds the leather up and I slip my arms in. It's heavy on my shoulders, but I love it.

"You are officially, my ol' lady."

I wrinkle my nose. "Can't I be called your woman or something like that?" I joke. Princess, Casey, and I talked about this term too, and I'm okay with it. I just didn't know when or if it would happen.

"No." His lips come down on mine, and I lose myself in my man.

Tug

ENTERING the clubhouse with my leather on Blaze, I can't take the stupid ass smile off my face. Music blares, but all attention is on us. Whoops, hollers, catcalls and congratulations ring through the room. I kiss my girl as she runs off with the other ol' ladies. I've seen her as one for a long damn time now. But I had to wait to get my rag then find out how to get hers. I just got it back early this morning. I was not waiting another moment to put it on her back.

"So, you finally claimed her?" Buzz nudges my shoulder.

"Fuck, man. I claimed her ass a long damn time ago." I grab a beer, taking a swig.

"I haven't got any more from the computer. But I'm going back to it after this." Buzz cracked through the first set of codes and it was quite eye-opening. Basic information on Ravage, T-Darts, Rabbit's Crew, Ransom, and a shit load of other clubs around the country. There was even information on Santos, that stupid motherfucker. It wasn't any kind of breakthrough. All basic. But we do have a list now of each member within each organization. That's a plus. He's not giving up though and I have every bit of confidence that he'll get it.

Drinking, dancing, and partying go on well into the night. It's the most fun I've had in a long-ass time.

At the door, a very attractive woman with fiery-red hair and a sexy body stands, looking around. I've never seen her here before and she seems to be searching for someone.

Dagger moves to the woman, who is now standing next to the bar where I am sitting. "Hey, beautiful. Where you been all my life?" Dagger coos. Damn brother, get a new line.

"That work with all the ladies?" she asks with a soft smile.

"Only when I want it to." Dagger places his hand on her hip, a predatory gleam sparking in his eye.

"Maybe you can help me." The woman's voice is sweet as honey.

Rhys comes up to the party, his eyes glazed with ferocious lust. Holy shit. Dagger and Rhys are going to go at it over the chick.

"I'll help you with whatever you need." Dagger takes a step forward, invading the woman's space. Rhys steps closer, the woman's eyes swinging to him. Her whole body trembles. She shakes her head, not in a 'no' but trying to clear it, and turns back to Dagger.

"Thanks. But I'm looking for Cameron Wagner." Dagger's grip tightens on the woman's hip and she winces from the touch.

"What do you need him for?" Dagger asks. Rhys has fury pouring off of him.

She looks around. "I'm Tanner. His daughter."

GET the next book in the series Inflame Me is available now!

ABOUT RYAN

Ryan Michele is the *Wall Street Journal* and *USA Today* **Bestselling author** of over 40 romantic suspense novels. She found her passion bringing fictional characters to life, being in an imaginative world where anything is possible. Her knack for the **unexpected twists and turns** will have you on the edge of your seat with each page. She is best known for **her alpha, bad boy bikers and strong, independent heroines who refuse to back down.** When she's not writing, you can find her on her swing, watching the water ripple in the pond and daydreaming about her next book.

Join my Reader Group: https://www.facebook.com/groups/RyansSultrySinners/
Sign Up for my https://www.subscribepage.com/918BackmatterSignUps

facebook.com/AuthorRyanMichele
twitter.com/Ryan_Michele
instagram.com/author_ryan_michele
BB bookbub.com/authors/ryan-michele

ACKNOWLEDGEMENTS

First, thank you to everyone that is reading this and who has read my books. I'm honored that you love the Ravage Family.

To my Facebook Hotties group, THANK YOU!!! I love that I can write a question and you guys help me answer it. *Fight Club* is all you guys! And for spreading the word about my books.

To my Ravages. I can't thank you enough for all the time and energy you put into promoting my books. Thank you. I <3 you hard.

My beta readers. There are so many of you and if I list them I know I will forget someone, so I'm just going to do general. Each of you helped make this book what it is today. Thank you for cutting it up and helping me find my path. I'm honored to have each of you in my life. I appreciate all of your time and hard work. THANK YOU!! And a huge shout out to The Indie Express.

Lori—Love you.

Lea. Thanks for taking me on and kicking my ass when I needed it. I'm honored to have you on my team.

Ena. What do I say? You... I just don't even know how to put into words. Thank you from the bottom of my heart. You are the glue holding me together. Lucky you. *wink*

Indie authors. I'm honored to be part of this community. I have made some wonderful friends, and you know who you are, hopefully. I thank you for the advice, strength and long conversations about nothing in particular that end up making so much sense. Some of you, I'll never be able to repay for the honesty and trust you have given me. I do not take that lightly and reciprocate it tenfold.

My family. I know I'm not around much when I'm in the heat of writing. That you have takeout more that you should and the clothes don't get folded and put away for weeks. I can't say that will change, but thank you for taking this journey with me. I love you.

~ Ryan

Editor: Lea Burn
    Proofreader: Julie Deaton
    Cover Artist: Cassy Roop, Pink Ink Designs

Thank you for reading!

Ryan
Michie